Graveyard of Metal

V. A. Trahan

To my seven brothers and sisters

PROLOGUE

June 1952

Burning metal, melting, charring to the core... The bone of iron. Stinking smells of well-done rat flesh permeating the already grease laden air. Rattling, clanging, opening the barbed chain link gate with his leathery, scarred hands, Whitey, the "Junkyard Man," always smiling until today. He propped a painted *closed* sign on a tire that leans adjacent to the entrance. He slams the clattering gate and kicks it closed tight. The rusty lock is a bear to click into place. "Damn."

Tickly, fuzzy, pine needle whiskers, covering, disguising, his blemished deep set lines that looked as if they brushed the outskirts of hell and back. His nostrils widened to the odorous stench of death. Devilish black dogs are growling and barking as they surround him. He curses under his breath. He swats the dogs away and points to a Hudson coup with a popped trunk filled with newspapers. They jumped in obediently and sit at attention.

Down the crude ash driveway, past the bone yard of cars, is a small unpainted grey wood house where a weeping woman is on the front porch. Whitey stares for a brief moment looking at Miriam, his despondent, fatigued wife. She barely stands, with one arm holding onto a flimsy wooden porch column. She holds a bundle while caressing and kissing its content. Matted long dishwater brown hair is half tied back, the other half dangling to one side of her pale face. Red and brown smears cover her legs and her bare feet stand in a puddle of blood.

Running toward his wife he shouts, "Mir!"

Whitey snatches the bundle away from Miriam. He walks along the driveway that leads behind the house. Miriam appears to be limping and struggles to barely follow behind.

The dogs begin barking again. *What's going on?* Dagwood Dooley carefully rolls over the left side of the lumpy mattress and swings his bum leg down, onto the freshly cleaned linoleum floor. He then pivots his body until he is able to get his sound leg over the edge of the bed and onto the floor where it can safely support his weight. He's then able to slowly and painfully get out of bed. *Why are those damn dogs barking this early. The sun is up but nobody else should be.* He limps over to the double window in his new apartment over the garage. The brilliance of the sun dazzles his robin's egg blue eyes. He looks down. *What is Whitey doing?*

Suddenly, like a swarm of insects, several stringy towhead children scurry barefoot across the ash and glass speckled driveway. All eight gravel girties ran to see what was causing the commotion.

Whitey is like a toreador chasing a bull. He thrashes at each one of them, shooing their skinny little bodies clear away. He hurries to the coal shed and flings out the pickax with one hand while awkwardly clutching the bundle to his chest with the other. Tattered and crying, his weary wife limps over to him attempting to catch a glimpse. Bloodstains and tears cover her worn, torn housedress.

With one hand, Whitey begins picking at the dirt. He starts to lose his grip on the soaking wet, rose flowered table cloth that surrounds the bundle. It is more than likely the finest they own. He hands the bundle to the weary, weeping woman without a word and continues picking at the dirt.

The oldest boy hands his struggling father a shovel. Scrambling to their mother, the kids strain to get a better look at this mysterious thing in her arms.

Cassie, the eldest daughter, tugs on her mother's dirty house dress. With innocent intention she cries, "Mommy, is that a baby?" The tired woman weeps harder. She ignores her eldest daughters' question.

Cassie remembers her pet calico cat, Sam, that died from eating rat poison, just the other day. Pop burned it in a shoe box along with some other trash. He dug a hole for the ashes. And that was that. The reek was still permeating the air. She begins sobbing.

When the hole was deep enough Whitey's marble blue eyes filled with tears. He looked straight at the youngest child, Dee Dee. No one knew why. She was barely six. He appeared to be reaching for an answer.

"So... Back away, that's it! The show is over. Now scat."

He looked at his bone weary wife and signaled. It was time. "Mir." He reached for the bundle but Miriam was not budging.

The kids all ran to their mother who has now tightened her grip on the bundle and is holding it close. Miriam looked at Whitey and began wailing, "No you don't!" The children never heard her yell at their father before. "Wait! Please George," she stammered.

Whitey grasped for the bundle. His normally demure wife was now wrestling with him. She may have been small framed, but she was strong. She was not letting go. Down she went, now he was winning. She let out a shriek and then there it was; a blood covered baby fell at their youngest child's feet, right there on the ground for all the kids to see. It was the size of and resembled a plucked chicken. She was small but a perfectly formed, dead sibling.

The Children's mouths were wide open, but no sound came out. Cassie began crying. Scared and curious, they knew to back off. Their pop looked mad as the dickens!

"Now look what you made me do!" Pop's voice is barking mad. Mom begins bawling. Blood is everywhere. She is reaching to touch her dead daughter. Pop pushes her away one more time.

He pauses when he sees his scared kid's faces. "Get back... Go in the house!" For a second he appears to be weeping. He shakes his head and mumbles under his breath. Suddenly, he grows at his eight frightened but curious offspring. "Go!"

They scatted away before Pop could look back at them with that glare of doom. They all ran into the house, the screen door snapped them into the kitchen. Then, those little stinkers snuck back out to peek one last time.

Suddenly Georgie, the oldest child, attempts to command what Pop would have wanted. He points to the door. There is no escape. Shrugging, the other seven stomp back into the house like marching soldiers.

The oldest sibling whispers so that the youngest two can't hear. But Bobby and Dee Dee hear them anyway. Pop is going to burn the little body and scoop her ashes into that hole.

This was an end; and a beginning. The ground around the hole has become dark and fertile. The soil has been turned and a robust garden has since brought them hope.

CHAPTER 1 The Bath

It was Sunday morning and cloudy. One ray of sunlight peaked through the single upstairs window, shining onto Cassie's eyes. She awakened and stood straight up. She wrangled her way off the crowded mattress, on to the splintered floor. She made it. She rose before Mommy called for everyone to get up. She couldn't get the dead baby out of her mind. It was difficult to erase the vision of that precious infant.

Sunday was church. Therefore, all eight of the kids had to get up and get their baths. Cassie was trying to make her way to the stairs by the time Mommy hollered. Her holler was quite forceful, sometimes threatening.

A loud shout out from Mommy came from the bottom of the steep staircase. "Get up!" She was back to normal pretty quick. She could be like a drill sergeant even when she was laid up. She had a serious look on her face today. Cassie was the first one down. Dee Dee and Bobby who were farting and giggling followed behind. The thunderous sounds of all the rest of the kids scampering could be heard. All headed down the echoey stairs, sputtering, and slapping each step with their bare feet and scattering all in different directions.

Bell Cook, the close friend and neighbor from across the street everyone called Cookie, was a tough cookie. She was every bit round... As a cookie. Sometimes she was even sweet... As a cookie. But on Sunday she was tough... As nails. Her rounded chubby stature gave the appearance of a softy, but don't kid yourself. Her bite was worse than her bark.

Her tightly permed short grey hair was never off, not a hair out of place. It was always perfect. She smelled of castile soap. She babbled when she was excited and was in a hurry. She was hard to follow. When her eyes squinted and she snorted, she was mad. It was important to follow her beck and call. So don't mess with Cookie.

Today, like every other Sunday, Cookie was pouring hot water from the stove into the grey galvanized steel bathtub that sat in the middle of the small dining room. The table was pushed against the wall and the child that was being washed had his or her own set of supplies. She set the baths up like a military exercise. She usually brought eight large bath towels for the children. They were folded and placed near the tub. After the baths were finished she would take the used wet towels to her home across the street to wash for the next week. She was quick and efficient. That was what Miriam appreciated.

Cookie arrived thirty minutes early. She was given the sad news of the birth of the baby. She said, "I'm sorry about the baby." Under her breadth, she muffled, "I'm sad about the loss, but I'm not sad you don't have another mouth to feed."

Bath day was right before church. Bobby pushed Dee Dee in front of the tub so she went first. The water was always *so* hot; the skin on the kids turned beet red. There was no escape, so Dee Dee had to go first. The saying *Don't throw the baby out with the bath water* dated back to the middle ages, but Cookie preferred 'Don't throw the baby in with the cold bath water.'

"Owww... Owww...Owww! ...It's too hot!"

Cookie laughed and said, "Oh stop. Don't be a sis."

Dee Dee never trusted Cookie ever since the day she visited when she had chicken pox. Cookie stopped by and saw the pox all over Dee Dee's body. Cookie had made her stand on the dining room table and take her clothes off. If that wasn't embarrassing enough, all her brothers and sisters were there watching. Cookie then wrangled up a dirty old dish cloth from the kitchen sink and poured alcohol on it. Each pox that was open was filled with puss and oozed. When she wiped with the rag all over the swollen poxes it burned like fire. There were so many poxes and they were on every part of her body. Absolutely everywhere! The pain was excruciating, kind of like a bee sting; but it felt like eighty two bee stings.

So when Cookie gave Dee Dee a bath, Dee Dee screamed whenever she could. Cookie worked fast, scrubbing Dee Dee's ears and neck. Sometimes she chuckled when Dee Dee screeched. Getting lava soap in her eyes was one of the most painful experiences this child ever had up to the age of six. She yelled at Cookie, "I want a towel right now!" She would press it tight over her eyes. When the shift in the color behind her eyelids occurred she knew she'd be okay. "I hate my bath," she pouted.

Bobby stared in fear knowing he was next. He imagined Cookie was the dragon and he was about to be burned alive by her. "No please don't burn me dragon."

Cookie, the dragon, looked at Bobbie and said, "Only weaklings are afraid of my fire."

Bobby imagined, "Yes, that's me! I'm the weakling. Send me away. I don't want to be brave!"

The older kids were last. They were so embarrassed when she washed their private parts, they protested, but to no avail. Cookie was known to swat them if they were too defiant. Once she actually looked at Georgie's penis and uttered to everyone in the room, "What is this?" Everyone tried to see his penis. It was soft and small. She said, "I never saw a penis as small as a peanut." She cackled loud thinking it was funny. Georgie was mortified.

Cookie was undoubtedly tough. She was there to do one thing and one thing only: Bathe Miriam's kids so they could go to church. Miriam would help by giving her buckets of rinse water, but poor Miriam was in no condition to exert herself too much today. She was still bleeding pretty heavy from a late term still birth.

"Miriam!" Sissy's proper name was Miriam, same as her mother's. Mommy called her that when she was in trouble. Sissy was the second oldest girl. She was given the most chores, and the least amount of respect. Today she had not finished her morning chores.

Miriam ranted, "What's wrong with you today? Look at those dishes." Sissy was the washer and dryer but today she was barely awake. It looked like every dish in the house was dirty. Sissy was going to be last today because she had so much to do. Pop hated seeing dirty dishes in the sink and Miriam would do anything to avoid his wrath.

Cassie and Georgie were carrying over-filled trash bags to the pop-made fireplace. The fire was still smoldering near where the baby had been incinerated. A large rock with a wilted flower in front of it was all that remained of that tiny dead baby.

June mornings were sometimes chilly, but this one was downright cold! The kids were outside with no sweaters as usual. Nancy, third in line of the girls to get a bath, jumped down from the tire swing and announced, "I'm not gettin' a bath. She hurts my ears." But Cookie's voice resonated through the house to the outside. Nancy hoped that if she hung out here Cookie would not be looking for her.

Cookie stuck her head out of the back door. and yelled, "Get in this house now! It's almost time to go to church."

All the other kids that were fooling around then suddenly and frantically ran toward the house. It was time to get their bath or get a whooping. Nancy stayed outside. She played within view of the rock and it was hard to get that tiny infant out of her mind. *Maybe she wasn't really dead,* she thought. She began crying for the poor baby.

Georgie walked outside and pulled Nancy by her skinny arm and said, "Come on, get in there. Cookie's waiting for your ears." He laughed. Nancy cried and fought him all the way.

Georgie and Billy demanded privacy today. Georgie announced, "I'll bathe myself. And I want every one out of the room while Bill and I bathe. Out!"

Billy agreed. "It's only fair." All the other kids walked out of the room.

Cookie smiled. "Okay... Fine... But wash your butts." She looked at Miriam and laughed, she made a silly face and went in the kitchen for a cup of coffee. Cookie poured a cup of coffee and sat with Miriam. They spoke quietly amongst themselves. Miriam asked Cookie if all the kids were ready to go. "Yep, all but one." She took a huge gulp of coffee. She could see Nancy trying to sneak away. She pointed at Nancy who walked slowly over to Cookie with a sour face.

The last thing Cookie elected to do for Miriam was to brush everyone's hair. She brushed all the knots out of each of the girl's hair. Because Nancy's hair was naturally curly, Cookie had to use a long thin poker pick to get out some of the knots. Her hair was still wet and was the worst! Cookie set their hair in tight pony tails, while ignoring their cries. Brylcreem was for the boy's hair. However the boys, all but Jimmy, just had gotten haircuts. Jimmy's hair was too long. He had a permanent alfalfa cowlick. Cookie smeared his hair with the cream so it looked neat. His two older brothers teased him and told him his hair looked greasy.

Mommy kissed each of the kids and made sure each one had a few cents to put in the offering. "Be polite and don't get dirty."

The three older boys waved and promised to keep an eye on the younger kids. "Come right home. No fishing." Jimmy looked at Mommy and shook his head while making a silly face. Georgie nodded and waved. As they all left they passed by the baked treats which sat on the kitchen table, observing their favorite coffee cakes. Bell Cook always brought baked goods on Sunday, but the kids never had the time to eat them before church. They were told to wait until after church. But by that time Pop had eaten most of the good treats.

The infamous horn honked three times today. Cookie's husband always seemed impatient. He took the kids to church every Sunday at the same time, eight twenty five, and expected them to be ready by eight thirty and no later. No one seemed to know Mr. Cook's first name. He never talked to anyone anyway. Cookie always did the talking for him. He was a burly old man with a head of thinning grey hair. The cigar that hung out of his mouth always had a stream of slimy brown tobacco that led to his chin. He would usually honk his horn once and Mommy would scoot the kids out of the house. They had to be at church by nine a.m. sharp. Mr. Cook was waiting out in his big, marvelous car. If it hadn't been for him they would have had to walk a mile both ways. Bobby and Dee Dee had always been a little afraid of him though because of that villainous mustache. Also, the smoke from his cigar drifted right through to the back seat where they sat. They thought he might just scream at them for no reason. That was the feeling they had when he glanced at them. When they arrived at church they jumped out and all but one turned to Mr. Cook. All together they said, "Thank you." He knew which one of them forgot to thank him. Mommy would always get the word and give them a shaking to beat the band.

When they saw the gaggle of children come through the door of the quaint little Church of the Advent the ushers would say, "Here come those King children," and always make them sit in the very back. Church was boring but they all liked to sing. Singing was the only thing they could hear since they sat in the very back. They were short and could barely see anything.

One very tall skinny usher gave them a mean, I'll-kill-you-if-you-make-one-sound look on his face. They were perfect angels for the most part. Bobby blew it once in a while; he couldn't help it. Dee Dee thought there was something horribly wrong with the kid. His loud farts stunk so bad and they were so loud they caused his siblings to burst into an uproarious laughter causing Skinny to toss all of them out with an I-told-you-so look. Oh well... That just prolonged their walk home a bit. They couldn't go home too early. After all… Mommy knew everything.

While walking home they had to cross a creek bridge. As part of the ritual Jimmy and Bobby would catch frogs and crayfish. Dee Dee wanted to tag along but she was wearing a dress. It sure sounded like fun. She said, "I hope Mommy doesn't find out."

Bobby looked at her and shook his head. "How will she find out? Unless you tell her." Dee Dee was a great tattle tale, but only when it didn't include her. She was afraid to get Mommy mad by getting her Sunday dress dirty. Mommy made most of their clothes and this dress was purple and a favorite. Bobby assured her everything would be just fine. He noticed Dee Dee's purple Sunday dress already had a tear from a sticker bush, but he didn't say anything. The boys wanted to bring the crayfish home so they elected Dee Dee to go find a coffee can. She had to run a block away to an old dump yard. *This wasn't fun*, she thought.

The older boys, Georgie and Billy, decided to sneak to the corner gas station and buy candy with the money that was meant for the church collection. They never told the girls about it for fear they would tattle. Especially Nancy or Cassie.

Jimmy secretly tip toed in the back door with his can of crayfish. He sneaked in the bathroom and set the can behind the toilet. He then ran to the boys bedroom, changed his clothes and ran back out to help Pop in the yard. And behind the toilet they remained... For three more days during which no one gave them any thought.

The two older boys had to quickly hide the candy, and change clothes to help Pop fill the big truck with metal. All the boys, even Bobby who was only about seven, were expected to do their share. They had to change their clothes and help pop. That was the rule. Some Sunday's the girls were asked to chip in. They didn't lift anything heavy like the boys, but they would find junk around the yard and help fill the big truck. They did that for several hours after church. Even Mommy had to pitch in when sales were slow. Georgie and Billy were the only helpers who worked on flattening the cars. They were trained to handle large equipment. They actually enjoyed it. This was all done before their Monday sale in Philadelphia.

Two hours later the boys came running into the house like hungry jackals. Georgie hollered, "Where's my coffee cake?"

Miriam could see the cake was gone. "You're too late. Your father had a few. First come first served. Eat the shortbread cookies. Oh by the way... I know you didn't thank Mr. Cook and you were kicked out of church."

Mommy did it again. It was like she was clairvoyant. Mommy shook her head but she didn't get mad today. She looked a bit sad.

Pop walked into the house exhausted, he also looked sad. He gathered all the boys and took them out for lunch.

Three days had passed. Miriam walked into the bathroom... *What the hell was that smell?* "Bobby..!!"

CHAPTER 2 Ivan

Alice was best friends with Miriam for many years. In fact, she helped with the birthing of Miriam's two youngest, Bobby and Dee Dee. She was often around cleaning and babysitting the kids. One day when she stopped by, Miriam noticed a big pot belly on her. She had been able to hide it up until then. Miriam knew immediately what it was, and it sure wasn't the result of an immaculate conception. Alice admitted to Miriam that she was eight months pregnant. The clincher was it was George's baby.

Miriam and Alice's mother helped her arrange a private adoption. George was in agreement and their own family doctor, Dr. Perry, who's wife could not have children, adopted the infant boy.

A year had passed and George and Miriam's relationship was not restored. George's affair was a lingering issue, especially since Alice, her once best friend, was still hiding the relationship that seemed to be permanent now. Alice was pregnant again. After that Miriam and George rarely had one civil word to say to each other.

Alice was now snappy and aloof when she stopped by to help with the kids. She was no longer the kind, sweet best friend Miriam once knew. She had become bossy and downright mean. None of the kids wanted to be around her. Miriam became so upset with this change in behavior she ended their friendship, this time for good.

Miriam heard a loud, rapid knock on her kitchen door. She said to herself, "Who in the hell is in that much of a hurry?

They could've knocked normal." She saw it was Cookie through the screen door and said, "Hi stranger," while wondering why she even knocked at all; she usually just walked in. Miriam was wondering why she hadn't seen hide nor hair of her in a week.

Cookie, hanging her head, replied softly, "Hi Mir. I'm bringing very sad news over to you." She pushed the door open. "I'm sorry I haven't been over lately. Ivan became ill last Sunday night. Mir... He died this morning! He was showing strange signs. He was confused and had to lay down early in the evening. It must have been six o'clock. I asked him, 'What in the hell is wrong Ivan?' He couldn't even answer me." Cookie, who had never cried in front of Miriam, began sniffling. Miriam pulled a kitchen chair away from the table and offered it for Cookie to sit down. Cookie sat down, showing signs of deep despair.

"Can I have some tea, Mir?"

"Do you want coffee?"

"No, thanks. I've been drinking tea for the past week, it's supposed to be calming, better for you when your upset."

Miriam filled the tea kettle with water and found one single tea bag. She reached an upper shelf where she brought down her finest Wedgewood china tea cup.

"So anyway... I tried to wake him to take his street clothes off and put his pajamas on. I tried and tried, but he wouldn't budge. I couldn't get him to even open his eyes. He had a pulse but I couldn't feel his breathing. I called the operator and told them I needed emergency help. I said to them, 'Now!' They sent an ambulance to the house and I rode with them. Mir, he looked blue. You know me, I never pray. But this time I began telling the Lord, 'I'm sorry for being such a bitch.' I then promised I would be better. Do you believe it? Me, praying. They thought he was dead when we got there. I'm sorry I haven't been around, but this was one helluva week. So... He had a stroke and we thought he would pull through. The blood to his brain had no oxygen. That's how they explained it to me. Then one of the blood vessels leading to his brain broke. They did everything they could, but he started bleeding, Mir. Unfortunately none of the best doctors around were able to save him. No one could help him Mir" She put her face in her hands and doing so, she accidently knocked over her tea breaking Miriam's favorite Wedgewood tea cup. "Sorry! Oh Mir... I'm so sorry." She began wiping the table leg and floor with her hanky. Miriam reached down and lightly smacked her hand. She first picked up several pieces of sharp china chards then with her apron she wiped up the tea on the floor.

"Bell, don't do anything else, just sit there. I'll get that." She called, "Miriam!"

Sissy ran into the kitchen. "Yes?"

"Go ask Woody if he has any tea." Sissy quickly walked out of the house. The screen door snapped back making a loud annoying sound. Miriam hollered, "Close the door quietly!"

Cookie said, "Mir, without Ivan, I feel like a tiny bird that fell from a tree." She started bawling. "I have no idea what I'm going to do. What am I going to do Mir?" Cookie walked over to the kitchen spigot and rinsed her hands. She stood there, leaning on the edge of the counter with both her hands, holding herself up.

"I'm torn about selling the house. But those damn medical bills are streaming in already, and becoming astronomical. He was only in the hospital for four days. And I got a bill already that would pop your eyes out. I can't take care of the house. I don't even drive. I have a funeral to pay for. Luckily, we both already have purchased coffins, plots and stones."

Miriam said, "I'll tell George and Maybe he'll buy it."

Sure enough... Whitey bought the house across the street from the junkyard. It had been Cookie's residence for fifteen years. It had three bedrooms and a full finished basement with a recreation room. There was one and a half baths. Miriam thought it was for her. She soon learned it was for *The Witch*. That was what Miriam had named Alice these days. *The Witch* was going to have Whitey's second child. This time she was determined to keep it. *And* she was getting a new house!

What a kick in the pants for Miriam!

Ivan's funeral was at Ferries Funeral Home in Westminster. It was quiet and beautiful. There were so many flowers they had to move some of the chairs to accommodate them. Miriam attended but George did not. He hated funerals. Also, he didn't want to be around Miriam until she calmed down from the divorce, and quite frankly, he hadn't known Ivan that well.

Poor Cookie. She sat near the casket alone. She had no children, no parents and no brothers or sisters. Ivan's brother and his family were there. They just didn't like Cookie. Dressed in her finest tailored black suit, she simply sat hands folded, no expression, eyes closed. Sadly, She became more of the main event than poor Ivan. A whispered comment that Miriam overheard was, "Poor thing, she won't survive without him."

Cookie moved into a beautiful retirement community called Living Vine Life Center two months after the funeral. The facility was surrounded by well manicured shrubs and flowered gardens with many shade trees and a large pavilion.

Beautiful walking trails drew affluent seniors in for a pleasurable, restful sanctuary. It was a place where your vista was their gift. It truly was spectacular. Especially the way their bedroom windows looked out toward the lake. The place had a host of activities that were offered. Not that Cookie found them interesting, but folks over sixty could expect 'Fun times in their final years'. That was how advertising drew her in.

She once told Miriam she didn't know how to have fun anymore. A week after Cookie had moved in, Miriam phoned her and promised she would visit soon. Unfortunately, Miriam, with her own crosses to bear, could not visit until three months later. When she got around to visiting, she saw that the grounds were like a park. Folks were walking on paths along the lake. The facility was neat and spacious. There was a family room with a fireplace. Beautiful paintings were on the walls. Fresh flowers were set on side tables. People were chatting with one another. One man walked up to Miriam and made a pass at her. He growled like a dog, and then grinned from ear to ear. There were folks playing checkers and cards on small gaming tables. People were playing ping pong. It gave Miriam a warm and fuzzy feeling that Cookie would love it here.

She looked around but couldn't seem to find Cookie. The Activities director said, "She may be in her room. She doesn't come out much."

The medicinal smell could not be concealed as Miriam opened the door of Cookie's room. Someone had just mopped and waxed the green and white linoleum floor so there was a slight shine that made the floor striking.

"Hi friend." Miriam looked at Cookie and attempted to tone down her greeting. "What a pretty room."

Cookie just sat in a chair. She was staring out the window expressionless.

Miriam asked her, "How are you doing?"

Cookie said, "Okay." Her hanky was held tightly in her hand.

Miriam brought her a crossword puzzle book. Cookie normally loved crossword puzzles.

She said, "Thanks," but didn't even look at it. She spoke like she wasn't Cookie anymore. She was in a trance like state.

Miriam brought a newspaper clipping about Georgie. He was one of Cookie's favorites. "Look Cookie. He's got an award from little old Westminster for changing an elderly woman's tire and then leading her to the grocery store. It was Acme. I thought everybody knew where that was. She was lucky Georgie was there because she was headed the wrong direction. Anyway....," Miriam forcibly laughed.

Cookie looked at the article and said, "Nice."

Miriam sat staring at Cookie for thirty minutes. Cookie blurted out, "The dirt under my fingernails wasn't enough for him. When the son of a bitch died he left me high and dry. Look where I am?"

Miriam looked around. She thought it was a wonderful retirement home. She said, "It's beautiful here."

Cookie said, "I couldn't do enough. The floors were never clean enough... His shirts were never pressed enough. The day he died he ate a shortbread cookie. It wasn't sweet enough. What did he want from me?"

Miriam walked over to Cookie and hugged her. She had a tissue in her pocket. She pulled it out and wiped Cookie's red, swollen eyes. "You were good to him my friend."

Miriam stood up, stretched her back and said, "Well today I'm going to be busy as hell. I have a part time job at a hosiery store in Willow Grove. So..." Miriam turned to leave. She bent down and wrapped her arms around Cookie to give her one last farewell hug. But Cookie was just broken. Somehow the spark was gone. Miriam could not fix her. So she had to leave.

Miriam drove the hour trip home feeling something was missing. It was awful, like she'd been slapped in the face. Cookie was her coffee buddy. Miriam remembered when she suspected George was fooling around with Alice and Cookie saying, "She's a witch, get her out of your house. She's after George's money. George is probably worth tons. And that woman is smelling it. Why was that jerk always laughing and fooling around with her? She's too young for him."

She and Cookie had talked for hours about just about everything. She remembered times when Cookie said she hated Ivan. She said one time, "He's a son of a bitch. I used to wish he would die." She remembered Cookie saying those very words, "Damn! Ivan will never die. He's too ornery." Now that he was gone Cookie couldn't seem to live without him.

Miriam thought about how sad she looked in her room. Life really threw her a curveball. Now Miriam was just coming up to bat with *her* life. So she told herself as she drove home, "Keep focused Mir. Divorce is the pits. You'll just have to deal with learning to live across the street from your ex-husband whose now married to your ex-best friend, Alice, *The Witch*. She is not your problem. You'll have to learn to live with it because you've got eight kids to love, all with mouths to feed."

CHAPTER 3 The Diner

Lingering rain clouds left over from an already wet October were hovering overhead and casting a shadow of doubt and confusion on those who were depressed and betrayed in this small country town outside of Philadelphia. November rain was getting much colder. Now it was biting, but just a preview of what was to come in the months ahead.

At the age of forty five Dagwood Dooley, who was known as Woody by most people, was abandoned for the second time in his life. As an infant he was left at an orphanage by his mother. This time he was left at a diner in

Westminster, Pennsylvania, by Sandy, his wife of sixteen years. She was five years his junior but she looked ten years younger. She left him stranded there for a younger man, Ernesto. It was all planned out. She went to the ladies room at Big Stop Diner where they arrived for breakfast and left through the side door without a trace.

Woody caught a glimpse of a newspaper opened to the funnies that had been left on the booth in front of him. Dagwood got the nickname Woody from reading Dagwood and Blondie in the funnies every day and loving Woody Woodpecker cartoons as a young boy. Did Sandy buy him a newspaper? He couldn't grasp what was taking her so long. She had been sprucing up in that ladies room forever. *Where are you Sandy?*

He ejected himself from the cushy booth seat that planted him. Looking straight into the eyes of Bob, the dishwasher that was bussing a nearby table. "Did you see where my wife went?"

Bob peered at the bathroom that was at the end of the long diner, near the entrance. "I ain't seen nothin' or no woman." He blurted out, "Gladys will go check if she's there." He gathered the dirty dishes and walked over to a tall grey haired elderly hostess who smiled at Woody. She teetered back to the ladies room.

A young, pretty, red haired waitress with a pin that said Nancy attached to her starched collar, heard part of Woody's story. As she was pouring his coffee she said, "As a matter of fact, I saw your lady friend. I heard she's missing... The lady who ran outta here. I saw her. I remember seeing a black truck in the parking lot. Umm... The skinny lady..."

He interrupted, "My wife."

She paused for a moment and cleared her throat. "A very pretty woman got into the truck." She stared at Dagwood's deep blue eyes. "The driver got out and seemed to poke a tire on the old grey truck over there." She pointed in the direction of Woody's truck. "I don't really know what he did. But it didn't look right. He jumped into his truck and then took off down the road like a bat outta hell."

Woody sank deep into the booth's green shiny covered seat and stared out the window in the direction where the waitress pointed. He then hid his face with his thick leathery hands. The break in his heart was a hollowing ache. His glum look took over his finely chiseled face. He'd been duped. She wouldn't do this to him, would she? A stray tear found its way to the table. He took a long swig of his strong black coffee, mumbling, "Damn! Damn you Sandy," quietly but loud enough that the waitress could hear. He whispered to the waitress when she walked by, "I think there must be a mistake here. She wouldn't do that..."

Nancy heard what he said but still walked over to the next customer and filled his coffee to the brim. She had to ignore Woody for the time being. The restaurant was now bustling and she was darting about from customer to customer. She grinned while carefully taking an order across from Woody. Her section seemed to be the busiest but she was smooth and undaunted.

She stopped, forcibly smiled at him and politely filled his coffee cup a third time. "You'll be fine. Can I get you something to eat sweetie?" she asked with soft concern.

The savory aroma of freshly cooked bacon and sausage was not enough of a draw for Woody. His appetite was gone. He shook his head.

He stared out the window at his truck but he didn't see anything, just the vision of Sandy's last fake smile before she zipped away. She was dressed to the hilt that morning. Today she was wearing her new crimson lipstick she bought just the other day. Her strange antics were making sense now. They had fought a bit earlier, bickering over Woody dressing too slowly on their way to breakfast. She snapped at him when he wasn't dressed quick enough. When they arrived she immediately left to spruce up in the rest room. The last thing she said was, "I'll be right back dear." Dear my ass!

A crusty middle aged man who was a regular known only as Whitey at the Big Stop Diner was in the booth next to Woody's. He awkwardly stood up and turned around, looking directly at Woody.

He asked, "Do you own that grey pickup out there?" pointing in the direction of Woody's parked truck.

Staring directly into eyes that reminded him of his own he replied, "Yes, why?"

"Well, I'm afraid you have a flat tire."

Woody thought *this can't be true*. He slid over to the window. His eyes became slits. He strained trying to see what Whitey was talking about. There... In plain sight... He was right! Woody's teeth clenched. He pounded the table with one full on fist. "Damn it!"

All eyes were on Woody. Whitey shook his head and then turned back around after Nancy whispered, "That poor guy."

Woody began to stand up then slouched due to the slippery seat pulling his weight back down. There were several tough looking dudes in the two booths in front of him. Nancy had spilled the beans to all the customers in her section and they all stared out the window mumbling and cursing. One guy actually laughed out loud.

Whitey loudly declared so that Nancy and the customers in the three booths could hear, "I'm paying for these two tables," pointing to the booths in front of Woody. He turned around and stated, "I've got your check too by the way."

"I'll get their ass! Don't worry," Woody erupted. Looking out the window, his face had become flame red.

Whitey pointed his finger at Woody's truck and said, "You should call the cops. That's a dirty crime." He turned and looked at Woody who appeared slightly embarrassed and lost.

Woody answered back, "No... They'll pay."

Whitey whipped back around and said, "You look like someone who could use a break." He reached over to Woody's table and grabbed his check.

"I guess I do, but I don't take charity."

Whitey snapped, "I've got it and that's that."

Nancy bent down and whispered to Woody, "It's only a cup of coffee and this is what he does." Woody gave in and nodded. As he left he thanked Whitey.

He was abandoned once before; he was left at an orphanage when he was three months old by his mother, Wanda Dooley, who wanted to keep him but was forced to relinquish the baby by her parents, because of the embarrassment of having a scandal in their family. He lived at The Pearl S. Buck Children's House of Hope in Bucks County, Pennsylvania. He grew up not ever having pizza, which he loved now and ate every Saturday. He didn't remember ever having been kissed goodnight as a kid, or having had a sleepover at a friend's, but most of all he didn't remember having had anyone that really loved him. Except his wife, he thought, who had just made a fool of him.

From the first time he met Sandy working at Bob's Beef n Ale, she was the one for him. She was only eighteen, everyone knew it, but nobody ever questioned her. She wore way too much makeup and was rough around the edges. But she kept her hour glass figure and that was all he ever wanted. Woody became accustomed to her short order cooking and his big belly was proof. Although they didn't have much, the apartment was always tidy.

In the past Woody had made ends meet. But recently they had found themselves living hand to mouth since he had lost his job as a mechanic at a gas station that had gone bust. Now all they owned was in storage while they looked for work. Most of their bickering wasn't due to money. It was because she could not have children. It was easier to blame him. Woody believed he was sterile.

"This can't be happening... Why?" Woody vocalized out loud in the parking lot. He stared at the tire. It had been grossly slashed. He got out the jack and lug wrench. He loosened the lug nuts and was already jacking up the old Chevy truck when he realized he didn't have a spare. He mumbled, "What the hell am I gonna do?" when he heard a now familiar voice. It was Whitey greeting him with a big smile.

"I got this buddy." He cumbersomely reached down and attempted to shake Woody's hand then patted him on his shoulder instead.

He said, "My name is George King. They call me Whitey. I own the junkyard in Westminster. King's Junk Yard."

Woody stammered, "I'm Dagwood Dooley... I'm called Woody. Oh... And thanks... Umm... For the coffee."

"Got a spare Mr. Woody?" Woody shook his head. "I figured." Whitey waved at two of his scrappers that had been waiting out by his truck and were now shuffling along toward him.

"You're the junkyard man. Something about you looked familiar. I could use a tire right about now." While he talked, he removed the lug nuts. He attempted to remove the wheel that had a slashed tire. Woody looked up at Whitey. "Yeah, I know the junkyard. I bought a rear view mirror from you once."

"Where did you grow up?" Whitey asked.

"When I was three months old my mother left me at an orphanage, The Buck House of Hope. Most people call it the Hope House"

"You're a Hoper?"

Woody nodded his head.

"You grew up at the orphanage?"

"Yep," Woody said trying to get the wheel off all the lugs. It finally popped off.

Both of Whitey's scrappers mumbled something to Whitey, then reach in the back of the tow truck. They pulled out a great looking full tread mounted tire. They began to jiggle the new tire's wheel onto the lugs. Woody backed away. "Thank you so much." The new tire was mounted and the lug nuts tightened in a jiff by Whitey's helpers who do this many times a day. They grabbed the old destroyed tire, still mounted on its wheel, and threw it up on the tow truck.

"Wow! Thanks... I can't believe you guys. I'm lost for words. How much?"

Whitey held his hand up and said, "I got this buddy."

"Thanks." Woody shook his head and stared at the tire.

Whitey smiled and said, "Glad to help. By the way, did you ever find out who your parents were?"

Woody nodded and said, "My mom's name was Wanda Dooley, but she's dead now. Why?"

Whitey stared at Woody with his marble blue eyes welling tears. "My friend... I do believe you're my brother."

CHAPTER 4 The Shopping Spree

Living in the junkyard for the past five years was very different than the two bedroom apartment Woody shared with Sandy in the city. Woody's one room apartment over the garage bay consisted of a room with a small sink, a one burner stove and a toilet that didn't flush very well. So Woody had to go down stairs to the garage office bathroom from time to time. He gave the place a fresh coat of paint and cleaned the cobwebs the best that he could. He had a comfortable bed that, because of his bum leg, was a struggle to climb out of. But he managed. He had a galvanized tub for taking a bath and a one burner stove with one pot to boil water. He remained grateful, though, for the courtesy his brother offered him when he was down and out. So as crude as his apartment sounded, it was a hell of a lot better than living on the street. When Sandy left she cleaned him out of their finances and valuables, but she did leave the storage shed full of furniture. His plan was to buy a house some day. So he was saving up for that rainy day... And hoping it would come soon. He was satisfied with what he had. He *really* appreciated the two large windows overlooking the entrance to the yard.

Woody was learning quite a bit about the history of his brother's junkyard. He found out it was started serendipitously. A friend of his gave him a car that didn't run very well and Whitey already had a car that sat useless on his property. This led to a neighbor down the road looking for a part that might be available from one of the two junk clunkers that just sat there. Friends and neighbors stopped by and unloaded a junk car, or what they thought was a junker, for a few bucks from Whitey. He'd then resell it at a profit. If it ran, he was lucky, or he'd strip anything he thought resalable out of it. It started to pay his bills.

The property that was now the junkyard was considered the very center of Westminster. It was once supposed to be a thirty-two acre race track one day. At least Reynolds, the owner, had planned to build one, but he ran out of money. George King bought Reynolds out for five hundred dollars in 1945. One of the cars that he was given at the sale was an old Rolls Royce. Whitey kept it for a while until someone made him an offer he couldn't refuse. And the rest was history.

Chilly December days had arrived. Although he had a heater in his apartment, Woody had to wear a coat even when he was inside. Cold drafts waft through on windy days. Even snow found its way in during blizzards. He strung a strand of lights across his double size windows giving the sense of Christmas.

He missed the smell of Christmas cookies and a fresh cut tree as he used to experience them at Christmas. He enjoyed covering the tree with tinsel and handmade decorations. He loved joining in the reindeer games with Sandy. They liked to slow dance to Silver Bells and White Christmas. He missed hanging mistletoe over the doorway and stealing a kiss from Sandy whenever he could. He would hide behind the door and call her. When she was in the doorframe under the mistletoe, he grabbed her for the requisite kiss. Now, five years had passed. He wondered if she was baking cookies today. He had an emptiness in the pit of his belly that wouldn't go away. She was always on his mind. Daydreams of Sandy played like a broken record over and over in his head. Singing Christmas carols and listening to music like Silent Night and We Three Kings went on almost every day after December first. But she was gone. His heart was left with the imprint of her smile that used to make his day come to light. That night, like many nights, he fell fast asleep before he had a chance to dream of what she may be doing. When he awoke the next morning down deep inside he wished he'd dreamed of her. He laid in bed for a few extra moments still thinking of her. He believed she must have found happiness by now.

The junkyard gave him some sense of peace. It was becoming more and more familiar. Even the smell of burning rubber was subtly becoming the norm. Woody and Whitey shared the newspaper and a cup of coffee every morning. Or sometimes they would run up to The Big Stop Diner for scrapple and eggs and the latest gossip. There, you could find out anything about anyone in Westminster. Although the two argued from time to time, mostly they enjoyed each other's company and worked well together opening up the junkyard at eight a.m. every morning.

Woody's start in life was so unfair. His father, George King Sr., had an affair with a woman named Wanda he met that worked at a local tire store. He used to drive her home once in a while. Their affair resulted in the birth of Dagwood Dooley.

Dagwood's mother kept him close for three months, long enough to feel hopelessly in love with this sweet boy. But her family wanted nothing to do with the illegitimate baby. Dagwood was an embarrassment. So Wanda's mother, Muriel, sent him to the orphanage, The Hope House. Wanda's father, Clyde, who was a distinguished banker during the great depression, was actually growing fond of the baby. However, Muriel did not want to embarrass the family that way. Her sister Ellen already was not talking to her.

Wanda was lost without her child and missed him terribly. A swirling sadness flooded her mind causing her to be on a downward spiral. The pain of loss was too much to bare. She begged her mother but Muriel was adamant about giving up the baby and that was that. Within six months Wanda became seriously ill. She died from an unknown ailment. The diagnosis was from natural causes, but some folks believe she died from a broken heart.

While living at the orphanage Woody contracted polio at the age of five. The disease left him with a bum leg. He could never play sports with one leg shorter than the other. But he was one of the survivors of polio that was able to walk fairly well. Other than a limp, he was strong as an ox, and quite handsome. His blonde hair the color of wheat and those blue eyes. He grew up with Gary Gleason, a friend at the orphanage, who was crippled from the disease. After graduating from the Hope House school with honors in 1933, he received a letter from Temple University inviting him to continue his studies there, apparently gratis. What he didn't know was that his grandparents had been paying the Hope House for his care all along and were now financing his education. Woody went on to get a Bachelor of Fine Arts degree. He was hoping to write his story someday, but his first job after graduation was at a local gas station where he stayed for ten years. He found working with cars was quite satisfying.

Woody living at the junkyard was great for Miriam's children. They seemed to enjoy Woody being around. It was like having your favorite goofy uncle living across the street from you. He told them jokes, taught them card tricks, how to whistle and draw a five-pointed star. He taught Bobby and Dee Dee to tie their shoes. The best was when he taught Dee Dee to ride her bike. That was a tough one. So many bruises and scraped knees!

Likewise, living there had many advantages for Woody. He didn't pay for rent or utilities. He was able to save some money for a few years. It was adding up. A whole fifteen thousand dollars that he kept locked in the glove compartment of an old junk car he named Plug. He used Plug for picking up supplies for Whitey. The car was kept next to the garage allowing Woody to keep a watchful eye on it.

What am I going to do with all that money? he thought. Since it was the week before Christmas he wanted to do something special for the kids at The Hope House. He took a thousand dollars and decided he was going to buy toys for the kids. Today he was taking Dee Dee and Bobby, Miriam's two youngest, shopping for toys. They were good at picking out all kinds of the latest toy trends. They knew all the great new toys; like dancing dolls, or a jack- in- the box, a great toy was a slinky. Even though they didn't have the luxury of owning any of them. When Whitey heard what they were doing he threw in an extra one hundred dollars and gave him the day off since he was only burning a few cars anyway. So off they went.

Woody remembered how his fellow roommates felt at the orphanage when some gifts from distant family members were received. They would send packages of things like toiletries and pajamas. It was downright sad. They all wanted toys. Wasn't that what Santa was supposed to bring from the North Pole?

After a long day of shopping at Woolworth's Five and Dime store, Woody and his two co-pilots picked up several pizzas from Gino's to bring home to their family, and also for The Hope House. This day was turning out great. He dropped off his two helpers, each getting a toy for their company and two large pizza pies for the rest of the family.

He drove over to the orphanage and walked in harboring a mixture of feelings, sadness and happiness. A familiar looking woman in her thirties held the door while he moved from his car to the kitchen with several loads of pizza pies. The cook was Bud, an unshaven and emotionless older guy that looked confused. He was not at all like the cook that Woody remembered, a sweet older woman named Betty that used to pat him on the shoulder and sometimes give him an extra dessert.

"I have some toys for the kids in my truck that I would like to bring in, okay?"

Bud the cook looked at Woody. He shrugged his shoulders and growled, "Go for it." Then he said, "Those pizza's smell pretty good! I haven't had pizza in ages."

Woody looked into Buds tired, squinty eyes and told him intently that the ten pizza pies were for the kids.

The woman that held the door for him was Jane, an old friend of Sandy's. He recognized her shapely legs.

She wasn't sure if it was Woody. "Is that you Mr. Blue Eyes?" Woody was dressed dapper in his new blue jeans and flannel red and grey shirt. The whiskers were gone and he sported a fresh new haircut.

Woody thought she looked familiar, but he didn't remember how he knew her. He continued bringing in packages through the kitchen side door while Jane held the door open with her foot. "Brrr, it's cold out here. Wow! You sure went all out," looking at the lined up boxes on the long counter. "Are those pizza's for everybody?"

"Well, they're for the kids. Whatever's left... Sure... For anyone. How are you Jane? Now, I remember you."

Jane smiled and said, "Just fine. You?"

He recognized it was Jane with a funny last name, the woman that Sandy always found time to go out with instead of staying home with him. Woody had questions for Jane but he still had at least a dozen more packages to bring in. One of the toys that must have been a jack-in-the-box made its *Pop Goes the Weasel* sound and scared the dickens out of Woody.

Jane looked at Woody gathering items from the truck. She felt a bit guilty. She shared a profound secret with Sandy, Woody's estranged wife, that she had promised never to divulge. She was here to visit David, Sandy's son, who had been taken from her after the accident and she knew that David was actually Woody's son. She knew she'd have to keep her guard up against any slip-ups while talking to Woody tonight. She realized why she hadn't recognized him. He actually was looking better than she remembered him. He lost his pot belly and those blue eyes sure drew you in. He was looking quite handsome.

Jane asked, "Are you living in Westminster?"

Woody replied, "Ah... Yeah."

An older, well dressed woman came to the door and held it for Jane. She looked at Jane and said, "Jane, Little David is waiting for your visit, and where is his mother today?"

Jane stared at Mrs. Lee without answering. Under her breadth she said, "Sick."

She turned to leave. "Good bye Woody. Nice seeing you. I'll see you again someday."

Woody was intrigued by the things Mrs. Lee had said to Jane, and by Jane's reply. Who was the mother? Why was Jane visiting a child here at The Hope House named David?

"Thank you so much Mr. Dagwood. The kids are going to be over the moon with joy. This is the first pizza some of these lonely children have ever had," Mrs. Lee said. "We haven't put up a Christmas tree yet. You're staying to see it and enjoy the pizza aren't you?" she asked courteously.

"Sure, but I have to run home first. Thanks. I'll be back pretty soon." Woody waved and left in a hurry. As he left he looked over at the clock in the cafeteria and skedaddled.

CHAPTER 5 David Dooley

Sandy had lived in a two bedroom apartment in Philadelphia with her boyfriend Ernesto for about a year, but when she had a blue eyed baby boy eight months into the relationship, Ernesto started shopping around for another girlfriend. By the time the baby, who she named David, had his first birthday Ernesto had flown the coop. He always suspected that David wasn't his. Finally, Sandy let it slip.

Sandy went back to work. She found a job as a waitress at Howard Johnson's. For a couple years Jane, her best friend in the world, watched David while she worked. Her hours were late and Jane couldn't watch David every day anymore. So Sandy asked her sister Amy to help out. She did, but unfortunately, Amy also came with a drinking problem which Sandy soon adopted. She began a drunken life living in filth and going out on late night binges. She soon lost her job. Alcohol had taken its hold on her. David was suffering the consequences.

Sandy joined her sister in daily partying. They both gradually became seriously addicted to the clutches of alcohol. Their bingeing showed in poor David's behavior. Always hungry... always lonely... All he knew was Mommy slept a lot and Aunt Amy screamed at Mommy and left.

One day Jane stopped by for a visit to see Sandy. She knocked hard and heard Sandy mumble, "Come in." It was eleven a.m. When Jane opened the door she saw Sandy was lying on a sofa, semi-passed out. An empty booze bottle, alongside a coffee can of dirty sand, filled to the top with ashes. Cigarette butts littered the floor. Clothes were strewn on the furniture and floor. There was a smoky stench that was the first impression she had. A record player was spinning around without a record.

"Where is David?"

Sandy pointed to his bedroom.

Jane called "Hey, David." She heard a soft cry. She slowly opened his bedroom door.

Putrid smells pervaded the room. As she walked in her heart sank. Sitting on the floor next to his bed, there he was, dirty face swollen and almost unrecognizable from crying. The four year old was covered in filth. His makeshift diaper was a filthy pillowcase smeared with diarrhea. His curdled milk cup added to the stench that permeated the room. Jane lifted the child into her arms, not paying attention to the dripping streams of putrid matter falling from him. David cried with desperation.

"You poor, poor boy. Aunt Jane's here. I'll help you sweetie."

Sandy slowly stumbled into David's room and acted surprised. "Hey, baby."

"Mommy wouldn't help me." David cried.

"What the hell... Oh my God! I'm here sweetie." David was in Jane's arms. His bed was covered with shit. "What in the world? Where are his diapers?" Jane snapped.

Sandy scratched her head looking around aimlessly. "I don't have any clean." She pointed to a huge pile of stinky laundry.

Jane said, "Are you kidding me? Why is he still in diapers, anyway? He's almost five."

"He won't go in the toilet," Sandy said and started bawling.

The child began screaming for his mother, "Mommy, I was calling you. Why didn't you hear me?" Sandy put her head down and shook it.

Jane held him close. "There... There..." She slowly laid David on the floor and carefully removed the pillowcase, wadding it into a ball. She found a paper bag sitting in the middle of the room and disposed of the mess. She couldn't find anything to clean him with so she carried his naked little body to the bathroom and placed him into the tub and ran warm water. She found some shampoo sitting on the floor next to the tub. The warm soapy water must have felt so wonderful. He stopped crying and finally relaxed, enjoying the feeling of care.

Sandy handed Jane a towel and cried softly. "I love him so much. He's my life you know Jane."

"This is not a life... Look at your son. Now get yourself together and we're going to feed this child right now."

"I don't have anything. Just old milk in the fridge. I'm outta everything..."

"You seem to have enough booze," Jane said sarcastically.

"Oh wait... I have peanut butter and a few crackers."

"Good. Anything. Just take care of him. Now!"

Jane dressed David without a diaper in a pair of pajama bottoms and a top that was very snug but was the only clean shirt she found. "There. Doesn't that feel better? Give Jane a kiss, I missed you."

David got up from the floor, kissed Jane and cried, "Don't go Aunty."

Jane hugged him. "I promise I'll be back buddy. I'm not leaving yet."

They walked into the kitchen. It was in total disrepair and filthy. Dirty dishes filled the sink. Food that had to have been fermenting and turning rancid sat on the stove. The refrigerator was empty. There was no place to sit at the table. It was covered with empty beer bottles, whiskey bottles and a half gallon of milk that had turned.

Sandy put two crackers on a plate with peanut butter and David ate them in a jiff. He morphed into a totally different child, happy and smiling. It wasn't much but he appeared content.

Jane moved all the booze bottles off the table into an empty milk box that was on the floor. One of the bottles wasn't quite empty. She hid it under the sink. The cabinet door wouldn't close properly; one hinge was hanging loose.

She used baking soda to remove the filth from old hard crusted dirty dishes and glasses. There wasn't any dish soap. She left the soaking pots and pans on the stove. David sat with his mother while he ate two more crackers with peanut butter and a glass of water.

"What are you doing here?" Jane asked full of curiosity and anger.

"Nothing, really! I don't have a job right now. It's not always like this. I'm in a lot of pain. You know? I just had a bad night. I can't get relief from my headaches. So my dad helped me out last week. He gave me rent money..."

Jane interrupted "I'm talking about David."

"Jane... I know, I know, it isn't like this normally. I've had a lot on my mind. My dad isn't doing too well himself. He has a bad heart, and arthritis real bad you know. He hasn't been working. I don't know what I'm going to do if I don't find a job. I tried to go back to Bob's."

"You're talking in circles. What about this child? Look... David needs you right now. More than ever. I'll go get a few things at the store and I'll wash your clothes, but the rest is up to you. Okay? I love you guys but I don't ever want to see anything like this again. Understand?"

"I love you too," Sandy responded looking at David.

"I wuv you Aunty. Mommy's sick." He looked up at his mother. Sandy hugged David and started to cry.

Jane looked at the coffee cans half filled with sand and full of stinky buts. Some on the floor. Ashes everywhere.

"I'll clean up," Sandy said.

"I thought you stopped smoking," Jane responded.

Sandy shook her head. "I stopped for a while. I know... I know..." Sandy walked over to the sink and searched through all the bottles.

"Where is my bourbon?" Sandy looked square in Jane's eyes. Jane looked down. "Where is it?" Jane pointed to where she had put it. Sandy noticed the cabinet door hanging open.

Jane shook her head in disgust while walking toward the door. "Well, I got to go! I'll pick up something for you guys to eat and some cleaning stuff. I'll be back."

Sandy stood at the sink and didn't turn around to say goodbye to Jane. Without looking she turned her hand backwards and waved good-bye.

David ran to the door. "Aunty, don't go." Jane hugged David and handed him a lifesaver candy. He was thrilled.

Jane returned around seven p.m. and knocked on Sandy's door. She thought she heard something but wasn't sure. When she looked for Sandy's car it wasn't there. Without a key she couldn't leave any food that was perishable, so she left a bag of dry beans and rice, Rice Crispies, powdered milk, canned fruit, a can of pineapple juice and a tasty cake. She also left a box of detergent on Sandy's front porch. Maybe she was at a restaurant, or visiting her dad with David. Or maybe she was out drinking... She thought, *Jane, why do you always fear the worst?*

CHAPTER 6 The Accident

Sandy suddenly heard a loud scrape and a bang. "Oh my God!" She found herself laying in an awkward position in her car. "What just happened?" She crawled toward the passenger door but her leg was stuck. She was in an accident! She wasn't in too much pain, just a serious headache. Blood was dripping into her eyes. She was mumbling, "David." She lay there scared and confused until an emergency unit arrived and pulled her out. She tried to get off the stretcher but her leg was in pain and bleeding. A police officer stopped her. He saw her car was totaled and noticed several broken bottles of bourbon on the floor of her car and she reeked of alcohol. It was simple. She was drunk and slammed into a utility pole.

Blood covered her face and her shirt was torn. She was going to the hospital whether she wanted to or not. "I just want to go home."

The police officer said, "This does not look good young lady. We'll get you checked out at the hospital first."

Suddenly she passed out.

As she awoke she realized she was in a hospital room and with an IV in her arm. "Oh no."

"Hello there missy. You are at North Philadelphia General Hospital. You were in a car accident. My name is Kathryn and I am your nurse for this evening. I need to take your blood pressure. They said your leg is not broken. I heard you had to be pulled out of the car. Your car was totaled so you're lucky. You have a few stitches and a sprained knee. So, you'll probably be on crutches. But no break. That's one injury you don't have to worry about. Your injuries could have been so much worse." The nurse continued to take Sandy's blood pressure.

"Wait... Wait... I can't stay here! I've got to go! My son... He's only four years old and he's at home. My sister Amy used to live with us but moved back with my dad last week."

"Well who is taking care of him?"

"No one. He's alone."

"Well, you've been here since seven p.m. and it's now midnight. That's five hours. Where's his father?"

"No father."

The nurse called Lucille, her supervisor, who made arrangements to pick up the boy at the apartment and take him to a temporary safe haven.

A little while later Kathryn came rushing into Sandy's room. "I just received word that your son is okay. He was taken temporarily to the Hope House. He'll be fine."

"Can I call him?"

"It's two a.m. girl! He's probably sound asleep. You know Sandy, you can't just leave a four year old alone for any length of time like that. That poor boy. The authorities found three bottles of booze in your car. You really messed up! You had a slew of tests and I believe they don't need any more tonight. So, get some rest."

At eight a.m. on the dot Dr. Harvey Livingston walked into Sandy's room with his clip board. He reached out his hand to shake Sandy's but she was barely awake. "Hello young lady. I was assigned your case. I just reviewed your head injury test results. I would like to go over them with you. I have some important information. Are you awake?"

Sandy nodded her head and yawned. "Sorry, I just need to get out of here... Now!"

"You have some minor injuries to your head from the accident, giving you a shiner. They stitched you up pretty good. Nothing to worry about there, however, we made a discovery while looking at your X-ray. You have a large amount of cancer covering the meninges of your brain. You have a serious looking tumor that could be terminal."

Sandy sat up. She moved her IV out of the way. "Well that sounds scary. Does that mean I'm going to die?"

"We don't know very much about this type of tumor. But, we do know it is terminal."

"So... That's a yes?" Sandy asked with concern.

"Yes. You may have a seizure from time to time. We prescribe medicine to help prevent them. We aren't able to predict anything for sure. Call our office if you have any questions. I can give you a prescription for medicines for headaches. Here is my contact information." He reached in his pocket and handed her a card.

"Can you operate? Can you take it out?"

"Unfortunately we can't operate, due to the location. But we will keep a close watch and keep you alerted of any spread."

"I think I had a seizure last month doctor. My headaches have been ruining my life for the past year. How long do I have? I have a four year old."

"It's hard to tell. But by the looks of the manifestation that we see on your tests you are lucky that you don't have more symptoms. You're lucky to be alive."

"Lucky?" She looked away.

"Look, you may live five years with this... Or more. My office will contact you when you can be released from the hospital."

She started a soft cry staring at the card. "Five?"

He turned and stared at her with concern.

"...Or more." He patted her on her shoulder. "I've got to go. It was nice meeting you. Sorry it was under these circumstances." Suddenly, before she could ask him anything else... He was gone. He left as quickly as he came in.

"What?" Sandy was sitting up when a young girl from the cafeteria came rushing in and slid a breakfast tray on her bed table.

"Coming through." A young female and male nurse technician came whizzing into the room at the same time with a stretcher.

"You can't have that." The male technician snapped. Sandy, still crying, shook her head and snapped back, "I don't want it anyway. Where am I going?"

"Tests."

Not long after the accident Sandy sobered up and seemed to be doing well. Her daily regimen of several pills twice a day became monotonous. She now realized that recovering from some painful injuries, like her cuts and sprained knee, kept her from going anywhere. She didn't have a car anyway. She often thought of Woody, and about calling him, but every time she picked up the phone she stopped short. *Who am I fooling?* It was becoming clear to her that she blew it. She caused Woody enough pain in his life... And what about David?

Sandy wondered if Dad was going to have a stroke when he found out she left David alone while she was out buying booze and was in a car accident. She stopped herself from calling him.

Amy, Sandy's sister, was the lost child that couldn't quite keep up with her sister. Amy was suddenly into Amy. No one could shake sense into her. She was selfish and bitter that Sandy was dad's favorite. She never got over it. She was mad at Sandy for some mundane reason and hadn't contacted her after the accident.

Sandy's father, Harry Schwartz, a potbellied, bearded, hard working pipe fitter, had worked at Standard Pressed Steel Company for twenty five long years. The company was doing a booming business, causing Harry to work more hours of overtime than his body could handle. He suffered from angina, high blood pressure, severe arthritis and very high cholesterol. Consequently he hadn't spent much time with his daughter and grandchild, who only lived two blocks away. He was spending his spare days at the doctor's office.

Harry's wife Cheryl died at the age of forty two from a heart attack leaving sixteen year old Sandy and fifteen year old Amy to pretty much fend for themselves. Because of their father's long hours they were alone and Amy often played hooky and hadn't attended much school. She and her boyfriend Gregory eloped to Georgia when she turned sixteen where they were married. Harry had no control of his daughters. Sandy was usually sensible and determined and could be trusted. Unfortunately, Harry was always tired and couldn't seem to keep track of either girl. Amy's marriage didn't last two years. She was homesick and at eighteen she moved back home.

The same year Sandy graduated high school she signed up for some classes at Temple University. During that period of her education she moved to an apartment closer to school. She found a job and was able to pay for her classes, without the help of her father. Harry often told her how proud he was of her. She was ambitious and ready to take on the world.

One night when Sandy was leaving work at Bob's Bar 'n' Grill her car wouldn't start. She ambitiously lifted the hood.

Woody was leaving Bob's with his to-go order when he saw Sandy under the hood of her car. She looked like she knew what she was doing. He peaked out his opened window and asked, "You okay?"

She said, "Oh hi. I am trying to get the butterfly on the carburetor open." This was something her dad had shown her once. But her car wouldn't quite turn over and it was now making sounds that the battery was winding down. She began talking loud. "Start you pile of metal!"

Her cute curly pony tail and great legs stopped Woody in his tracks. Woody parked his old truck next to her car and asked her if she needed a jump.

Giggling she said, "No, but my car does."

That was the beginning of a long deliriously happy relationship. That night she called him her cute knight in shining armor. She called him cute. That was a back handed compliment in his world. Cute meant small to him. He was six foot on good days, but his squared, John Wayne chiseled face and robin's egg blue eyes got him just enough compliments to keep him humble. Sandy noticed his limp, but she was mesmerized by those eyes and never again were any flaws a second thought.

Sandy and Woody were married after a brief courtship. Her dad was thrilled with an educated well mannered man like Woody. They used to talk for hours just about anything and everything.

Woody moved into Sandy's apartment and out of his old modest apartment across the street from Pop's Garage where he worked. Even though the drive to his work at Pop's was only five miles away, that was five miles further than he was accustom to... But it was worth it to be with Sandy.

They were so compatible that neither could stand being apart from the other for too many hours. Sandy was proud that Woody had graduated from Temple. She encouraged him to take some additional classes. After all, she thought, a degree in Liberal Arts was not going to take him anywhere. Literature was more like a hobby that he had in common with one of his counselors at school. The two used to meet up at older cemeteries and put together stories of the dead. They actually went all the way to Baltimore and found Poe's grave. Woody arrived back satisfied with his discovery but missing his wife.

Woody had broken down at a traffic light one day. He was lucky enough to be right across the street from a auto repair shop. He approached it and asked for help, and the guys from the garage and he were able to push his old clunker across the street and into the garage. Eventually, it turned out to be a simple timing problem. As part of the experience he met the owner. They became close friends.

The owner, who they call Pop, gave him a job. That was how he started his job at Pop's Gas Station and Auto Repair Shop. Woody was happy working there. He was learning everything there was to know about the engine of an automobile. And he was proud to work as a mechanic, an essential, much needed career that was often overlooked. That was what Sandy loved about him. He was humble. No frills or phoniness. He knew what he wanted to do in life.

Sandy on the other hand was beginning to get restless. Sandy continued her studies at Temple, kept her job at Bob's and Woody kept his job as the gas station resident mechanic. Everything in his life seemed perfect. But Sandy felt something was missing in her life. She wanted a baby for most of their sixteen years of marriage. Every time she went to the doctor and he said "I'm sorry you're not pregnant" became another chip in the rock of their marriage.

Sandy finally strayed, which left Woody at Big Stop Diner with a broken heart.

CHAPTER 7 The Will

There were only two people left in Sandy's life that cared about her well being now: her father and Jane, her very best friend. She now had to accept that she had no husband, no son, no booze, no transportation...This was what her life had been whittled down too.

Sandy's father wasn't told about her accident. He happened to read about it in the paper. He was floored! When he drove over to her nearby apartment he expected to see his grandson. Instead he arrived just as Child Protection left. Sandy just officially lost custody of David. The child that was the one thing that filled that empty spot was now gone.

Sandy was allowed to visit David once a week. According to the nice social worker, Bella, if she stayed clean for one year they would help her get David back. Her question was, did she have one year?

Harry, Sandy's father, couldn't believe Sandy had a drinking problem. He had no idea. He never saw the signs. He remembered her being a bit messy once or twice when he visited but there wasn't anything that jumped out at him. He felt guilty that he was blind to it all. She had always been such a loving mother and good person. How could she leave David alone while she went to the store? This stifled his mind... And just to buy booze was the kicker.

When he saw Sandy he told her he would do his best to help her get David back. He handed Sandy an envelope with money in it. She was very grateful. When she kissed her father they both sobbed.

"I'll be here in a snap the next time you need help sweetie. Just keep in touch." Before Harry left that day Sandy was planning on telling him about her cancer diagnosis, until she looked at his drawn, prematurely wrinkled face. Then she chose not to. He was one of the only boots on the ground solid elements left in her life. He'd do anything in the world for her. And she felt it. Just seeing him made her smile. He was the one person that loved her unconditionally and gave her the ambition to hang on.

Now that she had sobered up and was beginning to heal from her accident injuries she thought about getting in touch with Woody, but her shame was too great. And her seizures were increasing. He was once her rock, but pride ran her emotions now. How could she have told him she was pregnant when she left. She really screwed up her life... And his. Sandy knew how much he wanted a child. She didn't want to ruin his life anymore. She thought about what happened to him when he was young. And the irony! His son was in that same sad place. *I hope you can forgive me someday David.*

Sandy asked her close friend Jane to promise to keep the secret from him about her troubled life, but especially about David. Sandy toyed with the idea of telling Jane about her cancer diagnosis and worse, her prognosis. She feared it would be burdening her and she didn't want anything to come between her and her best friend.

Time was passing. She wondered how long she had. Would she survive a year? Would she ever be able to get David back? And this newly prescribed medicine which made her feel lethargic, would that interfere with getting custody of David?

Bella the Social Worker visited once a week. Her lively sessions with Sandy were welcome. It was like going to a pep rally rather than getting advice. They would both laugh and cry and the volume by the end was a blast, loud and full of belly laughs. Bella sometimes even told jokes. The whole hour was positive. Sandy actually looked forward to her counseling.

Jane was a kind soul who lived a monastic life. At first appearance she was striking with long bouncy, naturally highlighted hair. Her figure was of the type that women might say was a little overweight but men say was just right. What appealed to everyone was her personality. She would rather stay at home than be in a large crowd. Her kindness to anyone that was down and out was her best feature. She and Sandy were friends since High School. They loved the same music, had the same curious, exploring nature, and chased some of the same good looking boys. She worked hard but loved the simple life. Jane never married although she came close, but the man she loved cheated on her one too many times. She just told him to leave after several years of his playing around. After that, she never found a man that could make her happy.

Jane procured a job from a distant relative as caretaker of Grandview Cemetery in the middle of nowhere. It provided her with a small bungalow to live in and a measly salary. Only one other adult was permitted to reside there. No children were allowed. This wasn't much of a career for someone who had graduated from Penn State University, with a degree in Human Services. She believed that some day she would pursue her career, but for now, she was happy to live the simple life.

The day Jane moved into her pleasant new home she phoned Sandy remembering it was David's birthday. Her excitement was hard to contain, but it was stopped short. She said "Hello..." and then she heard a wailing cry that was extremely loud and so hard to understand. Not a word could be deciphered. The words were jumbled starting from the first sentence. Jane couldn't understand what she was talking about.

Jane said, "Sandy, slow down sweetie."

Sandy must have said, "Oh my God!" five times. Her words were all jumbled from her crying. Finally Jane heard, "My father died."

Sandy tried but couldn't stop crying on the phone. She finally became more intelligible. She said her father had died and she was trying to figure out Jane's phone number so she could call her to go to David's birthday celebration. She said she didn't have her new phone number and was afraid Jane might forget.

Jane said , "First, I want to offer my deepest sympathy. I am so sorry for the loss of your wonderful father. He was a good man. He treated me like family and I will miss him every day. I will be at your house in one hour. Got that?"

Sandy said, "Okay, but listen to this," She sniffled and told Jane that like the prodigal son, Amy was the prodigal daughter. He was leaving the house and the bulk of the money to her. Sandy's heaving sobs stopped.

She said, "Not only do I have to tell David that his grandfather died, someone he had loved and looked up to and thought could do no wrong, he left him a measly thousand dollars. And me... Not really anything. I can't believe it. Amy will go right through that money. He left me two thousand dollars and whatever the cost to have him cremated was going to be. That was it! He died Sunday and it's only Friday and she has the house on the market already. My dad would be rolling in his grave if he found out. I know he didn't want us to be burdened with an expensive funeral. But come on! His dying wishes were that Amy, who had made many bad choices in life, somehow benefits from that? What made him do that?"

Jane, sobbing uncontrollably, managed to say, "Sandy. I am so, so sorry. I can't imagine how you feel. I know he really loved you, Sandy. Maybe he felt that you'd do well in life, and she'll struggle more."

Sandy cried, "He just gave, gave, gave to Amy. Large sums of money that she borrowed from him. And then he rewards her with a large inheritance stipulating that any loans will be forgiven. I'm left with nothing. His first born. I am so upset over his dying and me feeling left out. I should be allowed to just grieve his death. David and I didn't matter to him." She started bawling

Jane said, "Look, just stay put. I'll be right there. Go cry as hard as you want. You're going to move in with me at the cemetery. "See you soon"

They both hung up.

Sandy shook her head. "The cemetery, huh? How appropriate."

An hour later Jane knocked on the door but there was no answer. She just spoke with Sandy and she knew Jane was coming over. Jane knocked louder, there was no response. She noticed the door was unlocked so she walked in to the foyer. She heard a loud banging sound coming from Sandy's bedroom.

"Oh my God! What's wrong?" She hurried into the bedroom and found Sandy lying half way on the floor and leaning on the wall. She was banging her whole body over and over. Foam was streaming out of her mouth.

"Oh no!" she said. "You're having a seizure!" Her arms were flailing and hitting the wall. "I'm here Sandy! Jane's here. I'll help you... What do I do? Your mouth! I have to put something in your mouth... I think. Oh my God! Please help me God?"

Sandy's was next to her bed on a rug, lying back against the wall. Her eyes had rolled back into her head. Jane held her arm so it couldn't bang the wall anymore and didn't break. She sat next to her on the floor. She propped Sandy's tense body across her lap with all her strength and reached up behind her and grabbed a pillow to put behind Sandy's head. Sandy's thrusting was powerful to Jane. She was heavy, though her weight was only a hundred and twenty pounds soaking wet. The convulsing was continuous and frightening. "There... There... There you go."

Drips of foam were hanging from Sandy's mouth. Her eyes were back to normal. She was now looking around.

As Sandy came around out of the seizure she smiled at Jane. In slurred words she said, "I knew it was coming this time. I actually felt it."

Jane looked confused. Sandy was now brave enough to divulge the truth about her brain cancer. She was getting tired of her fake stories to Jane. "I have cancer of the brain," Sandy said. "I know you think I've been avoiding you. It's just that I'm having a hard time accepting the truth myself." They hugged. Sandy's tragedies were consuming and hard to grip. After relaxing on the floor and regaining her strength, Sandy asked for a cup of tea. Jane carefully lifted her up, first onto the bed, then to her feet. She held Sandy and guided her into kitchen.

The death of Sandy's father had to be overwhelming and to have a terminal illness was hard to bare. Jane had never been exposed to a seizure before. It was frightening and she didn't want Sandy to leave the house today to go see David. What if she had another one?

Sandy told Jane she was slowly losing her speech, her coordination and the ability to think straight. Just today she said she had put a can of soup in the freezer. And she didn't know why.

"My seizures come on pretty quickly, but there is an aura that I feel right before the event. They don't last too long but... When the seizure is over, I feel so sick. I'm nauseous, cramps all over my body and totally clueless of where I am for a few minutes. My Aunt Martha had helped me out quite a bit. She picked up my prescriptions and brings over care packages with baked goods included. I love her shortbread cookies. She's the best. But she's in her eighties and hates to drive."

Jane was concerned about Sandy's seizures and asked, "Will they gradually go away?"

Sandy replied, "No. There is no cure Jane. I am dying. It's a meningioma blastoma of the brain. I was told there is nothing they could do for me. Maybe I have a month to live; if I'm lucky a year. I was told my brain looked like a basket weave of cancer intertwining my meninges. I'm doomed! I feel so devastated. All I can think of is my poor David."

"This conversation requires a cup of tea. We've been sitting here gabbing." Sandy smiled.

Jane said, "I have an hour." She stepped over to the stove and filled the tea pot with water. She reached up in Sandy's cabinet and found two red rose tea cups, she thought, *perfect*. She inspected them. She dropped in the tea bags and walked balancing both cups very carefully over to the table and said, "Tea for two. We can fix anything with a cup of tea. Especially in these two Alice in Wonderland cups. They're beautiful."

Sandy said softly, "Oh, they were my mom's. They go with a whole set my father had until..." Sandy sniffles, "Jane, the only things I have of my fathers are his ashes and a rabbits foot. Do you believe that? Amy's words were, 'I don't know what to do with them'. I wanted to scream at her. I don't think she ever found out I was dying, because then she said to me, 'You look like you're all better from your accident. I thought of you. I thought you might want dad's ashes. You would know what to do with them. You two were so close'."

"I said to her, 'Oh, thank you'. Like a fool, I just stood there and stared at her!"

She continued, "I'll keep them with me. Maybe she did that because I have Mom's ashes. Anyway, she gave me a key chain that Dad kept with a rabbit's foot on it. She removed the house and car keys. I guess she had his car. I *thanked* her, Jane! I swear she patted herself on the back. My Aunt Martha was there. She looked dumbfounded. She drove me over to the lawyers office while the will was being probated.

"The attorney's wife who's in real estate followed us to dad's house. She immediately pounded a sign into the ground with a hammer in front of his house. Then we went inside. I told Aunt Martha about my cancer. She already knew, she said, when she saw the medicine she was picking up for me. She is so sweet. She held my hand, like I was a little girl.

"We went in the house to see what Amy wanted to part with, if anything. Aunt Martha was as astonished as I was. I think Aunt Martha would have liked maybe some childhood pictures and their mother's china. She already had six of the tea set. These are the other two, and my dad implied many times he would leave that set to her. Amy said, 'I'm selling everything and moving.' Nothing else was said about it. She hadn't given Aunt Martha anything. Aunt Martha kissed Amy and said take care of yourself dear. Amy started talking about Amy, who else? She mentioned she was going to go to the Bahamas or Cancun. Amy is lucky; Aunt Martha just listened. I could feel she was fuming though, her demeanor had changed. But she stayed cool. Her only comment was, 'I only wish you would have told me my brother was sick'. Amy acted surprised. She said she had no idea he was sick. I felt sorry for Aunt Martha. For God's sake Amy lived with him. No idea?"

She looked up toward the ceiling. "Daddy... Look what's happening. She's selling everything, and I'm dying."

Jane walked over and hugged Sandy again and said, "Both your mom and dad are watching over you. They are going to make sure everything works out. You'll see."

Jane walked back over to her chair and held onto it tightly. She was not wanting to sit down. She stared at Sandy with deep sadness. Tears began welling in her eyes.

Sandy said, "I ache so, so bad right now. Oh my God! What do I do? I want to see David."

Jane said with concern, "I will tell him you are sick. He'll understand, he's five years old today."

Sandy held her mouth and shook her head. "Oh my God, your right he is."

"You're so pale, and weak you should stay home today. You had a rough seizure just now. What if you have another seizure?" With a bit more coaching Sandy agreed.

Jane looked at her watch and said, "Look at the time! I have to leave pretty quick. David will be expecting someone on his birthday."

Jane, still standing, took one more sip of tea and looked around the kitchen. Sandy remained sitting in the kitchen. She pointed toward the wrapped gift on the counter. Jane snatched it up and walked back over to Sandy. She patted her on the shoulder.

"I'll go now." Sandy nodded.

"Tell him Mommy loves him."

Jane asked Sandy if she wanted to go back into the bedroom. She shook her head. She pointed to the ice box."Don't forget the cake is in there." Jane gathered the cake and gift and took a giant deep breath. She kissed Sandy and left. After closing the door Jane could hear Sandy crying out loud, "David, I'm so sorry."

David was now five years old and potty trained. He felt so proud. He couldn't wait to tell his mom. He was a big boy now. He was in the recreation room waiting to join his mother and Jane for his birthday dinner. Twenty eight mixed aged children were lined up at the cafeteria waiting for a taste of something that was either a distant memory or something they had never experienced before. David did not remember the taste of pizza. But he did remember the promise from his mom that he would have pizza on his birthday. Today was the day!

CHAPTER 8 Plug

It was four thirty in the afternoon. A plume of black smoke was billowing over the junkyard. Woody pulled up to the entrance. It only took one pungent whiff; it was enough to cause him to hold his mouth. He realized Whitey had been busy clearing out junkers, probably along with some vermin. That happened once every couple of months. The last time there was a fire that large was when the local Westminster Fire Department practiced with volunteers and new employees, 'how to become a firefighter'. They had tons of people gathered around watching the huge fire and learning how to put fires out, safety measures, how to rescue someone in a fire, and measuring the time it took to put certain materials out. They loved the junkyard. The local police came to make sure some of the lookers were behaving themselves.

Although Woody normally closed the junkyard at five on the dot, and he was supposed to have had the day off, he decided out of the kindness of his heart to stop by and help his brother out. Closing wasn't the problem. But locking the yard too early when someone was left inside, milling about or trying to take a part off of one of the cars, was huge. Especially when Whitey wanted the devil dogs loose. He still had thirty minutes to waste.

A memory crossed his mind. One summer day when a young regular Whitey knew told him his Ford was turning over but wasn't firing ,Whitey said, "It may be your fuel pump." He told him there was an old Ford in the back corner of the yard and if he could remove the pump on his own before five o'clock he could have it free. But he had to use his own tools. Whitey's son Georgie closed at five on the dot. The kid apparently lost track of time and was having difficulty removing the mounting bolts from the pump because they were rusted. Georgie locked the yard five minutes early. He looked around and didn't see anyone milling about so he released the dogs. The kid could not find an escape route when he saw Zeus. He jumped into the Ford and fell fast asleep. The next day the dogs were sitting next to the car the kid was sleeping in. Whitey found him and he full on belly laughed. He helped the kid remove the fuel pump and drove him to his house.

Woody drove down the driveway and pulled up to the garage. Something was amiss. Smoke was like a cloud surrounding the yard. The rusty old sedan, Plug, that was normally parked next to the garage, wasn't there. Woody looked around but couldn't find the car that was being utilized as his bank. Where in the world was Plug? No one was around anywhere.

Suddenly, Bobby and Dee Dee came running out of their house. "Woody! Woody! Thanks for the pizza pies and my Sharp Shooter." Bobby shouted.

"Thanks for my dancing doll, Bonny." Dee Dee sang loud enough for Woody to hear. She danced with her Bonny doll over to Woody.

"Where is Plug?" Woody asked with concern.

Bobby responded, "Pop took it to the burn pile today. I think."

"What? Where is pop?"

Miriam called the kids to come back to the house and finish their chores.

"Okay Mom," Bobby answered. The two kids left throwing a kiss to Woody.

"Wait!" Woody yelled. The kids didn't hear him but Miriam did.

"What's up Woody?" Miriam asked.

"Oh nothing. I'm looking for that old sedan Whitey let me drive for parts."

"Oh, that thing. I think he burned it today. He's been burning all day. He told me the transmission was gone in it. It was a real junker, Woody. Why?"

"I left some personal belongings in it. Damn!"

"Well, you know George. He probably took everything out that had any value before he put it in the burn pile. I'm pretty sure."

"Yeah, you're probably right. But I have the key to the glove box. Okay, thanks. See ya Mir. I've got to go see where Whitey is right about now."

Miriam waved at Woody, "Well, you just missed him. He was called by *The Witch* to go eat."

"Oh, okay. Thanks."

Woody ran with a strong limp in the opposite direction of his brother's house. He hobbled toward the burning heap of cars. It was now getting dark and although a small flame was still burning underneath a couple of cars, he couldn't see much but a pile of dark steel shadows. Georgie came out of nowhere. His face was blackened covered with silt and his clothes were filthy.

"Hi Woody! He gave me the worst job on earth today! But I'm enlisting soon."

Woody was surprised. He said, "Enlisting?"

"Yeah! In the Navy."

"Georgie, you gotta help me... Where is Plug? You know, the car your pop lets me drive around town in."

"I don't know. I'm freezing out here." He threw a bucket of water on the flame. "I have to wait until all the flames are out before I can get outta here. It could be in that pile of metal over there," pointing to the smoldering pile of burnt cars. Woody looked around but it was now too dark to see much of anything. "There... It's out... Isn't it? I don't remember seeing it Woody. I think most of the fire is out, don't you?" The flames had all died down and Georgie turned and headed back to his house. "See ya."

Woody shook his head. "Bye." He limped with a deliberately slow pace down the driveway.

Miriam sent Billy over to Whiteys' house to inquire on Woody's behalf. Woody had just about given up when Billy found Woody limping around in the dark.

"Woody, I found out that the car was sold today to a kid we call Chicky. I don't know his last name. But he's got to come back to get the title transferred tomorrow. Pop said he couldn't get the glove box opened. He didn't have the key to the glove box."

Woody smiled. "Okay there Billy boy, you did good. Thanks." Woody took a deep breath and said, "I guess I'll close the place."

Billy said he would lock up so Woody could take off. Woody decided to drive back to the Hope House for dinner. A sigh of relief came over him. He hopped in his truck remembering that Jane was visiting one of the children that lived at the Hope House. 'Why?' was the question he was going to find out today.

He left with a weight off his shoulders but still a bit nervous thinking how stupid he was to keep his money in the glove box. As he turned onto the main highway he noticed a familiar sight. There it was on the side of Old York Rd. It was Plug. It hadn't gotten very far. He pulled up right behind the car. The kid must have had to walk home, wherever that is. Plug finally broke down. "Well... Well... Well," he chuckled.

No one was in the car, so Woody opened the unlocked door. He attempted to open the glove box but it was locked, just the way he left it. With his trusty key that he had in his pocket he opened the glove box. Walla! There was the envelope, money intact. Somehow luck had found him. He got back in his truck and continued on to the orphanage where he was originally headed.

Woody found a parking spot at the Hope House. Now he had fourteen thousand dollars in his truck glove box that didn't lock anymore. "Who's going to look in my old jalopy truck for money?" He asked himself.

Standing at the entrance to the cafeteria, Woody noticed almost everyone was finished eating. Mrs. Lee walked over and offered Woody a seat next to her. Woody accepted and sat down. He looked around and saw Jane sitting at the opposite side of the room. A small boy sat with her. A large slice of pizza was placed in front of Woody by Mrs. Lee.

"Is it hot?" she asked.

"Yes it is. Thanks! In fact it's delicious. Mrs. Lee, can I ask you a question?"

"Yes." Mrs. Lee nodded. "Please call me Ruth, if you don't mind."

Woody said, "Sure. Ruth, whose little boy is Jane sitting with over there?" pointing across the room.

Ruth looked away and noticed a balloon flying overhead and tried to get it. It floated over toward the kitchen entrance. She began chasing it. As she grabbed the balloon, everyone could hear Jane singing Happy Birthday to David. The whole roomful of kids began singing Happy Birthday. But the singing was a bit vague and disjointed.

"Okay everyone, let's all sing Happy Birthday to David." Ruth snapped her fingers to get their attention. She walked over interrupting their singing so they would start again. She began, "Happy Birthday to you..." as the rest of the room started to sing along, she handed David the balloon. Woody joined in the singing and then finished his pizza slice.

Woody walked over to wish the boy a happy birthday. "Hi Jane. Aren't you going to introduce me to your friend?" he asked.

Jane hesitated. "Oh... Ah... Hi Woody. This is David. Say hi to Mr. Woody, David."

David looked up at Woody and smiled. "Hi... Are you...?"

Jane wiped David's face and hands. She grabbed one of his hands and got up, then abruptly led him along and said, "Thanks everyone. Sorry, but we have to go right now." They began walking out of the cafeteria, through the corridor that led to the rooms. David turned and waved to Woody.

Woody called Jane, "Jane!" She didn't turn around and kept moving down the hallway.

Ruth noticed Woody hadn't eaten the second slice of pizza that the cook put on the table for him. "Mr. Woody, you didn't eat very much."

Woody continued staring as Jane hurried down toward one of the rooms.

Ruth blurted out, "Are you wondering about that little boy, David?" Woody nodded his head. "Well his mother was in an accident and left him alone. Poor boy. I understand she is very sick."

"Jane? Jane's sick?"

Ruth looked at Woody and shook her head. "No, his mother's name is Sandy."

CHAPTER 9 What's Scrapple?

Pink ladies slipper, wild strawberry, field pansy and wild radish were among some of the most beautiful wild flowers on the planet. They could be found right here in the center of Westminster at King's Junk Yard. A light April snow had melted and the day was a promise of good things to come.

Today was special for Woody because he would be meeting with a builder in about an hour who was a friend of Whiteys. They would be breaking ground soon and Woody was quite excited. He was about to have a house built which would afford him some privacy. Since young Georgie wanted to go into the military and leave all his belongings in Woody's small apartment, It would be way too cramped. Woody enjoyed his privacy and it was about time he had something to show for his own life.

Whitey deeded an acre to Woody with a stipulation: as long as he promised to keep it in the family. His house would be a simple cottage style. Room to eat, sit and sleep. Oh, of course, also a heated bathroom. He was getting tired of freezing his butt off at night, almost literally, since the apartment bathroom toilet mostly didn't work, so he had to go down to the dirty, cold garage.

He had just finished up building a small shed on the property without any help. Doing this in his spare time was quite the challenge, but Woody's proud to be just about finished.. There was a room in his new workshop where he could have privacy. He could read his morning paper and drink his coffee. It only needed painting and a window that he would be picking up later in the day. He was trying to fit all of his personal work in with his work around the junkyard. There was much to be done now that it was spring.

He heard his name being called by Cassie, "Woody... There is a lady that just came through the gate. She's been looking for you. She just said, 'I want to talk to Mr. Dagwood Dooley'."

"What's her name? Is she pretty? I only talk to pretty girls..." he said, toying with her.

Cassie laughed. "She's over there." She pointed toward the driveway entrance. "Oh... And Pop wants you to find a transmission in the yard for Chicky. The guy that bought Plug."

"Okay, thanks sweetie." As he walked across the grass past his sweet smelling crabapple tree he felt a wonderful sense of pride. The tree in his back yard was in its glorious full bloom beauty. Woody continued walking toward where Cassie was pointing. He was wearing a rancid t-shirt that was inside out. His dungarees were full of spackle and other benign substances. He wiped the crud off his hands onto his shiny, filthy jeans. It was difficult to watch him limp and shuffle along down the driveway. He was clearly in pain but he added a perkiness to his step when he saw she really *was* good looking.

"Hey there... What can I do for you young lady?" He reached to shake her hand but at the sight of his dirty hands she backed away.

He said apologetically, "I am so sorry! I'm filthy. I'm working... You need to talk with me?"

"My name is Barbara and I am from the Federal Government Census Bureau. I'm here to clear up some information. Do you have a few minutes?" she asked with a smile.

"Barbara, that's a nice name... I had a teacher with the first name Barbara. She's dead now. Let's go sit down by my new shed." They sat on a picnic bench seat.

"Do you own this property?" she asked with her pen ready to go.

"Yes ma'am... But just this acre," he said pointing to some separation from the junkyard.

"Where do you live right now?"

"Over there." He pointed to the garage. "It's only one room and belongs to my brother Whitey."

She smiled when a small kitten walked up to her and rubbed up against her leg. "Awww... You're so cute."

"You want her?"

"Whaaa... Oh no... We aren't allowed to take anything from anyone."

"Well, her name is Puff, and she really likes you. We have at least ten floating around," he said. "You could actually take your pick. We keep them because they kill all the rodents, and there are plenty. This kitten is the best! She loves people."

Woody was attracted to this lovely girl. She was slim, with shoulder length dark hair. Her dark brown eyes sparkle when she talked. And that smile was a gift. He completed all her questionnaires and began walking her to her car. "Barbara, would you like to go to breakfast tomorrow?"

Barbara was taken aback. "We aren't supposed to fraternize."

"I would never fraternize if you're not allowed. But a good hearty eggs and scrapple breakfast isn't going to hurt anyone."

Barbara laughed and said, "Sure. Actually, tomorrow is Saturday and I don't work. What time?"

"Seven a.m. Where can I find you?"

Without hesitation she rattled off her address, waved and left in her shiny new red Chevy.

The next morning Woody pulled up to a lovely brick home that was only a mile from The Big Stop Diner. His pickup was cleaner than usual and he had Puff purring on the seat next to him.

Barbara came running out in her little red skirt and patent leather shoes. She had a heavy winter grey coat on and a cute pair of red mittens that matched her skirt. She hugged herself. "Brrr.. It's cold for April."

She jumped in Woody's truck. "Hi! what do you have here? Awww... How adorable! I'm glad you brought her. Let me run her in to my house and show my mother." Barbara picked up Puff and took her into her house.

She jumped back into the truck and full of excitement said, "My mother loves her!" Woody smiled and off to the diner they went.

"Oh, by the way, can I ask you a question?"

"Sure," Woody said looking over at Barbara.

"What is scrapple?"

"That's just it. Nobody knows. It's whatever they don't use from the pig."

The diner was packed. Nancy, Woody's favorite server, waited on them. "Is this one of your nieces you brag about?"

Woody looked over at Barbara. "No, she's a friend." Woody and Barbara snicker.

Nancy gave them a stiff smile. "That's nice." She poured Woody coffee to the brim. She didn't look at either one of them. She looked at her order form. "Would you like tea or orange juice or pineapple juice or water?"

Barbara looked at Nancy and said, "Orange juice will be fine, thank you."

Nancy walked away and Woody and Barbara giggled. Woody looked at her intently. "Do you mind that I'm old enough to be your father?"

Barbara responded very matter-of-factly, "No... Do you mind that I'm young enough to be your daughter?"

"No... No... Age isn't important. But how old are you, just for the sake of knowing?"

"Twenty three... Twenty four in June."

"Wow, Just for the record, I'm twenty years older, but who's counting?"

It was six a.m. and Woody was sitting on a chair in his shed staring out the window. He was watching as a sliver of sun peaked over the horizon. He waited for that burst of morning. This time of day had always been his special time. He built his shed and placed the window facing the morning sun. He believed this was a glorious time of the day. His one little lamp that Miriam gave him did not offer him enough light to read by anyway. His instant coffee was cold and his newspaper was thrown in a mud puddle, so it was soaked. He knew not to walk up to the gate where Whitey's paper might be because Sampson and Zeus, the two Doberman Pinschers, the night watch dogs, might not recognize him so early. He had always been a little leery of them anyway. He has had many a nightmare of Zeus, the alpha dog, with his devilish eyes, tearing his throat out. That would not be a good way to start the day, so Woody decided to drive to Bud's, the local gas station, and pick up a paper.

There was a large glass display case with penny candies. Woody decided to buy two bubble gums for Bobby and Dee Dee. He wandered around inside the gas station and picked up a newspaper, a hot coffee and some warm cinnamon buns for everyone. Suddenly he was tapped on the back. It was Jane.

"Hi Woody. How are you?"

"Fine stranger. You?" Woody stared at her in delightful surprise. She was the same Jane but looked especially attractive today. Her natural beauty could be seen in her smile. He felt drawn in. Woody never noticed her alluring deep set brown eyes before. Somehow it was comforting just to see her.

"I'm good. I'm just picking up some coffee... I ran out. Those cinnamon buns sure do look good," Jane said, while looking at the box of buns Woody had nestled in his arms.

"Why don't you stop by and see my new house? I live just a block and a half down the road." Woody had a pleading look in his eyes.

"I'll follow those cinnamon buns anywhere." Jane laughed. She smiled and patted Woody on the back. "Good for you... Glad to hear it. I'll do that but we have to make it pretty quick. I'm taking care of someone that is sick, and she'll be expecting me."

"Umm... I have to open the yard for Whitey today and so... We won't be long. Follow me"

Jane walked out with her coffee and laughed. "I'd know that truck anywhere."

She got in her sedan and followed Woody to his new house. As Jane stepped out of her car the sun had fully risen and the crab apple tree blended in with the view of the black and white house. "Oh, wow! It's lovely."

Woody led Jane inside to a small kitchen painted soft green with pots and pans on the sink, but not *too* messy for a bachelor. "It's great Woody! I love it. How many bedrooms?"

"Just one." Jane walked into Woody's bedroom. She nodded her head and continued into his bathroom. He had a sink and a bathtub. The sink was a bit dirty. "Don't mind my bed. It's a mess, but it's comfortable." She saw a double bed with a homey looking patchwork quilt on it.

"Wow! I'm impressed Woody. You did good. I'm happy for you. Now let's have a cinnamon bun." They both headed over to the round maple table that Whitey gave him when he moved in. He stared at her beautifully shaped rose colored lips. He hadn't ever realized how pretty she was before. After a few moments laughter, nibbling cinnamon buns, and casual chit chat, Jane licked her fingers and said, "Woody I have a confession to make. The sick person that I'm taking care of is Sandy."

Woody took a long gulp of his stand up strong black coffee. He rose from his chair and looked out the kitchen window. "Why did you wait so long to tell me Jane? I wanted to talk to you last Christmas and you avoided me. Is she still with that guy?"

She shook her head.

Jane began to leave and poured a small amount of unfinished coffee in the sink. She shook her head again. "I know... I'm so sorry. Please understand I've been sworn to secrecy. Sandy has terminal brain cancer. She could hardly take care of herself anymore. She didn't want you to know. But she's having seizures every day now and they cause excruciating pain. I've been taking care of her for about six months."

"Oh my! What can I do to help? Does she need anything? Where is she? Jane... Can I go see her?"

Jane began walking out the door but turned and quietly said, "Listen... I'll have a talk with her and let you know. We can't push her."

"Tell her I still care about her. And I won't bother her if she doesn't want me to. I don't know what you should tell her. Just tell her I want to see her, or talk to her... Okay?"

Jane hugged Woody. She patted him on the shoulder and began stepping out the door. Woody stopped the door with his boot. "Wait... I'll give you my phone number... Wait..." Woody walked over to one of his cabinet drawers and found a pen and paper. He wrote his phone number down and ran toward Jane as she began walking to her car.

"Here Jane... Take this please." He handed Jane the piece of paper with his phone number on it. "Ask Sandy to give me a call. Just a call. It won't hurt to talk."

Jane took the paper and turned around facing Woody. "I'll talk to her Woody. I promise. I like your house. It's very nice. Oh... And thanks for the cinnamon bun. It was delish."

"Jane... Wait... Here... Take the box and share them with Sandy. That's the least I can do." Woody ran to her car with the box of buns. He handed them to her. He said, "Thanks for stopping by."

"Thanks Woody, you're the best."

CHAPTER 10 Cinnamon buns

Jane pulled up the cemetery road and reached the rock that prevents her from driving onto the flower bed. The garden she planted was being damaged when she sometimes found herself driving past the gravel end. She placed a large rock at the foot of the driveway to divide the driveway from the flower garden. There were colorful impatiens and a few petunias that were in full bloom. It was a lovely landscape to look at when you first arrived. The grounds were spectacular. The cottage was on a hill that looked over a beautiful park valley, hence the name of the cemetery, Grand View. Her job was to maintain the grounds by hiring and overseeing a landscaping company and also answering any questions a potential client may have about the plots. She loved her job and the splendor the job has offered her.

Sandy had adjusted well to her new abode. Although it was a one bedroom bungalow, she had her own twin bed. And she could practically step right into the bathroom from her bed.

Jane walked into the kitchen and set the box of cinnamon buns on the small table. She announced, "Hey Sandy, I have cinnamon buns."

Sandy walked into the kitchen to greet Jane. "Good morning... Umm, they smell good. I haven't had those forever. You really shouldn't have, but I am glad you did."

Jane put the previously prepared percolator coffee pot on the stove and sat down to talk to Sandy. She opened the box of cakes. "Guess who I saw at the gas station?"

"Woody?" Sandy guessed with a smile.

"Yep! Guess what else I saw?" Jane said excitedly.

"What... Or who?"

"What... I saw his new house. It's real cute. And he had a glorious crabapple tree in full bloom right beside it. He had an acre of land there. It's really nice."

"Where?" Sandy asked with interest.

"Behind King's Junkyard. There was a field there. That's where Woody's house was built. It's cute. Black and white. I love it. We can drive by one day," Jane said with excitement in her voice.

"It sounds nice. Did he ask about me?" Sandy inquired with hope in her eyes.

"He sure did. I told him you are single. He wants to see you Sandy! I have his phone number. He wants you to call him." Jane smiled.

Sandy took a big bite of the cinnamon bun and giggled a bit. "Wow! I would have to do something with my hair, and really clean myself up before I see him."

"Yes... Yes... Yes... I'll help you sweetie. You need to get out of the house." Jane reached across the small table and fixed a strand of Sandy's hair that was hanging in her eye. "There... There... My friend. Everything is going to be just fine."

"Jane, you are not replaceable, you know. You've taught me so much about being selfless," She said with sincerity. "You're my very best friend in the world. I truly don't know what I would do without you. Especially when you bring home cinnamon buns." They both laugh.

Later that evening Sandy had a grand mal seizure that lasted four minutes while, luckily, resting in her bed. Jane sat with her and made sure she didn't need to go to the hospital. This one was long and physically draining. Her neck had a dreadful cramp and she was having a hard time swallowing.

"Do I need to call Dr. Livingston?" Jane asked with serious concern. Sandy was still woozy and couldn't answer her question.

Jane sat on the side of Sandy's bed. "Are you okay sweetie?" Sandy was nauseous and needed to throw up. Jane grabbed a pot from the kitchen. Sandy filled it to the brim. Next time, she thought, she would find a bigger pot. The cinnamon buns she ate were disgusting now as Jane emptied them into the commode. Sandy apologized for seemingly expecting Jane to do so much work to take care of her. Jane patted Sandy's leg. "We'll get through this."

Sandy, exhausted and sore, looked at Jane. "I am just going to rest. I have such a headache. I know I was going to call Woody. I'll call Woody another day. Maybe tomorrow." She took two of her pills, curled up in her comfy bed and fell asleep.

Jane slept in the same bedroom with Sandy in a separate bed. She didn't want to disturb Sandy so she chose to sleep in the living room that night. This was because she was now wide awake and trying to sort out the feelings that were plaguing her. She decided to try and find Sandy's sister that was living out of town. She hadn't a clue where she was now. Jane began searching through the phone book without any luck.

Jane laid down on the sofa with a quilt her grandmother gave her when she was young. Her grandmother was her rock. Jane missed her terribly. Unfortunately, she had died a couple of years ago, but Jane talked to her at night. "Grandma, what am I going to do? I have to contact Jerry's Landscaping. I can't stay in this house and watch Sandy every minute. But someone has to keep an eye on her. Please help me. I miss you so much. Ground hogs are digging holes, one of the cemetery stones was knocked down and the back fence needs repair. Sandy needs medical help. She needs her doctor, she needs her family and she needs her husband. I can't do it all. What should I do Grandma... Just ride it out?"

Suddenly her side table lamp flickered. "Is that a sign? Grandma? Yep... Thank you." Sandy fell into a deep much needed sleep.

CHAPTER 11 The Arrest

Today, July tenth, was Woody's Birthday. He didn't have Barbara's phone number and he had a plan to ask her out on an official date. His dilemma was that he had to find a phone book. Miriam had several phone books, so Woody knocked on her kitchen door. It was early morning but he knew she got up at the crack of dawn.

Miriam was washing clothes in her sink with a washboard because her washing machine was not working. Her scrubbing made quite a racket so she did not hear Woody knocking on her door. Woody walked in. Miriam turned and almost jumped out of her skin. "Oh my gosh! You about scared me to death."

"Hi Mir. Sorry! I see your washing clothes the hard way."

Miriam gave Woody a disgruntled look. She kicked her washing machine hurting her foot. She hopped closer to Woody. "The damn thing broke down."

"Sorry, I see you're busy. I need to use your telephone book, please." Miriam pointed toward the top of her icebox.

Woody asked if she would help find the phone number of Barbara Barnes. He sat at Miriam's small kitchen table.

"Can I get you anything? A cup of coffee... Tea?" Woody shook his head. Miriam looked happy he had stopped by.

"I'm about to ask this girl out. I thought I would take her to supper for my birthday."

Miriam looked at Woody with a bit of a scowl. "That census girl? She's young enough to be your daughter." Mir shook her head. "It's your life." She looked into his eyes with deep concern. "Here it is, 695-4327."

"Thanks Mir."

"Happy birthday Woody."

Bobby came whipping around the corner. "It's your birthday?"

Dee Dee followed behind calling to the rest of the kids, "It's Woody's birthday."

Only Cassie and Sissy were in the house. They walked out, tired of ironing and folding clothes. "Happy birthday Woody," they both said unenthusiastically.

Woody walked out thanking Miriam. She turned and he could see she looked upset. "Mir, are you okay?"

"Yeah, why?" She wiped her eyes with a page of newspaper. He handed her his handkerchief.

"I don't know. Do you want me to look at that washing machine?"

"Do you mind?" Mir said correcting her facial expression. "That will help if you could get this damn thing to work." Mir kicked it, then pulled back her hair that had fallen in her eyes. "You know we're moving next month. Good lord." Mir shook her head. "We have so much junk. It's a big house. It's a two story with an apartment on the second floor. The house on the first floor has three bedrooms and a sun porch. It has a garage. I'll have to collect the rent from the guy that lives upstairs. This was what George wanted. Probably *The Witch* made him do it."

Woody bent over the washer and could see it was not plugged in. He pushed the plug into the wall outlet and announced, "Fixed!"

Miriam looked at Woody and chuckled. "I can't believe it! You are the best! Thank you Woody."

Woody left laughing and hollered, "I'll send you a bill ma'am."

Miriam hollered back with laughter, "Good luck."

Woody phoned Barbara. Her mother answered. "Good morning. The Barnes residence."

Woody said, "Hi Mrs. Barnes. This is Woody Dooley. Sorry to call so early."

"Oh, hi there Woody. You wouldn't believe how adorable this beautiful kitten is. She sits on my husband's shoulder every morning when he reads the paper. She purrs and just sits there. He has taken to her more than any of us."

Woody laughed and said he was happy they like the kitten. Barbara got on the line. "Good morning. Mother will talk your head off if you let her."

"Oh... That's alright. I was wondering if you'd like to go to supper this evening?"

"It's a work night so we'll have to go early, but I would love to. I'm just about to leave for work now. What time will you be picking me up?"

Woody, full of excitement, responded, "Six early enough?"

"How about five thirty?"

"Sure. Five thirty is perfect. I'll pick you up five thirty on the dot." He hung up wondering if he even said good-bye. He was on cloud nine. But he knew he had a lot to get done at work before he left so he took off without even having his morning coffee.

Billy met Woody on the walk toward the garage where Pop was waiting with his cup of coffee. "Hey brother. Morning to ya. Happy birthday."

Billy said, "Can I go in now, pop?" Whitey nodded.

Woody was surprised Whitey knew. "You know my birthday?"

Whitey laughed. "Cassie came over and told me you fixed Miriam's washing machine and told them it was your birthday."

"All I did was plug it in," he said matter-of-factly. "Have any more coffee Whitey?"

"No, but I'll treat if you run up to the gas station and get some coffee and some kind of breakfast cake. You can try out the Pontiac I picked up in Philly yesterday. It's for running around in. It's a bit stinky but in good shape."

Woody looked near the yard entrance. It was a clean looking old black Pontiac Silver Streak. "Nice paint job." Woody couldn't believe it. "It's great." Woody snapped up the keys, climbed in and made himself comfortable in the Pontiac. As he drove off he noticed a foul smell but ignored it.

It was a bit hard to shift but once it was in gear, the car was smooth. He pulled up to the gas station and stopped. He then noticed flashing lights from a police car behind him. He hesitated until a blast from the siren was heard. "What in the hell?" He began to exit, but the policeman told him to get back in the car. "What did I do?" Woody asked totally surprised.

"First, you were driving forty five in a thirty five mile an hour speed limit. And, you didn't signal when you turned left. I'll need to see your driver's license and registration." The officer was young and was taking his job very seriously.

Woody found his license in his wallet, but he couldn't find any paper work in the glove box of the car. He pulled out a sale slip on a napkin.

The officer looked at the car. "Nice looking Pontiac." He put his head up against the passenger window. "Ewww... What's that foul smell?"

Woody shrugged his shoulders. He reached over and handed the officer his license and the flimsy receipt. "Don't know sir."

The officer walked around the car and noticed something on the back fender that looked like blood. "Will you please open the trunk, sir," he asked with an authoritarian voice.

Woody got out of his car and opened the trunk. "Holy shit!"

The cop stared in the trunk and looked over at Woody. "Don't move an inch! You're under arrest."

Whitey opened the junkyard with Billy... No Woody in sight. He had been gone for over an hour. It was only two miles to the gas station. He was usually pretty quick with a small order of coffee and coffee cake. Whitey wondered if he broke down in the new car. He jumped in his tow truck to go check on him. "Billy, you're in charge until I get back. Got that?" Billy nodded.

Gus, the owner of the gas station, was pumping gas into a police car. There were several police cars at the gas station and several officers meandering around. Whitey could see the Pontiac in the center of a circle of officers and crime tape was surrounding the car. He was feeling uneasy. "What's going on officer?" Whitey hollered from his truck window to the cop that was having his car filled up.

"Keep going mister. We're taking care of everything."

"Well, where's the guy who was driving that car over there?"

"It's none of your business," the officer responded angrily.

"Yes it is my business. He's my brother."

Whitey pulled his tow truck over to park. He jumped out of the truck. The cop called him over. "Come here sir!" the officer demands. Whitey walked over to the officer. "Oh, hi Whitey. You own King's Junkyard, don't you?"

"Yes sir. What's going on?"

"Well, we arrested a guy by the name Dagwood Dooley. Is he related to you?"

"He's my brother. He has a different last name. There must be a mistake officer."

"Oh? Well, there was a dead body in the trunk of the car he was driving."

"Damn... You've got to be kidding!"

The officer looked down. "I'm afraid he's in big trouble."

"Where is he right now?"

"Jail. Follow me. He's at the local jail about a mile up the road."

Whitey got in his truck and followed the officer to the station. He could see Woody at the desk. He was in handcuffs and being processed to go to jail. "Whitey." Woody said with a sigh of relief.

"Hey bud."

The officer that led him to the police station stopped Whitey from walking over to where Woody was.

Whitey looked at the cop. "This is a big mistake here. I'll clear everything up."

Woody looked desperate. "Okay... I know you will."

The officer asked who just bought the car. Whitey said, "I bought it yesterday at Dodd's Junkyard and Auto Yard in South Philly. It was a steal. I mean Dodd's wife only asked fifty bucks for it in good condition."

A handsome, clean cut detective walked over to Whitey and asked if he would follow him to his office to answer a few questions. Whitey asked if he could stop by the junkyard to help his young son Billy who was currently there alone. "I'll just close it for the day and come right back."

That satisfied the detective. Whitey called over to Woody, "I'll be back. I'll bring *The Horse* to make sure I keep things straight. Oh and Woody, Happy Birthday."

Woody watched as Whitey walked away. The horse? "Okay... I'll be right here."

Whitey pulled up to the junkyard. There was a strange guy walking down the driveway in a very expensive suit. Billy was beside him. They headed over to Miriam's house. Whitey called, "Billy, What's going on?"

Billy quickly turned toward his father. "This guy, Mr. Pool, wants to ask questions about the junkyard. I was taking him to talk to Mom."

"That's okay," Whitey announced from the window of his truck. "I got this."

He Jumped out of his truck and approached the man. They shake hands. "Hello, my name is Ray Pool, I'm with the IRS."

Whitey stared at the guy and shook his head. "What the hell is going on?"

"You must be George H. King, the owner of the King's Junkyard."

"Yeah." He stared at Mr. Pool with serious concern, "Are you here about the body in the Pontiac car?"

"No... Huh? ...Body? ...No, no. I don't know anything about a body in a car." he stated emphatically. He nervously fiddled with his tie. "Actually I'm here to ask you a few questions about your transactions with a company out of Philadelphia, Dodd's Junkyard. Do you recall doing business with them?"

"Yeah. That's where the body came from." Mr. Pool frowns.

Whitey asked Mr. Pool to follow him into the garage where he had a small makeshift office. He offered Mr. Pool a seat. Mr. Pool removed a handkerchief out of his pocket and wiped the seat off.

"Actually Mr. King, I am here about your taxes that were not paid in 1950 through and including 1958." Mr. Pool pulled out his notebook where there were accounting figures. The bottom line figure was in red. He said, This is what we have calculated that you owe the IRS as of today." He showed Whitey.

Whitey laughed at Mr. Pool. "Where do you think I'm going to get that kind of money?"

Mr. Pool did not laugh. Whitey stood up and walked around taking his hat off, scratching his head and putting his hat back on. He shook his head and stared at Mr. Pool. "When does it have to be paid?" Whitey asked with concern.

"You have sixty days to come up with funds or face incarceration and leans on your current properties, along with interest and fines."

Billy peeked his head in the garage and said, "I just made fifty bucks on all those tires you were going to throw away pop."

Mr. Pool looked at Whitey and said sarcastically, "You have a young child working for you and you do mostly a cash business. That's interesting."

"He's my sixteen year old son and that's how a junkyard runs Mr. Pool. Yes. We do mostly a cash business. Anything else I can do for you?"

"No, thank you very much. I'm sure we'll be in touch." Mr. Pool handed Whitey a card with his phone number on it. Whitey started to follow him. He turned and said, "Pleased to meet you Mr. King. I'll see myself out." Whitey followed him to his black Chevrolet. He nodded at Mr. Pool and walked away. As he watched the car drive away he waited for the customer that Billy took care of then closed the yard for the day.

Clang! Bang! Crash! Slam! Bang! The sounds of jail were similar to the sounds of the Janitor at the Hope House once a month when he was doing a major cleaning. It was loud and scary. That was what Woody was hearing as he sat in his cell. There was an older man in the cell beside him that seemed quite drunk. He was lying on the floor next to his chair, mumbling something. His arms were tightly wrapped around himself and he was lying in a fetal position. He looked cold, Woody thought.

It was early morning and Woody was missing his new house, his newspaper and a cup of strong black coffee. He realized he was in a mess. How did that body get in the car?

Was it Dodd that was in the trunk? It sort of looked like him. Woody didn't remember if he had a beard or not. Who killed him? His wife sold Whitey the car. Whitey better get him out of this mess.

The guy next to him began moaning. Woody, looking concerned, said, "Hey bud, are you alright? Do you need a blanket?" The guy looked up at Woody and mumbled something that sounded like a bible parable. He then dropped his head back down on the cement floor and started to cry and gurgle at the same time.

Woody saw the guard and asked if he would get the poor guy a blanket. "No blankets around here. This is a Jail, not the Ritz." The guard looked at the guy. "You're lying right under the air conditioner. Move over." He pointed toward the front of the cell. "Nobody else is cold. I'll have them turn the air off." The guy didn't move. He called his assistant, "Hey Bob, this guy is sick. Help me get him to the infirmary." A tall heavy set man with an angry look on his face went into the sick man's cell. The two carried him out and down a long hall and out of sight.

Now Woody was totally alone and felt anxiety filling his thoughts. It was nine in the morning. Why was Whitey taking so long? He should be getting me out of this place.

There was a change of shifts at the jail causing much commotion. Someone was cleaning the floor and emptying trash. Woody couldn't see the activity but could hear it. He heard someone say the guy that was in the cell next to the murderer died last night. Woody felt sick to his stomach. Damn! Why hadn't someone helped him sooner? He felt nauseous.

He could faintly hear the TV in the guard's office. He heard anchor man Chuck Billings, who he was familiar with from the morning news, report Dodd Miller as the dead body that was found in the trunk of a Pontiac driven by Dagwood Dooley.

"But I didn't kill anybody." he said under his breath. And then he said it out loud. "I didn't kill anybody."

The news caster added, "They have him in custody and are looking into another person of interest by the name of Michelle Miller, Dodd Miller's wife." He paused, then began again, "A man, Reginald Gross, was picked up for intoxication at a local tavern. He was found dead in his cell from natural causes. More to come in the next hour."

"What? That's a lie too." Woody said out loud so that whoever could hear him understood. "That guy should have been given medical treatment right away, not when they finally got around to it."

Ivy town, Pennsylvania, was where shady attorney Joe Palermo's office was located, just about five miles up the road from the junkyard. Joe had been his attorney for ten years. He had always reminded Whitey of a horse due to his long face and prominent teeth. Without question, he seemed to like 'the green stuff' more than any other attorney Whitey knew, so he called him *The Horse*. Whitey sat in a waiting room on fancy modern office furniture. He had a lot on his mind now. First he needed to get Woody out of jail. And because he owns the car he had to make sure his butt's clear, also. The tax stuff would have to wait.

The pretty secretary escorted Whitey into a beautifully decorated office and announced him to Joe.

"Hi George, how are you?"

"I'm just fine, but my brother Woody is in jail for something he didn't do."

"Wait... I heard something about that this morning. Dagwood Dooley is your brother? "

"Yes. I gotta get him out of the can."

Joe turned, walked over to the television and turned it on. "I got a glimpse of that story on your brother earlier. Let's see what they are saying now."

Chuck Billings was broadcasting a picture of Dagwood Dooley's arrest yesterday. "Here is the latest on that story in Westminster. Nothing like this had ever happened in this small mom and pop town. Dagwood Dooley, half brother of the junkyard man George King, was arrested during a routine traffic stop. The officer noticed a foul smell was coming from the trunk. When Mr. Dooley opened the trunk of the car, a dead body was found. Later it was disclosed that it was the body of Dodd Miller who owned Dodd's Junkyard in South Philadelphia. The investigation is ongoing. More to come on the noontime news watch."

Damn! Whitey stared at the television. "That's a friend of mine. I wondered where he was when I bought that car yesterday. The car did stink, but I didn't think anything about it. A nice looking Pontiac. His wife said he went on a trip. He went on a trip alright."

"So you bought a car from Mr. Miller?"

"No. From Mrs. Miller. Mr. Miller was in the trunk, dead."

"Did you get a receipt?"

"Yeah, but it was on a napkin. We were going to take care of everything the next day. I've been buying crap from them for twenty years. I never liked her. She was a bitch. I'll bet she had something to do with the murder."

"What time did you buy the car yesterday? We're going to have to deal with facts. Nothing but facts."

Barbara woke up wondering why Woody hadn't shown up for his birthday dinner. She was ready and dressed in her favorite pink sweater. He hadn't even called. She was about to leave for work, she didn't have time for breakfast. She walked over to pet Puff the kitten who was sitting on her father's shoulder at the kitchen table. Her father looked at her curiously. "What's Dagwood's last name?"

Barbara started to leave. She was worried about being late. She hesitated and looked over at her dad. "Dooley, why?"

"He's on the front page. It say's he was arrested for murder."

Barbara backed up, and said, "No, that can't be dad." She walked over to her father and looked over his shoulder. The headlines said in bold print, "Body found in the trunk of a car in Westminster." The first line in the article read, "A Westminster man was nabbed during a traffic violation stop. The officer asked Dagwood Dooley to open his trunk due to a foul smell. There, the body of Dodd Miller, shot in the head with a small caliber pistol, was found. Investigation is currently underway."

Barbara sat down next to her dad. "Oh my, I went to breakfast with a killer."

Her father looked at her. "You never know. You've got to be more careful. He seemed like such a nice man. Too old for you, but he seemed so polite. That shows you can never be too careful."

"Well that's scary. I have to go to work. Bye dad." Barbara gave her dad a kiss and left in a hurry.

On the other side of town in Grandview Jane was outside on the lawn trying to water her flowers at the top of her driveway. She heard a scream coming from inside the house. She ran in and found Sandy in front of the TV covering her mouth. She looked over at Jane and pointed to the TV.

"Look... It's Woody. He murdered someone."

Jane couldn't believe what she was hearing. She turned the volume up. "What in the world? Woody wouldn't hurt a flea," Jane said. She listened to the whole report and the two women hugged and decided they would contact Whitey to get the correct information.

"Woody's in jail? I can't believe it."

Sandy cried, "He couldn't have done that. He's a gentle soul."

"They have the wrong man," Jane stated. Jane called the number Woody gave her but there was no answer. "Look... I'll call his brother Whitey later. Right now he's probably bailing him out. In the mean time don't forget to take your medicine. Today is Friday and we have to go visit David in a couple hours."

Sandy went into the bathroom to take a shower. Jane walked outside to pay Jerry the landscaper for mowing the lawn for the cemetery. Jerry was waiting at the flower garden admiring Jane's flowers.

"They look very nice he said." Jane paid their agreed upon price and smiled.

"Thanks Jerry. I put them together myself. You like them?"

"I think you better water them because this afternoon is going to be hot and no rain in sight."

"Okay, Jerry thanks. See you in two weeks?"

"Okay, Miss Jane. Oh, don't forget... I'll fix the fence when I get the supplies, I also just hired somebody that has done fencing work before. Okay?"

Jane shouted, "Okay!" and watched as he quickly trotted to his truck. They both waved.

Two hours later Jane and Sandy wait in the lobby of the Hope House to see David. Mrs. Lee greeted them and asked if the girls had seen the news about Woody. Jane told Mrs. Lee she was sure that it was a mistake. But Mrs. Lee looked in her eyes. "He's a bit suspicious. Don't you think?"

Sandy shook her head. "Mrs. Lee, Woody didn't have a mean bone in his body. I assure you he had nothing to do with that murder."

"Well, let me go get that sweet child who has been counting the hours until your visit."

Sandy laughed and said, "I can't wait."

From where the girls sat in the comfortable soft chairs in the waiting area they could see David come running down the hall. "Don't run David." Mrs. Lee hollered. David walked fast and laughed as Sandy opened her arms wide to catch him.

"Mommy and Aunty Jane."

Sandy and Jane call in unison, "David." They all hugged for the comforting feeling they were all longing for, which was love. The visit seemed short because Sandy had to leave thirty minutes early to see her doctor. But Mrs. Lee promised they would get a thirty minute longer visit the next time.

An hour later Jane and Sandy were sitting in Dr. Livingston's office. The visit was brief because he didn't usually have office visits on a Friday. Sandy would have to come by Monday for an X-ray to see the growth of the tumor. Doctor Livingston noticed some slight changes in Sandy's gate and strength of her right side. The seizures concerned him but he was glad to see she was up and getting around.

As they headed home the girls picked up a pizza pie for dinner. "This is a real treat," Sandy said. "Now let's go home and see if we can get in touch with Woody's brother Whitey." As they exit the car Sandy fell onto the gravel driveway. Jane ran around and pulled her up. Sandy laughed, looking at the funny way she had fallen.

"It's not funny." Jane said with a slightly serious look. Together they walked into the house arm in arm.

Woody sat in Jail alone worried he would be in prison for the rest of his life. A guard entered, handcuffed him and walked him toward the interrogation room.

Detective Hall came down the long hallway meeting Woody halfway. Joe Palermo, the attorney, was sitting and waited for them. "Hello Mr. Dooley. Remember me?" Joe said addressing Woody.

"Yes... And I'm sure you know by now that I'm innocent," Woody said matter-of-factly.

Joe nodded. "Yes you are. We both know that. We are here to prove that to the detective." He turned toward Detective Hall. "Hello detective. As I said, we're here to prove that Dagwood Dooley had nothing to do with that murder."

Detective Hall smiled at Joe. "Whoa there... Slow down. We'll see. I'll ask questions and you and your client will answer them."

Joe looked unmoved. "That's fair."

Detective Hall put his serious face on. "Okay... You've been finger printed and your personal information has been recorded. Let's start with this. What time did you get up yesterday morning and what did you do?"

"Six thirty... Or maybe ten minutes later I got up. I grabbed my news paper on my front porch. I didn't have coffee yet. It was my birthday. I called a friend at about seven thirty. We arranged to have a date that evening to have supper together. I lost track of time and it was getting late so I skipped my cup of coffee and thought I would see if Whitey, my brother, had any extra at his garage. He didn't so he told me to go pick up two coffees and a Tasty Cake up at the gas station. He told me he bought a new car to run around in for the junkyard use. He told me try it out. He was being nice to me since it was my birthday. I was stopped because I was speeding a bit but the station is only two miles away. Anyway... I tried to use my turn signal. The turn signal light bulb must have been bad. That's when the cop stopped me. He thought the car smelled real bad... I did too, so he asked me if I would open the trunk. I didn't resist. I wanted to see what smelled so bad myself. Well... There it was... A body. He arrested me. That is everything."

"We know that your brother Whitey collaborates your story. But what did you do the day before? Let's say from the time your brother arrived back from Dodd's?"

Woody squinted in concentration and looked a bit concerned. Joe noticed this and took Woody aside. "You just have to tell him the truth. Whitey said you weren't around when he parked the car in that vacant spot. You didn't see the car until the morning of the tenth... Right?"

"Right," Woody responded. He turned back to the detective and said, "I was at home, that's all I remember. I didn't see any car that day. The next morning... Like I already said, I saw the car. I drove the car. I saw the body. Then I was arrested."

Detective Hall jotted something in the ubiquitous cop's notebook and left.

Joe remarked, "Hey... You're doing fine. I believe you. I'm going to try and get you out of here pretty quick."

"I told him everything that transpired. I never saw that car before I drove it to get coffee. I love my brother and I believe that he bought it with a dead body in it. He said he towed it from Dodd's so he didn't get a very good whiff of that thing or he would have looked in the trunk."

The guard walked Woody out of the interrogation room and into his cell. Woody collapsed on the small cot for a nap.

Detective Hall stared at his notes knowing full well Dagwood hadn't done it but decided to keep him in custody while he covered all bases and got the right person before it was too late. He walked to Woody's cell. He noticed he was lying on the cot. "Thank you Mr. Dooley, I'll get back with you real soon." Woody held his hand up in recognition.

It was noon. The television was on at Barbara's home. She and her father were listening to Chuck Billing's news report. "Today they continue to question Dagwood Dooley for the brutal murder of fifty year old Dodd Miller. Miller leaves behind his wife and sixteen year old son. Authorities continue the investigation. Questions are beginning to emerge. More to come on the evening report. "

"That poor young man doesn't have a father now. That's awful. I just lost my appetite," Barbara said with disgust. She had only a short time for lunch. She was ten minutes from her office but only had forty five minutes to eat.

Her father got up off his chair. He walked into the kitchen and opened the icebox. "Here is some soup your mother made. I made us some tuna fish salad. How about it?"

Barbara shook her head. She picked up an apple off the counter top and bit down. She held her hand up, waved to her dad and walked out of the house. She took off without saying a word about Woody.

Detective Hall arrived at Westminster Police Department with part of the puzzle on the Dodd murder in his mind. He just finished coordinating with Leon Rein from the Philadelphia Police Department. "He feels she's guilty as sin..." he said out loud.

Leon had uncovered a hundred thousand dollar insurance policy that Michelle purchased just two months ago. Just yesterday she put in her claim.

"That's pretty quick for a grieving widow I'd say." Detective Hall looked over at his assistant Ron. "It seems Dodd was having financial problems and Michelle was having an affair. So that gave gives us plenty of motive. Now we've got 'em all: motive, method and opportunity."

CHAPTER 12 Bubble Gum

Jane and Sandy were sitting in Dr. Livingston's office waiting to see the results of a recent test. Jane held Sandy's hand. "It's going to be okay, my friend." The patient room was all white and the floor was black linoleum, very plain, but very clean. His diploma showed he received a degree from the very prestigious University of Pennsylvania School of Medicine.

"Your hand is so cold," Jane said with care in her voice. "Are you okay?" Sandy nodded. She looked infirm and pale.

The smell of disinfectant was strong but left a positive feeling that this guy knew about germs.

"You didn't get enough sleep last night, I'll bet. Oh... I think I hear him coming."

A knock at the door and Dr. Livingston entered with a straight face. "Good morning." He did not smile. He looked at both girls and questioned who Sandy's friend is. And then it happened... Sandy fell off her chair and began convulsing. Jane immediately threw herself down onto the floor and held Sandy's head. Dr. Livingston called his nurse. "Betty!" She came into the room and ran back out. She returned bringing in a couple other nurses.

Betty yelled to one of the other nurses, "Get a blanket!" She grabbed a tongue depressor. Dr. Livingston and one of the other nurses lift Sandy up onto the examining table while she thrashed around. The doctor called an emergency number and an ambulance took Sandy to the hospital.

Jane followed behind in her car. She began crying. "Dear God, please keep Sandy safe. Help us all."

As they all arrived at the Grandview Hospital the emergency room people were darting back and forth getting Sandy onto a stretcher and whisking her away. Jane filled out important information as she checked Sandy into the hospital.

An hour passed. Jane was worried about Sandy so she inquired at a desk where a young blonde haired girl was jotting down information. She was waiting to get the blonde's attention when a grey haired nurse with a kind face walked up to her and asked, "Is there a Jane Rathgeb here?"

"I think it's that girl," she said, pointing to Jane.

The nurse greeted Jane and asked if she would like to visit with Sandy. "Yes, Please." Jane was glad she was able to go see her good friend. Sandy was finally being treated. The nurse led Jane to Sandy's temporary emergency bedroom. Sandy was hooked up to IV tubes and oxygen. It looked scary to Jane. "Oh you poor, poor dear." She bent down to hold and kiss Sandy's hand.

The nurse that was taking care of Sandy whispered, "Shhh... She just fell asleep. I'll let the doctor know you're here." Then she asked pointedly, "Are you a relative?"

Jane fibbed, "Ah... Yes." Quietly Jane said, "She's been through a lot... She has brain cancer."

Jane sat on the small chair next to Sandy's bed. She folded her hands as if she was praying. The nurse closed the curtain that surrounded the bed. Sandy whispered, "Thank you." and the nurse left.

Whitey was sitting at Miriam's kitchen table. He just arrived from talking to his attorney about Woody and his involvement in the murder case. He was given advice on how to handle the problem he was having due to his not paying taxes for six years. He would have to dip into his safe for some serious money.

"Well Mir, you know that I can't buy you that house on York Road right away. The tax man got me." Whitey laughed. "I was served papers from the IRS. And I have to pay Palermo for legal fees. It's going to be rough for a while."

"George... You know that damn toilet doesn't flush and the kids are all growing and need new coats for the winter." She looked at him shaking her head. She gave him a glass of lemonade.

"I know... I know. Here..." He pulled out a wad of money and handed it to Miriam. She took it and put it in a cracked cup she kept on an eye level window sill.

"How much is it?" Miriam asked quizzically.

"I have no idea. You can count it when I leave. Buy yourself some shoes please." He looked down at her dirty bare feet. "I'll let you know how Woody is after I see him tomorrow. He might be coming home."

Miriam offered a forced smile and walked Whitey to the door. Georgie had just arrived and grabbed the door to enter. "Oh, hi dad."

"Georgie, you'll have to work the yard tomorrow too. Got that?"

"Pop... I have to see the Recruiter tomorrow. Can't Billy do it?"

"Jimmy can help and if a problem comes up they can send the customer to me," Miriam said sternly. "He has an appointment tomorrow."

"Oh, okay... You're really signing up?"

"I already did. I thought you knew. I need you to drop me off at the train station, pop."

"What time?"

Miriam answered, "Eight in the morning. He has to be in Philadelphia by nine. I told you last week, George."

"I didn't think it was the real thing, I thought you were just talking about it. Okay then. What's in Philadelphia?"

"I have to pass a physical and then I'll be leaving for boot camp next Tuesday." Georgie looked super excited.

"See you on the dot." Whitey left. Under his breath he mumbled, "Hmmm... a real man now."

"Bye."

The two youngest kids were at the door and watched their father leave. "Bye pop."

Miriam counted the money and looked at her feet. "Wow! Two hundred." She quietly said, "*The Witch* must not know about this. Okay, let's get ready for supper. Who's turn to set the table?"

Nancy and Cassie walked up to Gus's Sinclair gas station to buy bread for the family. And, of course, their pop gave them a quarter each, since penny candies were always fun to choose from Gus's showcase. While they were standing there Barbara Barnes, the Census worker, arrived at the gas station. She stared at Cassie while standing in the bread aisle.

"Hi there," Barbara said with uncertainty in her eyes.

Cassie turned and said, "Hi." She then looked at Nancy, and gave her a crazy signal and remarked, "Who in the world is that?" Nancy shrugged her shoulders, paid for her bubble gum choice and began chewing loud and obnoxiously. Cassie pushed her and said, "That's Woody's friend, remember?"

Nancy looked up at Barbara as she blew a large bubble. It broke and got all over her hair. Barbara walked away smirking. She mumbled, "You blew that one." Then, looking directly at Nancy she said, "Your mother isn't going to be very happy."

Barbara paid for her bread. There was still a loaf sitting on the counter. She then turned and looked at Cassie one last time. "You're the girl from the junkyard, aren't you?" Cassie nodded and began chewing on a piece of licorice. "I knew you looked familiar."

Nancy started crying. "Mommy is going to get be so mad at me."

Cassie and Nancy left quickly forgetting their bread. Barbara ran out of the store and handed the bread to the girls. Cassie thanked Barbara and added, "You know Woody's coming home tomorrow."

Barbara stared at Cassie, nodded her head, waved and walked to her car. She slammed the door and said quietly to herself, "I could care less."

It was eight a.m. on the dot. Whitey had just pulled up the driveway. Georgie looked around but he didn't see his mother. He walked out of the house with one loud, "Bye Mom." The door snapped shut. As the car pulled away Miriam hurried to try to catch him. She wanted to give him a twenty dollar bill but it was too late. They were gone. She could see they were already on their way. She mumbled, "Give your son some money you cheap SOB."

Billy ran into the house to tell his mother Jimmy peed his pants. "He's fifteen years old! Tell him to get in here and change his clothes or he'll get a whooping. You keep an eye on the yard."

"Okay Mom, but there's two weirdoes out in that old Mercedes."

"What are they doing?"

"They're just sitting in it. I forget what Pop wants for it."

"Nobody knows. Not even your father. If they ask you, make sure you tell them it doesn't run? They won't want it. Tell them to come back on Saturday, if they want it."

"Okay Mom." Billy ran out to the yard and didn't come back for an hour. When he walked into the kitchen, he glared at his younger brother Jimmy. "Where have you been?"

"Mommy washed my clothes and we're waiting for them to dry."

Billy mimics his brother, "Mommy has to change my diaper."

Jimmy yelled, "Mom... He's teasing me again."

Billy shook his head and laughed. "Ask Mommy if you can come out and play, little boy."

Billy pushed Jimmy who was only wearing underpants. He pushed him until he fell on the floor. Jimmy ran to his mother. She came storming out and pointed at Billy. "You go outside. Are those Weirdoes still there?"

Billy shook his head and ran out to the garage away from the total unfairness that he just saw. Billy could see something black in the back area of the yard, but on the other side of the fence. He hollered, "Mom! Zeus is loose." He looked at the area of the yard that contains both dogs. Samson was still in his pen. He could clearly see that the black dog that was running around the back behind the fence was their very aggressive Doberman Pinscher watch dog that would bite if provoked.

Miriam was hanging clothes out on the line when she heard Zeus barking in the distance. She turned and could see him through the fence near Millie Lewis's house, a neighbor she had known for years.

The large vicious watchdog was running toward the back of the yard. Billy had to run all the way around the thirty acres of the junkyard to get to the other side. He made it, panting heavily. Millie, who was a bit of a crazy old lady, but nice with animals and sometimes kids, could be seen feeding Zeus candy as she tried to catch him for Billy.

"Millie, don't touch him... He bites."

She hadn't heard him. Billy could see she was still petting him. He licked her hand and continued to beg for the tasty hard candy Millie was sharing with him.

Miriam was right behind Billy with a dog collar and leash, "Here... I'll take him."

"Hi Miriam. He's a sweetheart." Millie petted Zeus.

Miriam put the choker chain on Zeus and he followed her without a fuss. No one knew he could be so tame.

When they arrived back at the house, Carol and Nancy were there with bubble gum all over their hair and clothes. Miriam glared at them, then turned her attention back to Billy. She told him to take the dog to his pen and make sure they both had plenty of water. As he was leaving she said, "Close the gate and make sure it clicks into place."

When he got to the pen he found it was secured but the latch was not closed all the way. Luckily, Samson didn't get out. A bit frightened, Billy cautiously walked Zeus back into his pen and made sure the latch connected. He fixed the problem by turning the screws tighter using his pocket knife. He felt confident that his father would be proud of him.

Jimmy came running out with a clean pair of trousers and glared at his brother. "Mommy said she made you a peanut butter sandwich. I ate mine She said if you don't come in and get it I can eat yours too."

"You touch it and you're dead."

Billy squinted and laughed at Jimmy. "Thanks baby boy. I hope you enjoyed your bottle that Mommy gave you with your peanut butter. "

Jimmy chased Billy and started crying until Billy turned. "Okay, I'll stop." He laughed at him again. "Now shut up and close your barn door."

CHAPTER 13 Released

Whitey and Woody pulled up to the junkyard in the tow truck. It was four forty five and although the yard entrance was not locked, Billy had already leaned the *closed* sign up against the gate. He waved and ran up to welcome Woody home. Pop got out of the truck and could see a customer was walking toward him.

"Hi there. Are you Whitey King? I'm interested in one of your junkers."

Whitey replied, "That's me! One of the junkers, huh?"

"Your son here told me I would have to wait and talk to you about buying the Mercedes."

Whitey laughed. "You know it's sold as is... And I haven't had my supper yet. My wife is waiting for me. Look, I would like to sell it, but I will have to check it out in order to give you a fair price. We close at five."

"What would a fair price be?"

"A million dollars... I don't know! I have to look at it." He laughed. "There you go. I don't know yet. Call me tomorrow. I ain't gonna sell it to nobody else. Okay?"

"Okay... Here is my name and phone number." He handed Whitey a piece of paper. "My name is Bob Bourdage."

"Like I said, I haven't eaten my supper. Call me in the morning. We open at eight. The yard is closed right now. I won't sell it to nobody else."

"Okay..." he whined. "Just don't sell it! I love that car. It's real sharp looking. Okay... Bye." He drove away in a Ford Ranchero.

Woody was still talking to Billy and Jimmy. He thanked Whitey and limped toward his house just a foot ball field away, but a long way when you had a bum leg. He turned around before he was out of view. "Thanks Whitey. You're my favorite brother."

Woody walked into his house through the front porch while picking up a pile of newspapers and a couple notes that were stuck in his door on the way. When he opened the door he noticed he left his kitchen light on all the time he was gone. "Damn! I have to get a loan to pay the electric bill. It's going to be through the roof." He shook his head. He talked to himself as he looked at the front page of a couple of the newspapers. "Well Mr. Dooley, you're a star. You hit the big time." He read aloud, "Local man Dagwood Dooley arrested for the brutal killing of a well known forty eight year old man from West Oak Lane, Philadelphia." He spoke very quizzically, "I did not kill anybody."

Whitey was exhausted. He walked into his house and Alice was standing with her hands on her hips. "Dinner was ready at four, when you said you'd be home. Well, it's five and we already ate. I didn't know what time you would get home George."

"Come on... Don't be mad. I had a busy day. I brought Woody home." He noticed what looked like a kitten run past him in the kitchen into the baby's room. He ignored it.

"Woody... Woody... Woody... That's all I hear. He's caused nothing but trouble." Alice took Whitey's tray out of the oven. "Here, you bought those chops, you couldn't wait to eat them, but now they're probably cold and dry."

"Shut up." Whitey was quickly getting irritated by Alice's complaining. "Alice, Stop fussing and get me a glass of milk."

"I'm not a maid you know." She started slamming pots and pans around. The kitten walked past Whitey but he did not see it.

"I'll take care of myself here." Whitey looked around for the newspaper. It was on the counter. He caught a glimpse of the cute little tabby kitten. "What in the hell is this?" He pointed at the kitten. It was now playing with his shoelace.

Alice made a face and poured Whitey a glass of milk. "Here. It's yesterday's paper."

Whitey grabbed the newspaper and sat at the kitchen table ignoring Alice's silly faces that she continued to make at him. He was so hungry he didn't care that the food was not very warm. When he finished he asked for more pork chops. He continued reading the paper. He mumbled, "Woody's an innocent man. I could tell by Michelle's smirk on that mug she did it. She is a son of a B. She's gonna burn in hell."

Yesterday's paper said *Dagwood Dooley was acquitted when the wife of Todd Miller confessed to the killing*. The paper went on to also identify her brother Raymond Caruso as being the one who pulled the trigger. The motive was money. Whitey and Woody were at their own homes reading the same article in the paper at the same time.

Whitey looked around the kitchen for the current paper. "Where's today's paper?"

"I had to use something for the cat box. We found a kitten. Sharon named it Tiger, because of the stripes."

Whitey shook his head. "No cats Alice. Get that cat out of this house."

"Oh, I see. Are you going to take it away from your daughter?" Whitey looked at Alice mad but defeated.

"I better not smell that cat. You're taking care of it! You hear?"

Woody read the article aloud. He sat on the easy chair that Whitey bought him and fell asleep with newspapers surrounding him on a side table and the floor. He didn't awaken until six in the morning when the paperboy threw the paper at Woody's porch and hit the door. Woody snatched the paper and read the headlines. "Local steel prices rise offering more jobs for Bethlehem Steel." He proclaimed, "Good! My stardom days are over."

CHAPTER 14 The Transfusion

Dr. Grayson was the doctor on duty. He was waiting in emergency to speak with Dr. Livingston before he admitted Sandy into the hospital. "Sandy will need to receive blood. Her count is dangerously low. Because of her blood type they are going to admit Sandy into the hospital for a couple of days so she can receive a much needed transfusion and an IV to boost her strength. She is too weak from all her seizures. We are also looking at all her organs."

Dr. Livingston and Dr Grayson enter Sandy's room. They focus on Jane. Dr. Livingston addressed her, "We understand you are her sister and her husband is not in the picture anymore. I'm sorry to say Sandy's cancer is growing very rapidly in areas that may show in a disabling way. She may not be able to speak or she may start slurring her words..."

Jane interrupted, "Yes... She sometimes will try and say something and she can't get the word out. Then she'll say the wrong word slow and slurred. She is convulsing more. She had several this week." Dr. Livingston nodded his head.

He continued with his concerns, "Because of her blood type she needs to stay here for now. We'll send her up to a room as soon as one is available." Jane nodded. "Will you be able to admit Sandy? The nurse will be in to take the pertinent information?" Jane nodded again. "We'll probably keep her for a couple of days and tomorrow start with a transfusion followed by some more testing. She isn't going to be very talkative right now anyway. She is going to be resting and sleeping for awhile. She'll have pain relief medicine that will make her comfortable..."

Jane interrupted again, "When she comes home, will she be able to walk?"

"She'll probably be able to walk but may be slower or need assistance. More so than she does now because the cancer is growing. We just don't know. We can prescribe a wheel chair or a walker."

Jane pondered the situation and then said, "I live in a four room house that is probably too narrow for a wheel chair. I would have to check."

Dr. Grayson also responded, "Will she have someone helping her throughout the day?"

Jane nodded, "Yes... That will be me... And night."

Dr. Livingston nodded. He added, "She is lucky to have a sister like you. Sandy is showing signs of weakness on her right side. You may have to lift her from time to time. Are you okay with that?" Jane nodded. "I've told her before but you need to know... We can't operate." Jane nodded. He asked her if she had a religious pastor or priest... Or rabbi that could talk with her.

Jane said, "I don't know but I'll talk with her about it. She's Catholic... But Sandy will let me know. I have one more question. Will she need diapers?"

Dr. Livingston stopped in his tracks. He glanced at Sandy's chart. He looked up at her and said, "The nurse may be able to answer some of your questions about her care. But... Not yet. That day will come.

"This is a meningioma blastoma stage four and they are fast growing and devastating. My job is to give you the facts in such a way that you can understand them. I have to run to the patient across the hall. If you need me for anything or you have questions have the nurse get in touch with me." He shook Jane's hand.

She said, "Thank you."

Jane walked over to Sandy who was sleeping and looked so peaceful. She said quietly, "I'm here for you, friend. We're in this together."

The nurse was working on her IV. Jane asked her what she was doing. She said, "We're getting ready to give her a blood transfusion. She is showing signs that there is bleeding. We just don't know where. I have recommended increasing the amount of her Phenobarbital seizure medication because her seizures are increasing. The doctor also wants to keep her pain free. She told me that her painful headaches rate at about a nine. We're going to try and keep her pain free. Well, Dr. Grayson and I are going to examine her and set a plan for the next two days that she will be with us."

Dr. Grayson was at the doorway to Sandy's room. "I just spoke to Dr. Livingston and we're in agreement about her transfusion. So if you just step out into the waiting room. We'll call you in when she's finished." He shook her hand. "There's a cafeteria around the corner that has coffee and donuts if you're hungry. We are going to take good care of your sister and the nurses will let you know when they have a room ready. She's in a well established facility for brain tumors. Dr. Livingston is one of the finest Neurosurgeons around. So nice meeting you. I'm sorry it's under these unfortunate circumstances. Your sister is in good hands, I assure you."

Jane sighed and turned. "Thank you." She started to walk out of the room, then she paused and said, "Do I need to go see the nurses first or can I go get a cup of coffee? How will I get back in?"

"Get your coffee and then come back and speak with Gale the admitting nurse," Dr. Grayson said in a comforting tone of voice.

Jane walked down the hall, but didn't see where to go. She looked across the parking lot. She remembered a donut shop across from the hospital but wondered if it was still there. She walked across the parking lot to Yum Yum Donut Shop and plopped herself down on a bar stool. She felt weary and scared for Sandy.

"One black coffee and one cream filled donut, please."

Hours had passed. Jane was now sitting in an empty room at Grandview Hospital waiting for Sandy to be wheeled in. She was falling asleep. Clang... Bang... A gurney was wheeled into room 506. Sandy was wide awake talking to the two guys that were pushing her like it was a speed race. Laughter was heard.

"Hi Stranger." Jane said while stretching and yawning. "I was ready to get in your bed and go to sleep myself."

Sandy was slipped into her bed smoothly and without much effort. The IV's were switched over to her room's set up and the nurse smiled at Sandy. One of the two fellows handed a clipboard to the nurse who smiled and joked with him. She signed a piece of paper, handed it to the animated gurney guy and they all disperse into the hallway. Sandy looked cold but wide awake.

"Do you need a blanket Sandy?" Jane asked.

She nodded her head. Jane headed out into the hall asking the nurse who was laughing and joking with the gurney guy for a blanket. The nurse pointed in the room toward the closet. Jane found a blanket and covered Sandy with it. She kissed her on the head. "Well, you've been to hell and back today. Are you okay?"

Sandy looked over at Jane. She smiled and started to cry. "You are my... My... My... You know..."

"I'm your friend, that's what I am," Jane said with sincerity. Sandy cried loudly. The nurse came running into the room. A light was blinking at the nurse's station. Jane apologized and said, "Oh sorry, I leaned on the button."

"Is everything okay?" They both nod. The nurse firmly said, "If you need anything at all here is the button on your bed. Just call me." Sandy nodded. "I'll be right back to take your vitals Sandy." She looked at Sandy with a smile. "Now don't go anywhere." They all smiled.

CHAPTER 15 The Mercedes

Woody woke up at five in the morning. His own bed felt so comfortable he stayed there for a few more minutes thinking of contacting Barbara. He said aloud, "She's too damn young." He rolled over and put the pillow over his head.

An hour passed before Woody crawled out of bed. He looked for the two notes that he found attached to his door. One was from the paperboy wanting to collect, the other one was from Jane. It said, *Woody, Call me when you get this note.* It had her telephone number on it. He wondered if maybe it's about Sandy. He grabbed the newspaper and walked out to the shed carrying his coffee. It was still dark. The morning was a bit damp with a chilly wind indicating rain was on the way. One of Cassie's kittens began rubbing up against his leg. Woody reached down and picked him up.

He gave him a soft kiss and began petting him. He stared at his little face with just a smudge of black next to his nose. "You have a funny looking smudge on your face. I guess that's what I'll call you... Smudge."

It was eight a.m. Woody walked toward the yard and entered the gate. He called Zeus who barked and then ran up to him full throttle and slammed into Woody, full of excitement. "Okay, okay. Where's Sampson?" He found Sampson drinking dirty water that was in an old tire. He shoos Sampson away and filled their bucket with clean fresh water from the garage spigot. He carried the bucket over to their pens limping in pain the whole way.

Billy came running up behind Woody. "I have their dog food." He's carrying a bag of dry dog food. "Hi Woody."

Woody patted Billy on the back. "Hi my friend. Thanks pal." Woody walked over to the junkyard gate. He noticed a sweet looking Ranchero parked nearby with the engine running. He ignored it and walked back toward the garage office. Without warning, the Ranchero pulled up right behind him and parked next to the garage. Woody limped over to the driver's side of the car.

The driver rolled his window down, "Hi my name is Bob Bourdage. Whitey's expecting me. We talked yesterday. He's going to give me a price on that Mercedes in the back lot."

Woody had a strained look in his face. He leaned on the wall of the garage. His bum leg was hurting. Woody looked in at the guy. He laughed, "Whitey's eating breakfast right now and has an appointment sometime this morning. Maybe I can give you a price."

Bob reacted happily. "Whoever wants to help me it's fine."

Billy walked up to Woody and said quietly, "That guy was here for over an hour yesterday."

"One hundred dollars. That's a good price." Woody looked into the guy's eyes. "...As is."

The guy said "Fine... Sold."

Billy looked at Woody with a frightened look. "I'm glad *you* said it. That's what I would have sold it for, but Pop would have screamed at me."

Bob pulled one hundred dollars out of his wallet and smiled. "I love that car." They all walked into the garage and Woody wrote up a receipt.

"Billy, will you go and clean it out?" Billy nodded and ran over to the car.

Whitey came fast walking down the driveway and into the garage. He said to Woody, "I see my friend is here."

Woody said, "I'll let you talk to him. I just gave him a price on that black Mercedes in the back."

Whitey whispered to Woody, "How much?"

"A Ben Franklin. I figured, since there's a lot of rust and dents."

"What! I was going to ask for two."

Woody looked at Whitey. "Let's just get that thing out of here. It's growing grass on the floor board. Cats and rats pissed in it."

"Okay... Okay."

Bob held his hundred-dollar bill out to Woody. Whitey grabbed the money. "Thank you. You gotta get that car outta here by tomorrow." Woody handed Whitey the receipt for the guy.

"I'll have my guy pick it up today." Whitey handed him a receipt.

Woody sat on an old cushioned chair that he used to relax on. He propped his feet on an old car seat. "Ahhh... That's good."

Jimmy, Cassie, Nancy, and Sissy came running into the garage. "Woody... Woody... Woody! We missed you." Nancy yelled, full of excitement.

Cassie said with glee, "We're moving soon. We have a new house across from the funeral parlor."

"I'm going to miss you," Nancy said with a sigh.

He grabbed each one of them and gave them a hug. "No... I'm going to miss all of you little squirts."

Jimmy looked at Woody and said quietly, "What was jail like?"

"It was like the worst place I've ever been. The food was awful! I don't plan on ever going back to a place like that... Ever!...And I was an innocent man."

Whitey laughed and threw an oily rag onto Jimmy's head. Jimmy put his mad face on.

"If you don't stop wetting the bed you're heading to that place."

Jimmy said, "Shush pop! They don't put you in jail if you wet the bed."

Whitey laughed and said jokingly, "If you get married your wife will divorce you if you're still wetting the bed." Everyone except Woody and Jimmy laughed.

Jimmy looked into his father's face. "I don't wet the bed anymore."

Pop was still laughing. "Right... Right..." He continued to laugh.

Jimmy was very embarrassed and kicked a stone on the driveway. It boomerangs and hit a car. Pop got up mad as the dickens and chased him. He hollered at him, "There better not be a scratch on that car or *I'll* put you in the can."

CHAPTER 16 The Reconciliation

Woody was sitting in the family waiting room next to the chapel. There was a desk next to a single window in the room. No one was sitting there. He was nervous as hell since he hadn't seen Sandy in over six years. The smell of disinfectant was strong, obviously due to a janitor mopping the floor just a few steps away. Woody walked into the empty attached lavatory and stared into the mirror. He asked himself, *What the hell are you doing here?* Someone attempted to use the bathroom, trying to open the locked door. He turned the water on. He combed his hair. He practices, "Hi Sandy, I hope you're feeling okay." *That was stupid.* "Hi Sandy, I am so sorry you're here at the hospital." *Damn! That was worse.* Someone attempted to get into the room again. The handle was turning back and forth.

He walked out and sat on the closest seat. The Janitor swished the mop over by where Woody was sitting. Woody got up, walked about circling the room and paced out into the hall trying not to ruin the man's clean floor. He waited a couple beats and stepped back into the small waiting room looking a bit frazzled. An elderly woman walked into the lavatory. A few minutes later she emerged and sat at the desk. She made a phone call. Woody heard his name. He noticed Jane entering the room. She headed his way. The two see each other then hugged for what seemed like forever.

"I'm so glad you're here Woody. We've both been so worried about you. We knew you weren't guilty."

"It was terrible! It's good to see you too, Jane. It was hell. I'll tell you about it later. So... What's going on with Sandy?"

Jane looked around the room and spotted two seats together in the corner. "Let's go sit over there," pointing to the chairs. "We can have a more private conversation there." After they sat down Jane started out telling Woody about the doctor appointment and how they arrived at the hospital. "She is having a blood transfusion right now. She'll be back in her room in about an hour. We could go get a cup of coffee and a donut." Woody nodded. "The doctors are saying she doesn't have much time. The cancer is growing fast. Her speech is changing, all in one week. She's getting confused. She isn't eating. She still has her sense of humor but she is sleeping most of the time... When she isn't seizuring. Maybe you can brighten her spirits."

They both got up, left the hospital, hopped in Jane's car and headed to Yum Yum Donuts across the street. They both got a favorite: cream for Jane and jelly for Woody. Jane asked for two black coffees and two glasses of water, one with ice.

Jane filled Woody in about Sandy and how she was still in love with him. He closed his mouth tightly and shook his head. He sat silently for a minute. "I've been thinking about her for a long time, Jane. But time is tough; you get to remember things that can't be undone." Jelly dropped out of his donut onto his clean, crisp white shirt. Woody wets a napkin and tried to get the stain out. Jane grabbed hold of a napkin and picked an ice cube out of her glass. She used the ice cube on the stain and it was almost completely gone. "Thanks." Woody said with a smile, "It's probably been an hour. What do you say? Let's go see how everything went."

They arrived back at the hospital's waiting room. The elderly woman asked if they were the Rathgeb's. Jane nodded. Woody replied, "Under Dooley."

"My name is Jane Rathgeb."

"Oh, that's right... The funny last name." Jane looked at Woody and smiled and asked the woman about Sandy.

"It says here she is ready to see her family now."

Woody looked at Jane. "Family?"

Jane looked back at Woody. "Ah... Yeah... He's the husband. I'm the sister." She nudged Woody's side.

"Yep."

The elderly woman unlocked the door to the aisle where seriously ill patients are. She told them she was in room 308.

Jane walked into Sandy's room first. "Hello." Jane said. She walked over and kissed Sandy. Sandy asked what time it is. Jane said, "It's eleven thirty in the morning. I have a visitor for you." Sandy looked confused.

Woody walked in and kissed Sandy, to her surprise. She stared at him and asked where he had been all her life. "Right here! He said with sincerity. Waiting for you." He looked around the room. She had IVs and oxygen next to her. She looked very pale and much older than he remembered her, but it was his Sandy and he was glad to see her. He noticed her blinds were shut. He asked, "Do you want me to open your blinds?"

She didn't answer him. She just stared at him. "You're my uncle, right? I'm trying to figure out how I know you." Woody looked at Jane with confusion.

Jane walked close to Sandy and held her hand. "Sandy, that's Woody. He's come to visit you. He's your husband."

Sandy asked, "Can I have a drink of water?"

Woody went over to the nurse and asked, "Is she allowed to have water?" She nodded and said she would get it.

The nurse brought Sandy a cup of water with a straw. Sandy knocked it off her table with one swoop of her arm. The nurse looked at everybody and said, "She's got a bit of anxiety, so we'll have to ask the two of you to leave for a few minutes, if you don't mind."

Sandy yelled, "No... No... No! It's okay." The nurse put some medication in her IV.

"She needs to rest. She'll be okay later."

Woody and Jane left quickly and sat in the waiting room. Jane started crying and Woody comforted her. "I'll help you get through this Jane. It's going to be okay."

Jane looked up into Woody's eyes. "She's dying Woody, it will never be okay."

Early in the morning Georgie ran out of the house into the junkyard to say good-bye to Woody. He was getting ready to leave for Illinois. He was headed for boot camp. He looked as if he had just been released from jail. He yelled, "Yahoo! I'm gonna be a Navy man, just like pop."

Billy followed behind him and hollered, "I'm going into the Army! I'm gonna be an Army man."

Georgie looked over at him and made a mean face. "Navy's the best."

"We'll see."

Woody peeked his head out of the garage, "Come here you two." He handed Georgie a twenty dollar bill and said, "Write us letters buddy." He looked over at Billy and said with a serious face, "You're gonna miss him." Billy shook his head. Woody said, "You'll see."

"Where's boot camp?" Woody asked.

"Great Lakes, Illinois."

"Well, good luck bud."

Whitey was walking toward Georgie. "Did you get everything out of your mother's house and into the apartment?"

"Yes I did. All but my bike."

Billy piped in, "He said I could use it."

Whitey looked at Billy. "If it's okay with your brother."

Georgie remarked proudly to his father, "I got my license today so I don't need my bike anymore. I've been driving since I was ten."

"Well you gotta have a car to drive."

"I know pop. You'll give me one."

Whitey shook his head and with a bit of laughter he said, "Well I'll be damned." He laughed a full belly laugh. "I'll give you the Pontiac over there. He pointed to the car that the cops just brought back that had the body in it." Everybody laughed, including Georgie.

Miriam came out of the house calling to Georgie to hurry and get ready to go. His new friend John was on his way to pick him up. Georgie hugged his dad and Woody. Billy and Jimmy wave. Bobby and Dee Dee were running up to him from the house to hug him. Whitey watched his boy hugging his family. "He's ready to make a big change in his life. He's a grown man now."

Woody nodded. And said with sincerity, "Whitey, You did good. I mean it. You should be proud of yourself. I'm gonna leave early now to visit Sandy at the hospital."

Whitey looked surprised. "She's still in the hospital?"

"Yes. And things don't look too good."

Whitey nodded. "Okay. Any time you need to take off."

An hour later Woody walked into Sandy's room. Jane was not there. A different nurse came into the room. "Are you a relative?"

"Ah... Yes. I'm her husband."

"Oh, okay. I didn't think she was married."

The nurse bent down and spoke quietly, "Sandy your husband is here."

Sandy opened her eyes and looked over at Woody, "Oh... Hi there." The nurse walked out of the room. Woody proceeded to walk over to Sandy. He bent down and kissed her on the forehead. Tears began welling in both her eyes.

Sandy said, "I've missed you."

Woody looked into her big brown eyes and said, "I'm here now. Do you need anything?"

Sandy said very quietly, "No thanks. I'm so sorry for what I did to you Woody." She looked away from him. "I've ruined your liii..."

Woody shook his head. He held her hand and patted it. "You didn't do anything. I wasn't giving you any attention. All I thought about was myself. But I'm a changed man now. My family helped me see what was important. I thought of you every day."

Sandy began crying. "I did, I ruined your liii..."

"My life?" Woody asked. Sandy nodded.

"No." Woody shook his head.

Jane walked into the room. "I brought you a candy bar. Oh, hi Woody."

Woody walked over and hugged and kissed Jane hello. Sandy stared at Woody and looked away. Jane walked over and kissed Sandy, "How are you feeling?"

Sandy pulled away and said, "Like a Mack Truck just hit me."

Jane saw Sandy's foot was hanging out. She fixed her pillow and covered her better. "You're having a headache?"

"Massive! But when Woody came in it started to go away, until you came in just now."

Jane stared at Sandy who was looking away.

The nurse came back into the room. "I have good news, you're going home tomorrow." She turned the light on. "I'll be back for your vitals. Okay?"

Jane clapped softly, "Great Sandy." Woody also said good to hear, but the atmosphere had changed in the room.

Sandy was looking at Jane with a stiff upper lip. "So where are you two going for dinner tonight?"

Jane looked directly at Sandy and said, "I beg your pardon? Sandy, what are you talking about? I'm going home and Woody will probably go to his house. Why did you ask me that?"

Woody patted Sandy on the hand, kissed her on the forehead and said, "I'm leaving right now, Sandy. I'm beat and I have to open the junkyard in the morning. I'm going to pick up a couple pizza pies for my brother's kids." He walked over and said goodbye to Jane and just patted her on her shoulder. "See you Jane. Thanks for taking such good care of Sandy."

Jane nodded, and said, "Bye."

When Woody had left Sandy cried, "I'm so sorry Jane. I didn't mean anything by it. I just thought..."

"You thought Woody and I... How could you? You know me better than that. Woody was a great guy Sandy but I would never ruin our relationship for any man." They both start crying and Jane hugged Sandy. Jane said, "Friends for life girl."

Woody arrived back at the yard at five thirty. The yard was closed. Whitey was long gone to his new family with, as Miriam called her, *The Witch*. He knocked on Miriam's door. She answered. She looked like she might have been crying. "Hi Woody."

"Do you guys need a pizza pie?"

Miriam looked at Woody. "Yes, now that Georgie's gone we need to get happy and by the looks of their hungry faces a pizza will sure help. Thanks."

Everybody jumped up and down shouting, "Thanks Woody."

CHAPTER 17 Lucy

Jane woke up six a.m. She stretched... She yawned. "If this is the crack of dawn I should have gotten up before it cracked." Her mind stared into space at the sea of things she had to accomplish. She hadn't planned on Sandy coming home until tomorrow. So now she had to ramp up her schedule with no time to spare. She got up and made a small pot of coffee. She set food out on her stoop for several feral cats that keep the mouse population down at the cemetery.

A fence contractor promised he would be at her house by seven thirty a.m. and she said she would give him the information that he needed to finish the job. She had to be at the hospital by eight thirty when the doctor was supposed to arrive. She wanted to hear what he had to say. Of course, she had to bring Sandy home at or around nine.

Her laundry had become a job in itself. The sheets were washed and she had them hanging on a clothesline from tree to tree which wasn't allowed, but she was not even worried about getting caught. She ran outside to check on them and they were not dry yet. She decided to use a different set of sheets. The fitted sheet was for a larger bed, but she would make it work. She ran from room to room vacuuming, dusting and putting dishes away that were sitting on her sink. She wanted Sandy to feel good and be happy when she walked into the house.

Seven fifteen her phone rang. Who could be calling this early? "Hello..."

"Woody? Good morning. Do I need help, well... Let me see. Hmmm... No, I've got everything covered." She nodded her head and laughed to herself thinking, *He can't see you Jane.* "No Woody. Thanks... She's fine. We are best buddies. I'll call when she's home and everything is hunky dory. Okay? Thank you from the bottom of my heart Mr. Dooley. Okay... Bye."

That was sweet of him. He was definitely a sweetheart. Her mind wandered. Hmmm... I remember when he hated me. Maybe he didn't. I just know he's the best. She walked over to her kitchen sink to put dishes away. *Keep things cool Jane* she thought. She peeked outside. It was still dark but she could see a sliver of daylight. *Okay Jane, now focus!*

Eight a.m. Woody opened the junkyard like every other day. No one was around and he walked over to the garage. He walked in and noticed Whitey's newspaper wasn't there next to the gate. Someone was in that dirty old bathroom. Suddenly the door opened. It was Jimmy. He had the paper opened to the funnies and he had just made a dump.

"Hi Woody. Our bathroom is clogged up again. We aren't allowed to use it except to pee."

"Okay there buddy. I understand. Go back to what you were doing."

"I'm done." He ran out of the bathroom leaving the newspaper on the floor. The toilet wasn't flushed, he hadn't washed his hands and he left the light on.

Woody could see Jimmy looking around for Zeus and Sampson. He grabbed Zeus and began walking him to his pen. Sampson followed. They loved walking back to their pen since that was when breakfast usually arrived.

Woody cleaned up the bathroom and gathered the paper putting it back together. The headline showed Michelle

Miller and her brother Robert Caruso were indicted for the July tenth murder of Dodd Miller. "Good, you money hungry son of a bitch." The junkyard phone rang. Before he picked up the phone, he said out loud, "Who the hell needs a part this early?" He answered, "Hello. King's."

"Woody... Oh hi. It's Jane. My car won't start. I think the battery's dead."

Woody said, "Don't worry. I'll be there as soon as I get relief." She said thanks.

Billy came running out and told Woody he was going shopping with his mom today. Woody snapped back at him, "You gotta to stay here for just about two hours first so I can go help Jane get her car started."

Billy whined, "Ohhh... Woody... Please. I'll be back real soon."

"Tell your dad he has to get over here right away."

"He won't come. Don't go Woody."

Woody was already in his truck. "I'll be back soon."

Woody pulled up the driveway. Jane was talking to someone who was writing on a clipboard.

"Hi Woody. Thanks for coming."

"Hi Jane. We can fix your car later. Don't you have to pick Sandy up now?"

Jane waved to the guy who was now walking behind her house with two other workers. She hopped in the truck. "Thank you, thank you, thank you. They're putting in a new fence in the back of the cemetery. We have had some vandalism in the past year and hopefully this will help."

They pulled into the busy hospital parking lot. It was a bustling Monday morning. Jane got out and said, "After you find a parking spot I'll be checking Sandy out. So just come in."

It was nine fifteen and Sandy was dressed and sitting in a chair. Her IV's were still attached to her arm but her bed was already clean and ready for the next patient. She had a bad night which caused the nurse to give her a strong dose of medicine so she was a bit drowsy.

"Hi Jane." she said with slurred words.

"I'm taking you home sweet girl."

Sandy looked at her and said sleepily, "Thank God."

The nurse came in and sent Jane to the desk to get the information that the doctor left with Sandy's discharge papers including a long list of prescriptions. A candy striper had already brought a wheelchair up for leaving.

Just in time Woody walked in the room with a smile. "Hey Sandy. You're taking a ride in Lucy, the old grey tank." Sandy smiled. Woody limped away to retrieve the truck from the parking lot. His leg was sore making his limp more obvious.

The nurse said goodbye to Sandy and told her to not run around the house too much. They all smiled and left. Lucy was cleaner than usual, and Sandy was smiling ear to ear.

CHAPTER 18 The Transmission

September mornings could be quite nippy. Today Woody could see frost already on the grass. One single stream of sun had burst across his front yard melting the ice crystals where the sunbeam streamed. Zeus and Sampson were waiting for Woody at the gate to his home. He usually brought them some small treat when he entered the yard. Today Woody had run out of treats so he brought them both a piece of his favorite cheese.

"I hope you two are happy. That was my last piece of cheese." Woody limped over to their pens without dog food. He walked back over to Miriam's large covered porch and opened the lid to the galvanized trash can that held the dog food. It was down to less than a cup per dog. "That's not going to work." He scooped the small amount and sadly gave each dog a pittance of their normal share, but they were so hungry they didn't notice. "I'll pick some dog food up for you guys," he said apologetically. He began limping over to the gate. Whitey was there earlier and beat him to the punch. He was already reading the paper and on his second cup of coffee.

"Good morning boss," Woody said as he plopped himself on the comfy chair. "I have to pick up some dog food for those devil dogs."

Whitey shook his head. "That son of a bitch is only going to the slammer for twenty five years." Woody stood up and reached to see the article. Whitey handed the whole paper to him. "We have to scrap today. I need to pick up some money. Billy will be out after he has his breakfast. I want all the cars on Ivy Street side flattened and put on that old geezer truck. Jimmy will be out to help."

"Okay, we'll get it done," Woody said reassuringly.

Miriam hollered for Jimmy to come back to the house to get a jacket on, but he said he was okay. Jimmy walked up to Woody. He looked up at him. "Chicky said he's coming up here to beat me up if we don't give him a transmission. His dad hates us even more. He's going to beat Pop up if we don't do something."

"Don't you worry. Nobody's going to beat you up. Anyway, his transmission is waiting for him in the garage."

"Oh, good. Thanks Woody." Jimmy ran to the garage and hollered, "Hip hip hooray."

Woody shouted, "We're not putting it in though." Jimmy stopped and looked back at Woody with bewilderment. Just as Woody said that Chicky walked up to Woody and asked about the transmission. "Hi Chicky. We have your transmission here. Just what you asked for. Do you have a truck to take it home in?"

His father came walking around the corner behind Chicky. "My name is Charles Lee and I want to speak with George King."

Woody said, "I'll be able to help you. I'm his brother."

"Well, I want a damn transmission for the car we bought from you."

"It's been sitting in the garage waiting for you," Woody said innocently. "Come with me, I'll show you what has to be done." The two men walked to the garage and laughter could be heard. Chicky was staring at Jimmy pissed and ready to pounce on him.

"Well, I got to get going. My dad is filling our scrap truck with smashed cars."

"What's a scrap truck?" Chicky asked.

"It's a large truck big enough to take about twenty cars that are flattened to the scrap yard and they weigh the truck with the steel in it and then they take the cars off the truck and weigh the empty truck and that determines how much money to pay my dad. He makes good money that way... And I've got to help. Bye." Jimmy took off to the other side of the yard. Chicky watched as Jimmy ran away.

Chicky noticed his father and Woody were lifting the transmission on to Woody's truck. Woody drove over to where Whitey was working and told him he had to deliver the transmission to Chicky's house just down the road a piece and maybe Jimmy could watch for any customers. Whitey waved and Woody followed Charles to his house.

Several hours later Woody pulled in and quickly Jumped out of his truck. He was greasy and had a panicked look on his face. "What time is it Whitey?"

"Three, why?"

"I have to pick up a prescription for Jane... I mean Sandy."

Whitey laughed at his excitement. "What time are you supposed to take it to her?"

"Well... Hours ago. I didn't pick up dog food or those snacks the store has for dogs either."

Whitey looked at Woody, "I'll go get the dog food. But snacks? You've gotta be kidding." He laughed. He then shook his head and said, "No one called today. If she was in need of the medicine wouldn't she have called?" Whitey said, "Snacks huh?"

"Well, maybe she tried to call me at home. I have to leave early again today."

Whitey waved him on. "Go, go, go." Woody jumped back in his truck and drove it to his house around the block. He called Jane.

"Hello Jane. I got caught up in a transmission. I'm sorry."

"That's okay, I ran out and picked it up when the pharmacy called. Everything's fine here. No worries. Why don't you come over for an early dinner? I made Spaghetti."

"Sure. How is Sandy?"

"Fine. She's sitting up right now watching some game show. You want to speak with her?"

"Ah... No, but tell her I'll see her. When do you want me to come over?"

"Why don't you come whenever you can get here? She'll be thrilled."

"Okay, I'll be right there."

Woody jumped in the shower. He scrubs using a floor scrub brush but the grease still wasn't coming off very well. "Damn." He hurried and got dressed. He left a small smudge next to his nose. When he looked in the mirror he laughed, "Well, anyone can tell smudge is my cat." He laughed again, a full belly laugh just like his brother.

CHAPTER 19 The Murmur

"One hundred fifty eight thousand dollars is what they want Alice! I don't have that kind of money." Whitey stormed out of his house. The door slammed shut. "Money don't grow on trees."

Alice, in her robe, stepped out on the front porch which was on the second floor. Her face was red and her eyes were swollen from crying. "George, you'll go to jail if you don't pay it."

"Well, I won't get cold eggs there." She cried harder. He looked up at Alice. "They don't want to put me in jail. I have eleven kids. Go in the house and get some clothes on."

Alice turned and waved some papers. "You forgot your papers."

Whitey had already finished walking down the steps. He grumbled, "Those damn people. Son of a B." He climbed back up and grabbed the papers from her hand. "Stop your damn crying." Alice went back in the house and slammed the door.

An hour later Whitey was sitting in Joe Palermo's office. "The only thing you have to worry about Whitey are death and taxes."

Whitey stared at Joe. "I'm not throwing away my hard earned money."

"Do you have it Mr. King?"

"Maybe, but they're not gettin' it! Can't you stop this?"

"I'm not a tax lawyer Whitey. Look, I have a friend I went to college with who is a tax attorney. I call him Mickey. His name is Michael Gaines. I'll call him today and get back with you."

"Don't forget or I'll be in the can! Tomorrow they will be at the yard. They could shut it down! What can I do?"

"Whitey, go to work like any other day. You have to earn a living. You have to pay your bills like I do." He chuckled. "I'll call you tomorrow."

Whitey stood up, reached in his pocket, and pulled out a wad of money. "Here, I think it's all there."

Joe stared at the wad sitting on his desk. "I'm sure it is." He nodded his head. "You're one in a million Whitey... One in a million."

As Whitey pulled up the drive way he noticed that the yard seemed to be bustling with customers. Billy was driving around in an Alpha Romeo sports car showing a customer. Woody was throwing some tires up onto someone's truck. Bobby and Dee Dee were sitting in the middle of the driveway next to their house half dressed and barefoot. They seem to have rocks and toy soldiers scattered about. Whitey pulled up right next to where they were playing. "What in the world are you two doing?"

Miriam came flying out of the house. "I told them to play on the porch. They're going to the doctor's today. Bobby, go finish getting dressed. Wear your brown trousers." He was dressed in his pajama bottoms. "Dee Dee, you have to wear the dress I made you. One of you move those soldiers off the driveway."

"Ah Mommy, I don't like that dress. It makes me look skinny." Dee Dee started slowly picking up the soldiers.

"You're wearing it and that's that."

"Miriam, if the IRS comes by... Tell them..."

"Tell them what? I won't be here. I have to take these two kids to see Dr. Perry today. I won't be home. Have Alice come over."

Whitey shook his head. "Who will be left here in the house?"

"Your three oldest daughters. What do they want from me anyway? I don't have anything to do with the IRS."

"They might want to talk with you."

"George, that's ridiculous. I'm not employed and you're not married to me anymore. What would they want from me?"

"The house you're living in is in my name."

"Of course, *everything* is in your name."

"Mir, I thought I put the land in your name when we were married. Everything *else* is in my name."

"No, you did not. You said you were going to... I know you didn't. I already checked that out."

George looked down. "Maybe you're right."

"Well, you are the one they are looking for George, not little old housewife me." Miriam hurried back into the house.

Whitey was standing on the porch. He grabbed a hold of Dee Dee and gave her a big bear hug. His whiskers hurt like a scrub brush. But she just laughed at him. She escaped his hold on her and ran into the house. "Owww... He hurts."

An hour later at Dr. Perry's Office the waiting room was packed with kids.

"Virginia King..."

"That's me. My name is Dee Dee."

Miriam got up and told Bobby to stay put. She took Dee Dee's hand and walked into the examining room. "Her formal name is Virginia but we're so used to calling her by her nick name." The nurse measured her height and weight.

She asked, "Why do they call you Dee Dee?" And added, "You're going to have to eat more meat and potatoes, Virginia."

Dee Dee looked at the nurse and made a funny face. "You can call me Dee Dee."

The nurse took her temperature. "You have a bit of a fever."

Miriam shook her head. "She's fine. I know when she's sick."

Dee Dee said, "My brother Bobby named me when he was a baby and learning to talk he called me a Day Day instead of baby. So, that's how I got the name Dee Dee."

Dr. Perry walked into the room and Miriam sat in the chair. She smiled and nodded at him. "Miriam. Who do we have here today?"

"This is Dee Dee." She smiled at Dr. Perry.

" Oh I know who you are, you're the one born on Christmas day. Dee Dee nodded her heard. "Hmmm..." He washed his hands in the sink.

"So that's what they call you, huh?" He threw the wet linen towel into a container. He walked over to Dee Dee and examined her. "Open your mouth and say 'Ah'." He looked in her ears. "How many potatoes do I see?"

Dee Dee looked at him and said, "What?"

He listened to her heart. It seemed like forever. He looked over at her mother with serious concern on his face. "Did you know she has a very prominent heart murmur?" We should do an EKG on her just to be on the safe side." The nurse was in the room with them. He whispered something in her ear. She nodded her head.

"This can be the result of a very high fever. Remember two years ago when you had me come out to your house? She had rheumatic fever. She also had strep. Sometimes the heart valves can be permanently damaged. We'll arrange for her to go see a specialist. You don't want to wait too long. Now, the nurse will have her change into a gown and we're going to do an EKG on her. *If* our machine is working. Otherwise I'll send you to a Dr. Bisetti who has several machines. He'll be able to check her out."

"No," Miriam shook her head rapidly. Miriam leaned in to speak with Dr. Perry so Dee Dee couldn't hear. "Is that serious?"

Dr. Perry whispered back, "We'll talk in my office." Miriam nodded.

A few minutes later she was alone in Dr. Perry's office.

"I don't know how serious her murmur is. I'll refer you to a fine cardiologist who is the best in the area. Dr. Frank Bisetti. He's one of the finest in his field. He's trained in valves. So there's no charge for you today Miriam, but Dr. Bisetti may charge a pretty exorbitant amount. You might want to tell your husband."

"My ex? Her father. Believe me I'll let him know as soon as I get home."

CHAPTER 20 Dinosaurs

It was Friday and the day that Sandy and Jane typically visited David. Sandy had been having a bad day so Jane decided they couldn't go. But Jane remembered she promised

David she would bring him a book on dinosaurs. The book was in the back seat of Jane's car. Woody was on his way over. He was bringing some soup that Miriam had prepared for Sandy and Jane. When woody arrived the girls were having a hard time with personal stuff: bathing, finding Sandy's tooth brush, and figuring out pills.

"I can run and get you guys some ice cream for later if you want," Woody called into the bedroom.

Jane called back, "Woody, I do want to ask you for a favor."

"Anything... Well almost anything."

Jane ran out to her car and back into the house with the book. She held her hand up and said with excitement, "I'll be right back." She ran into Sandy's bedroom.

Jane came running out and told Woody, "I need feminine pads... And ice cream would be great. But the biggest favor would be for you to drop off a book to little David, Sandy's son at the Hope House. You know, that little birthday boy. His name is David Dooley. Here... I wrapped it. He loves to unwrap things."

"She used my last name?"

"That's Sandy's last name too. You two are still married, you know."

"But... David is her boyfriend's child right?"

Jane looked at Woody with hesitation. "Umm... Listen. The guy wasn't interested in David. Sandy's last name is still Dooley. Sooo... Do you get it? She didn't want to change her name, especially since that jerk didn't want to get married or have anything to do with David."

"Yeah, he was a jerk alright! Yeah, I'll take the book to David, no problem. Oh, by the way, what brand pads?"

Jane laughed. "Whatever is the cheapest or whatever you find. Don't forget to get chocolate ice cream for me and..."

Woody said, "Vanilla for Sandy. I remember very well. I better get going. Do I have to tell David anything special?"

Sandy came out in her robe. "Sorry, I was eavesdropping. Tell him Mommy loves him."

Woody stared at Sandy. "I will definitely tell him that." Woody left with the package that Jane gave him for David. The dinosaur book was neatly wrapped.

A half hour later Woody walked into the Hope House. Mrs. Lee was there. "Well hello Mr. Woody, how are you? What brings you here this afternoon?"

"Hello Mrs. Lee, I mean Ruth. I am here to deliver a gift for David Dooley from his mother who is sick."

Mrs. Lee with confusion said, "She's sick again? Sign in here Mr. Woody."

Woody signed Dagwood Dooley. As *Reason for the visit* he wrote *Want to drop off a gift*. "Well, yes. She has cancer you know."

Mrs. Lee's attitude changed immediately and she shook her head. "Oh my, so sad." She looked at the sign-in sheet. "You're related to Sandy and David?"

"Kind of," he said. "Which way do I go?" Mrs. Lee asked how he was related to Sandy. Woody said, "She's my wife."

"I am so, so sorry Mr. Woody, I mean Mr. Dooley. You don't have to explain anything else from now on. I'll walk you to his room right away. He'll be so happy to see you, I'm sure."

They walked down the familiar hallway. Mrs. Lee knocked on David's door. "David, I have a special visitor for you."

Both Woody and Mrs. Lee could hear David through the door say, "Mommy and Aunty, hooray." When the door opened David looked disappointed and asked Mrs. Lee why that man was here and not Aunty or Mommy.

Mrs. Lee looked at Woody. "This child doesn't know who you are."

David looked at Mrs. Lee, "Yes I do. I know him. Aunty said he's a friend. Mommy's friend and he bought the pizza pies at Christmas for everybody. He bought everybody toys and sang Happy Birthday at my party. But I wanted my mommy to be here. I miss Mommy and Aunty."

Woody spoke with careful concern, "Your mommy is sick today. Your Aunty and Mommy asked me to bring you something." He handed David the gift. David was sulking but took the present without hesitation.

"Do you mind if I just sit with you for a moment or two while you open the gift?"

David shook his head. "I mean..." He quickly nodded his head.

Mrs. Lee asked David if he would like to go into the activity room with Mr. Woody. "Sorry, I mean Mr. Dooley?"

David looked at Woody with surprise. "You have the same last name as me."

Woody replied, "Yep! And I really like my last name."

The three walked out of David's room and down the hall to an activity room. Mrs. Lee waved at Woody and said, "I'll be right down the hall at the front desk if you need me." Both Woody and David seemed to be preoccupied with the gift.

David sat in a chair at one of the tables. He smiled from ear to ear. "I hope it's what I think it is."

Mrs. Lee peeked in at the two of them, smiled and walked away.

David quickly tore at the package frantically. "It's the dinosaur book I wanted. "Yay." David hugged Woody and it was a feeling that Woody could not believe. There was an instant spark, a connection with this child. He kissed David and sat with him, going over every page multiple times, exploring this new relationship that surprised both of them.

Woody was paging through all the pictures in the book. David showed how smart he was by naming each dinosaur. Woody showed a great surprise and interest. David hugged Woody.

Looking into David's bright blue eyes, Woody said, "Was it just what you were hoping for?"

David nodded rapidly, and smiled.

CHAPTER 21 The Doctor's Office

Coughing, and suffering one of her worst headaches ever left Sandy yearning for the comfort of her own soft pillow. The doctor's office waiting room where she was sitting was well air conditioned and brighter than usual causing Sandy to have a sensation of spinning. Throbbing pain intensified as she coughed. Jane planted her there so she could run an errand a block away to pick up several prescriptions. "I'll be right back," Jane said as she left.

Sandy was alone in the waiting room but found a way to lay across several empty chairs. She wrapped herself in her sweater like a cocoon.

The door opened. "Mommy, I don't want to go in there." A young girl entered holding a sweet little doll. Her mother walked in and sat on the other side of the waiting room. The child continued to cry.

Sandy sat up and apologized. She stared into the child's frightened eyes. "I didn't mean to scare you sweetie. I'm feeling sick today. I sometimes have to lie down when my head aches."

The child's mother responded, "You didn't scare her. She just doesn't want to have any more tests."

Sandy looked at the mother and said, "I get bad headaches. I feel yucky when they won't go away. I hate them." Sandy stood up, put her sweater on and sat a bit closer to the child. She said quietly, "But you know what? I have to find out how to fix whatever's causing these bad headaches." Sandy took a deep breath, then continued, "How old are you? My name is Sandy."

The little girl hid in her mother's arms and tried to get on her lap. Her mother moved her to the chair next to her.

"Sit there Anna. Mommy can't carry you anymore. Her name, since she won't talk to you, is Anna, and she is six years old."

Anna whispered to her mother, "I'm almost seven."

Her mother responded in a whisper, "But you *are* still six."

"My little boy is five, and he can't wait until he's six."

Anna asked, "What's his name?"

"David. He's only afraid of spiders. He told me nothing makes him afraid... Just spiders." Sandy coughed for a short time, apologized and held her head with both hands. "Sorry."

"Isn't he afraid of snakes?" Anna asked getting closer. Close enough that Sandy could see an area of her hair that had been shaved.

"Well, the only snake he ever saw was a friendly garter snake in his grand pop's garden. And they are our friends. They eat bad bugs that try to eat our plants. So I taught him to leave them alone. They are not dangerous. However there are many very dangerous snakes in the world." Sandy smiled.

"Where is David?" Anna asked quizzically.

With a tear in her eye Sandy tried to answer Anna's question. She hesitated, and coughed.

The nurse slid the window to the waiting room open. "Anna Smith?"

Sandy got up first, then realized the nurse was calling for Anna. She sat back down. "That's you sweetheart." she said.

Anna grabbed hold of her mother's hand. "Mommy, I don't want to go in there."

Anna's mother walked into the examination room. Her daughter followed behind pouting in defiance. Finally she was in. The door slammed shut.

Sandy began a soft cry. "I don't know how to answer that child." She held her head on both sides and looked up. "Dear God, please help me. I want to see David."

Fifteen minutes had passed. The door of the examination room opened and the little girl came out. Looking at Sandy she said, "I don't need any more tests." The mother followed behind slowly sobbing.

Doctor Livingston followed behind her. "I'm so sorry Mrs. Smith. I wish I had better news for you."

Mrs. Smith turned and looked square in his eyes. "There must be someone that can help her. I'm not stopping here. She is my life."

"Wait Mrs. Smith. I have the name of a doctor at the University of Pennsylvania who has been doing research on that particular type of tumor." She grabbed the card from the doctor and with her other hand tightly held on to her daughter's. They walked out. Mrs. Smith could be heard sobbing. The door slammed shut.

Dr. Livingston walked over to Sandy, shook her hand and gestured to follow him into the examination room. Jane arrived while Sandy was being examined. She could see a little girls doll on one of the chairs and took it to the nurse. "Oh thank you. That must be Anna's Smith's doll. I'll make sure she gets it. Thank you."

"Dr. Livingston. I can't endure much more of this pain! I'm coughing all the time now and it causes me to want to throw up. My headaches are also intensified."

"Well, I suspect you have pneumonia from the wheezing I hear in your lungs. You have a fever. But I'll have to send you next door to the hospital to get a chest X-ray as soon as possible. The prognosis will most likely be to rest until the infection is gone. So let me say good bye for now. Head over to the hospital. They'll send me the results and I'll prescribe a strong antibiotic to get rid of the infection. How have your seizures been?"

"I haven't had one today at all. And the day before I had a very mild one," Sandy said. He shook her hand and walked her to the door. Jane was sitting facing the door.

"Jane, we have to run next door. I have to get a chest X-ray. He thinks I might have pneumonia." Two hours later they drove over to the doctor's office to find out if it was pneumonia. Sandy wanted to go into the office to get the information herself. As she was walking in, Mrs. Smith and Anna were leaving with her little doll in hand.

"Thank you Miss Sandy." Anna smiled. "Thanks for saving Mary my doll."

CHAPTER 22 The IRS

By the week before labor day Miriam had saved quite a stash of cash for her children's school clothes. She would make it a two part shop. She wanted to bring the younger kids first because they grew so tall over the summer. Nancy, Bobby and Dee Dee were getting ready to go. Mommy liked them to wear clean clothes. That may be a challenge. Today especially since the wash had been building up. Miriam had saved her money this year by sewing dresses for the girls and a pair of trousers for bobby. The temperature was in the 90's. It felt strange to be shopping for winter coats. The soles of Bobby and Dee Dee's shoes had holes and had been flapping. Miriam looked at their feet. She was in a good mood. She whispered, "New shoes at last." Whitey expected Miriam to take the bus but today he had softened a bit. He had offered her one of the junkers that he had been trying to sell. She was thrilled. It would take forever to complete this chore by bus.

Miriam liked to pick dresses that were plain beige and browns. Dee Dee tried to persuade her to buy bright colors. Once in a while she would succeed. But for the most part it was almost impossible. Miriam usually had the last word. She liked to keep it simple and use basic colors because she could match them easier and she could get away with not washing them longer. She liked to buy material in bulk and make their clothes. But all the girls were getting tired of the same material. Their clothes looked like uniforms. Luckily, today Whitey gave Miriam some extra 'going back to school shopping bucks'.

Whitey asked, "How's Dee Dee? You said she had to see a cardiologist."

Miriam said, "She's fine for now. She'll need to be checked every year the cardiologist said. Thanks for the money. You know he charges twenty dollars more than Perry?"

Whitey reached in his wallet and flipped out a twenty dollar bill and handed it to Miriam. "There."

Miriam walked away with a Cheshire Cat smile.

Woody had filled the car with gas and cleaned it out for her. It had been full of tools, tires and trash. It was an old beat up Studebaker. Miriam was thrilled to simply not have to wait for a bus with three in tow.

Georgie was back from boot camp and would be flying to Rota, Spain, in a couple weeks where he would await further assignment. Today was his last day to work at the junkyard.

He would then be busy with the normal stuff required to prepare for going overseas. He would have to get his new uniforms and all his shots. Mostly he was anxious to bring his girlfriend around to meet the family.

Whitey would be joining Georgie for a last smashed car-truck weighing. He wanted to take him to their favorite cheese steak sandwich shop in South Philly on their way home. Georgie was annoyed with his father for suddenly taking a last ditch interest in a father and son camaraderie. Whitey had been pushing him from morning to night for the last year. Georgie was exhausted.

"You don't have to go with me pop," Georgie said with more confidence than ever.

"I'm going, and that's that," he said with a smile.

Billy, along with Woody, was assigned to watch the operation of the yard. Today was special for Billy; his brother who he was close to was gaining a great lunch and the greatest escape too. He felt a bit envious. He wanted to go but Whitey would not have it. Instead he was asked to clean up the dog pens. One of the worst, and most disgusting jobs of all. Woody asked Jimmy, Sissy, and Cassie to help him. They protested but they liked Woody so much they all agreed.

Without warning four black ominous cars pulled up the driveway all the way to the house. A fifth car pulled inside the junkyard entrance. It stopped and a man in a dark suit swung open his car door with complete calm. He closed the gate. The kids were milling around on their front porch dressed neatly waiting to go shopping. They began staring as if something nefarious was about to unfold. The man at the gate spotted the *closed* sign and propped it so that it could be clearly seen.

Mr. Pool from the IRS got out of one of the cars and walked toward Whitey. Last night's rain puddled the driveway. It splattered on Mr. Pool's clean starched trousers. With his hanky he wiped the mud quickly. He waited for Whitey to meet him halfway.

A camera man was at the gate. He spoke to Billy but he wouldn't answer any of his questions. The camera man was not let in so he stood on his car. The flash of several pictures made everyone curious. At the same time they were perplexed as to how the media knew the IRS would be there at that moment. The cameraman took more pictures.

Woody limped up the driveway toward the house and locked eyes with Whitey whose reddened, chiseled face was now etched with distress. Georgie walked over to the two little kids standing on the porch and sat on a round wooden electrical cable spool. He attempted to hold Dee Dee's hand but she pulled away and ran into the house.

"Mommy, is Daddy going to jail? I'm scared." The dogs began barking.

Mr. Pool was followed by two official looking men with guns. "George H. King. Is that your correct name?"

Whitey began a nervous laughter. "Now, you know my name," he said sarcastically. "We met before. Yes?"

Mr. Pool read a paper that sounded very official. He was with Internal Revenue Service and was here to collect one hundred and fifty eight thousand dollars. Whitey grimaced and shook his head. "I can give you half of that but I haven't been able to come up with that full amount." He began to shake like none of the kids had ever seen him before. His eyes teared up. "My attorney sent you a letter, didn't he? Can I have a few more weeks?"

"Mr. King, you were given sixty days. You assured us you would be able to produce the funds to get you caught up for the tax years of 1950 through 1958. The amount was one hundred fifty eight thousand dollars. Penalties will be added by the court. You are now under arrest."

"Will you let me make a phone call first?" The two IRS police were cuffing Whitey. Sweat rolled down the side of his face. He exuded the look of a guilty man that thought he could get away with anything.

Woody said, "I'll call *The Horse*. He'll get you released."

Miriam tried to shield Bobby and Nancy who started to cry. "Go in the house." Billy, Jimmy and Georgie tried to look in the darkened car window. They all waved to their dad.

Miriam tried to get a glimpse of her ex-husband. "Yes George. I'll take care of it. I know what I have to do." Miriam teared up.

The kids followed the strange black cars while the IRS man unlocked the gate then gave the key to Georgie, the oldest boy. The agent said, "This business is closed as of this moment until further notice." All four cars left while the media took pictures of the kids and the cars leaving for the federal courthouse in Philadelphia.

CHAPTER 23 The Fly

Sandy was awake. It was nine a.m. and she had the world on her shoulders. She had been lying in bed for over an hour contemplating the possibility of a future with Woody.

Secrets that fester and lay dormant for too long could cause more damage to the person hiding ones hidden story. Once a secret was revealed the truth would truly set you free. Those thoughts have helped many including Sandy understand that it was not the fabrication but the withholding of knowledge from people that may permanently destroy them. On the other hand, this may give peace to someone who already knew the information. What if they had been given a lie and the secret was with the storyteller? This information was swirling in Sandy's head. She wanted to confront Woody. She had every intention of telling him the truth about how she met Ernesto. She wanted most importantly to tell Woody about David, but he was already introduced to the boy. Why hurt him? *You've already hurt him,* she said to herself. This was her biggest fear. He believed the boy was some other man's child. He has found out how very sweet David is already. He enjoyed talking to the boy. He gloated about his visit with him. Maybe Woody already knew. Maybe when he looked into David's eyes he could tell. After all, David was the spitting image of Woody physically and Sandy believed mentally also.

It was the same time at the Hope House. The staff was attempting to gather pictures and information for their annual yearbook. Mrs. Lee was leafing through some old pictures from way back when and found a photo of Dagwood Dooley that was the spitting image of little David. He had just turned six. She stood up at her desk and called her assistant Glenda Rhine to verify what she had found and how absolutely amazing the resemblance was to the photo of David that would be in the current year book.

Glenda was floored. She replied, "It's his doppelganger. They *must* be related. There is no other explanation."

Sandy had fallen back to sleep for two more hours. Now it was eleven a.m. and she was waking up and feeling pretty good. Her coughing had subsided but she was weak and felt a bit nauseous. It was time to try and feel alive. Her headaches were there but not severe. She stood up and gazed at the vista out the window. You could see for miles because they were on a hill. It truly was a 'Grand View'. She couldn't see Jane, but she could see the beautiful grounds that she maintained. Jane had worked tirelessly and was outside somewhere soaking shrubs and sprinkling flowers. It was the last week in August and Sandy was on a mission to get herself well enough to sit out under that beautiful maple tree where the picnic table was and where she could feel close to nature.

Jane walked into the bedroom. "Hi there Sandy! Good morning. Glad you're up." Jane looked at Sandy with a curious expression. "You're up to something. I can tell. Are you coming in the kitchen to eat breakfast?" Sandy nodded. "Are you feeling better?" Jane clapped her hands and said, "Let's have our favorite... Pancakes."

Sandy looked at Jane and blurted, "Okay, let's do it." They both giggled.

Jane added, "And... We'll eat at the picnic table this lovely morning. Okay?"

Sandy vigorously nodded.

An hour later Sandy and Jane were still sitting under the maple tree. Sandy was smiling and looked over at Jane. "Paradise." Jane made a high stack of pancakes. Both the view and the pancakes sopped in butter and warm maple syrup were exquisite. One single fly was diving about like it was playing a game. It was switching from Sandy's pancakes to Jane's. Jane swatted at it and said, "You're not getting mine."

Sandy laughed and said, "Nor mine."

Both girls attempted to cover their pancakes with their hands. Then it was back. Jane had a fly swatter but being outside made it a bit difficult. The fly had the advantage. She methodically brushed it away from the sticky bottle of maple syrup which was its target. She was in a race with it for the tacky potion that was slathered on both stacks of pancakes and the bottle. It was definitely the maple syrup it was after. She focused on the sticky lid of the maple syrup bottle. She knew the fly would land there sooner or later. Sure enough... It alighted on the lid. As soon as she aimed, the fly did too. Jane was determined to strike it on the tacky lid. The fly had two eyes sprinkled with thousands more covering them in case they were needed. In this case... They were. It saw her coming. Jane slapped at the bottle's lid but hung up the swatter on the gumminess of the neck of the bottle. The lid teetered. The fly had tricked her. There it was on the top of Jane's stack. The girls laughed. This was going to be a good day.

Jane was finishing up her cold coffee. She said, "Isn't this view worth being here? I have enjoyed this place as if it were my own. I can't get enough of that view."

"Jane... Jane..." Sandy tried to get her complete attention. "I'm going to have a talk with Woody. I'm going to tell him everything... Everything! I want him to know everything about how I messed up. I believe I'm still in love with him. I mean I *am* in love with him."

Jane nodded, and stammered, "Good... Good." Jane thought about Woody and how hurt he must have been.

"I want to tell him all the sweet things about David that a father needs to know. And... I'm going to tell him that I have always loved him." All of a sudden, without warning, everything Sandy ate was barfed onto the ground next to the picnic table, including her sun glasses which were plopped in the middle of the mess.

Jane jumped up and ran over to Sandy. She wiped throw up off her pajama top and escorted her back into the house. "We tried, sweetie. One too many pancakes will do it." She continued fussing over Sandy who began crying.

She pushed Jane away and snapped, "I can clean myself, Jane. Give me a moment. I'm okay now, please."

Sandy flopped on her bed. Jane sat at the kitchen table shaking her head. She reached for her cleaning bucket and filled it with water and bleach. She looked at sputum that had made a drip path to where Sandy was headed back to the bathroom. She felt deflated. The phone rang. Jane answered. It was Bella from Social Services. She was on her way out to visit with Sandy.

One hour later Bella was at the door. Sandy had cleaned herself off and was sitting in the living room waiting while dozing in the lounge chair. When Bella arrived Sandy was in full sleep mode and very comfortable looking.

Jane called her, "Sandy, Bella is here."

Sandy was drowsy but woke up feeling much refreshed. "Hello Bella."

Sandy sat down at the kitchen table and they chit-chatted for a while about how beautiful the landscape was here and how it has been over a year that Bella had been working on getting David back. Today was the day they were working on a plan. Sandy was so excited she could hardly contain herself. She felt suddenly like she was on cloud nine. She wanted to move outside to sit on the picnic table but feared Bella would be sickened by the dried vomit still there.

With a bit of excitement Bella said, "I'll be representing you for the State. Today we are just going to fill out the paperwork that will have to be presented to the courts. It will state that we feel you are not a threat to do any harm or to neglect your child and that you are not drinking or using any type of recreational drugs. We also conclude that this lovely home is the best place anyone could ask to raise a child in." She laughed. "Even though there are some dead bodies all around you." She laughed again.

Jane looked at Sandy with a disappointed stare. Sandy whispered to Jane, "I'll get my own place. It'll work."

Bella looked at them. "Is everything okay?" She fidgeted with her clip board.

Jane looked down at the floor. "Well, the only problem is that children are not allowed here. You have to be eighteen or older." Sandy looked over at Jane and shook her head.

Bella addressed Sandy with concern, "We have thirty days to come up with a suitable living arrangement. So not to worry. I'll give you a couple of weeks to come up with a plan that we can all agree on. How does that sound?"

Sandy looked happier than Jane had ever seen her. They all smiled and watched Bella walk past the picnic table toward her car. She looked around and shook her head. "There's a funny smell out here. Kind of like pancakes." They all laughed.

CHAPTER 24 The Jail

It was eight a.m. on a Friday morning. George H. King sat in an eight foot by six foot jail cell. He was waiting for some sort of activity... Anything. The small bunk bed that he slept on had a flimsy striped mattress with no sheet. There were visible urine stains and a flat pillow without a case that caused his neck to feel quite stiff. There was a toilet next to the bed with no seat and a sink without any soap. There was no place to sit except the bed. A bible was on the window sill that was so high that Whitey couldn't reach it if he wanted to. He laid down and yelled, "Get me coffee, please."

A guard was standing in front of his cell gate. "Breakfast is at nine a.m. The janitor service will be in today at nine thirty and your attorney, Mr. Palermo, called to let you know he will be here at eleven a.m." The guard walked away shaking his head.

Whitey barked back at him, "That's it!? Damn you! What the hell am I supposed to do here? Am I supposed to rot here? Just get me a damn cup of coffee! Can't you give me a damn chair to sit on? I'm not a murderer."

Back at the junkyard, after talking to *The Horse*, Woody had opened for business with Billy and Jimmy in tow. They were learning more important things about selling banged up cars than jumping in them and crashing into other junkers.

"You two are going to have to get tough and just do the work. One of you is going to run this place some day."

They both looked at each other. Billy looked at Woody. "I'm joining the Army next year."

Woody looked at Jimmy who was looking at a blister on his leg. "I don't care. I'm not running this shit hole! I'll just be a bank robber if I have to."

Woody spun him around. "You better wise up because if your pop is in prison for any length of time you'll have to, whether you want to or not."

Jimmy looked up at his uncle. "Sorry. I just hate it here. I'm glad to go back to school next week. I never thought I would ever say those words. I want to go hang out with my friends like other kids do. All we do is work."

"You'll be able to. Just help your pop out now. He needs you two guys more than ever. Make him proud. Things will get better."

Billy Stopped Woody in his tracks. "Why is he in jail, Woody?"

"Because he broke the law. He chose not to pay taxes. That is a federal offense. Your dad has to change the way he sells parts. When somebody wants to buy a radio out of a junker, if it cost ten dollars you'll have to charge them ten dollars and forty cents. You can't put the money in your pocket anymore. That forty cents goes to Uncle Sam. You'll have to put pop's money in one shoe box and Uncle Sam's money in another. Get it?"

Jimmy looked a bit confused. "Who's Uncle Sam?"

Woody smiled and walked on toward the dog pens.

Scrubbing the dog pens had resulted in the kids managing to get half of the filth onto themselves, so Woody sent them home early. He had a few regular customers to take care of and then he would close. He limped back to his house where smudge was waiting for her bowl of milk. "Hi there my friend. I haven't forgotten you." He reached down to pat his soft little pet on the head. He stepped out on his back stoop and as soon as he put the kitten's milk down the phone rang.

Sandy was on the phone. She invited Woody to dinner. "At the Hope House? I would love to go with you. I just need to get a quick shower."

A short time later at Jane's house as Woody pulled up the drive way he could see a dark blue truck parked where he usually parked. He parked beside it and scooted up to the door. He knocked and a man answered. "Who are you?"

Woody smiled and said, "Hi." He reached to shake the guys hand, but the guy looked away. Woody pulled his hand shake back. "I'm Woody." The guy didn't say anything.

Jane stood up next to the kitchen table. "Hi Woody. This is Michael Long. Michael, meet Woody Dooley."

Michael nodded his head but looked away again. He didn't seem to want anything to do with Woody.

Woody nodded. "Pleased to meet you. Who all is coming to dinner?"

Jane took Woody aside and quietly said, "I'm inviting Michael. He doesn't know it yet. He has some more work to do. The gate was scraping the grass. When he's finished, I'm going to ask him to dinner."

Michael said, "Well... I'll be back with the bill Jane." Jane waved.

Jane darted around the kitchen like a kid with a balloon. She stirred the spaghetti.

"Okay. Just you and Sandy are joining David for dinner at the Hope House. They are celebrating Labor Day early and invited relatives and friends for dinner. Hot dogs and hamburgers. I think they have French fries too." Jane said with lots of excitement, "David is going to be so happy to see you two!"

Woody smiled. "You look a bit too happy. So... Who is he?"

Jane smiled. "He's cute, isn't he? I actually don't know anything about him." She laughed.

"Well, he sounds okay, I guess. Why don't you know anything about the guy?" Woody inquired. He had a strange, uneasy feeling about him.

Sandy came walking into the kitchen and gave Woody a kiss on his cheek. "Hi!" Woody held her arm so she didn't fall. She was walking slowly and awkwardly.

Sandy said, "Woody, I'm not quite ready. I'll be right back." She headed back to the bedroom and laid on the bed fully dressed and ready to go. All but her hair.

Woody walked over to Jane wanting to finish the conversation. He looked at Jane who was now flitting around the kitchen. She was filling a very large pot with water.

Jane said, "Michael works with my contractor that's building our fence in the back. They're doing an amazing job. We're going to hang out here together and maybe take a walk exploring the cemetery stones after dinner, and... Who knows."

Woody said, "I'm going to go sit on that comfortable lounge chair. I hope you know what you're doing. We won't be gone too late."

He saw the paper on a kitchen chair and picked it up and moved into the living room. Jane looked out her kitchen window, smiled and shook her head.

She said, "Okey dokey."

Jane was standing outside waiting for the bill from Michael Long. He was sitting in his truck when a cloud burst opened up and the rains were pouring on Jane. She dashed to her stoop at her back door that had a small awning. Michael met her on the stoop. Rain was spitting on them both. They were elbow to elbow. "This is awkward." Jane laughed and invited Michael inside to keep dry.

Laughing, Michael said, "Wow! That was good timing. That job was finished five minutes ago. The gate no longer scrapes the grass. So, it looked like you're in luck."

Jane grabbed a dishtowel. "Do you need to dry off? Step into the kitchen." He stepped in the doorway. He looked at his boots.

"No," Michael said. I was in my truck most of the time. "I'm dry, you're the one who must be drenched." He looked at her wet shirt revealing her breasts. Michael looked around the kitchen. He could see Woody sitting in the next room on a chair seemingly reading a newspaper.

"Yes. I am," She laughed. He took the towel from Jane and he wiped her hair back off her face.

Jane was mesmerized. They locked eyes. Michael looked at Jane. "Umm... What smells so good?" He notice a large pot on the stove.

"I'm making spaghetti."

Michael said, "Yum..."

"You need to have dinner with me. It will be ready in an hour. We could take a walk around the sacred grounds of the dead people afterwards." Jane giggled.

Woody listened to the flirting in the kitchen. He continued to read the paper.

Michael said to Jane, "Sure. Is that a date?" Michael smiled and handed the invoice to Jane. Jane barely looked at it. She usually paid for the work and then got reimbursed from the family that hired her to live there.

Jane snickered. "I guess it is. I'm asking you to dinner." Woody heard the whole exchange.

Michael was tall and muscular. His face was chiseled and distinctive. He looked much younger than Jane which didn't seem to bother her.

They both laughed and Jane said, "I'll pay you when you come back."

Michael nodded and smiled. "I'll be back. So... Dinner in an hour? It sure does smell great in here." Michael turned and walked out of the house. A moment later Jane could hear stones rattling against the bottom of his truck.

After Michael left, Sandy came out into the kitchen asking Jane if she wouldn't mind fixing her hair. "Who were you talking with in the kitchen?"

"My date for tonight." They both shrieked one big uproarious, "Yes!"

Sandy hugged Jane. "Goody goody gum drops. And he's so cute."

Woody slapped the newspaper down and stomped outside standing under the awning just watching the rain. He was feeling sad and awkward, but somehow the rain had the ability to drown it all out.

Jane gave Sandy a pretty French Twist type hairdo. The dress attire tonight was casual but Sandy almost never went out so she was going to wear a classy black dress. It was getting late so Jane jumped in the shower. When she got out she styled her own hair and put her favorite rose colored lipstick on. She was still thinking about Sandy's evening out and was wondering if she was well enough to go to The Hope House dinner.

Jane realized she forgot to wrap David's personal items. Because he loved to open things that come from home the girls always wrap them. Today they don't have wrapping paper so Jane put his personals in a bag and wrapped the bag in foil. She put a pretty red bow on the top. Sandy took her pills with Jane's coaxing. She wanted to avoid the one pill that made her feel a bit tired because she was afraid she might fall asleep.

Jane said to her, "You have to try and avoid a seizure at all cost." She looked at Sandy. "You look so pretty. If you fall asleep, so be it." Woody will be with you to save the day." The girls hugged one last time.

Sandy said, "Thank you Jane."

Jane had to tend to her spaghetti and meatballs to assure everything was perfect. She made a fresh salad. She mumbled out loud, "I wonder, are the meatballs any good?" Jane and Sandy looked at each other with a smile and sat down at the kitchen table to eat a meatball just to test it and make sure it was up to par.

Jane could see Woody standing on the stoop. She said, "Woody come in. We're testing the meatballs." He stepped inside.

"I'll pass, thanks. I'm going to go back and rest on that comfy chair. I haven't read the funnies yet."

The girls had a fun filled time laughing and talking about how young Michael might be.

Sandy asked, "Is he married?"

Jane replied quickly, "Ah... No. At least I don't think so. He better not be."

"What if he is?"

Jane looked at her intently. "I'll boot him out. Don't worry."

They heard a car pulling up the driveway. "Hurry Jane. He's here."

Jane looked confused. "That was quick. He must live nearby."

Sandy said, "I'll make myself invisible." She walked back to the bedroom.

Jane looked outside and smiled when she saw Michael petting one of her outside cats. She opened the door. "Hi Michael. Meet Bob and following close behind him is Boo Kitty, my first black cat." Michael petted Boo Kitty.

"I had a cat too, named Spackle. The cat was found at a construction site, it was a new house build. The poor guy was covered with spackle, from the workers there. I took him home and washed the spackle off. "

Jane grabbed a half full glass of milk from the table. She poured milk into their bowls. "That's sad. How did you get the spackle off of him?"

"Good old fashioned soap and water. It took me hours but I managed. He's the best cat I ever had; a great mouser." Michael entered the kitchen. "Can I help you in any way?"

"Sure. Why don't you keep an eye on the sauce and just stir it once in a while. I'm going to make sure my roommate is doing okay. She is going out in a few minutes."

"I think I saw her once. But I wasn't sure who she was."

Jane ran back and re-applied her lipstick. She was nervous.

Sandy looked at her. "You look beautiful and everything is going to be fine."

Jane hugged Sandy one last time.

"Why don't you come and officially meet Michael before you go?"

The two girls walked out arm in arm. "Michael I want you to meet Sandy, my very best friend, and Sandy I want you to meet Michael, a fine man who likes cats."

Woody got up from the lounge chair and Jane stared at him for a moment. He said to Michael, "Hi again. I see it stopped raining."

Michael nodded at Sandy and totally ignored Woody. He turned and like a goofy kid smelled the spaghetti sauce and stirred it once more. "Yum!"

Jane smiled nervously and, trying to distract his behavior, said, "Ok then..."

Sandy scurried over to give Woody a kiss. He looked at her approvingly, "You look great!"

She smiled and thanked him.

Jane smiled and said, "So... You two have a real good time. I know David will be so excited to see both of you."

Sandy turned before she walked out with Woody. "Have fun," she said very quietly.

"We will," Jane said with a giddy demeanor. "Tell David I love him and miss him and I'll see him next Friday."

As they were pulling out of the long driveway Sandy said, "I think that guy's cute, don't you?"

Woody looked straight ahead and very blankly replied, "If you say so."

CHAPTER 25 The Seizure

Woody was pulling up the driveway of The Hope House. It clearly brought back memories. He remembered his best friend Gary Gleason who had been in a wheel chair. The two of them would sit in the Activity room that had a tall window allowing a clear view of the visitors arriving and leaving. They made a game of it. The boys would gaze out the window and daydream that the people arriving were there looking to adopt one of them. A very special child like me or Gary. It was a guessing game. The game went like this:

Woody announced that a car was arriving. It had two people in it. "Maybe it's for me, because I have a blue ribbon for best kept room for the month. They like neat children."

"They are looking for a boy that is smart in math," Gary would say, "And someone that is a good reader. I have read more books than you or anyone here."

Woody would laugh and say, "But I am strong and can lift heavy packages. Oh... And and I can win at Canasta and Gin Rummy."

Then they would laugh because Gary won more than anyone at those games. They would talk about their dreams in which they were adopted by a loving family that had a dog and a cat.

Gary would say, "Cats are the best. They will sit all day on your lap and feel all warm and cozy."

Then Woody would say, "I want a dog to play catch with. But I'll take a cat. They like to sleep in your bed sometimes. I want to hear them purr, and to feel that fur next to my pillow."

Sandy, who had initially been very talkative, gradually fell asleep. As they arrived in the parking lot Woody noticed that the flower garden was gone and the path that led to it from the main building was overgrown. *How sad*, he thought. *It used to be so pretty to look at.*

"We're here Sandy."

She looked over at Woody as if she was trying to figure out where she was, then she quickly perked up and said, "Oh... Sorry. I am trying not to sleep so much, but now every time I ride in a vehicle I fall fast asleep."

"Let me come around and help you out." Woody opened Sandy's door and helped her, then he carried the package for her. Woody added a slinky to the package in an opened part of the aluminum foil that covered the personal items they'd brought for David. As they walked into the vestibule Mrs. Lee was speaking to a couple that was interested in adopting and has had their eyes on one particular child. They had been visiting that child for the past month, every Friday.

"Hello Mrs. Dooley and Mr. Dooley." Woody nodded and helped Sandy who was walking very slowly. They both gestured to Mrs. Lee. Sandy looked up at Woody. "She said our names correctly."

Woody laughed. "Yeah, she didn't call me Mr. Woody." They both signed in and headed to the cafeteria.

"Mommy!" David hollered from down the hall. He came running and hugged his mother full of excitement. Sandy started crying and hugging... And crying... And hugging. He leaned over to Woody and said "The dinosaur book is sitting on my wardrobe." Woody could see how very much Sandy loved her son. Woody reached over to shake David's hand. David took Woody's hand and kissed it and smiled. "I'm happy you're both here. But... Somebody's missing." He looked around the room. "Where is Aunty Jane?"

Sandy said very happily, "Jane found a boyfriend, but she told me to tell you she'll see you next time, and that she loves you very much."

"I know," David said and looked over at Woody. "What's in the package?"

Sandy nodded and said, "You can open it, it's yours."

David laughed. "Oh wow! I wanted one of these. It's a slinky. And lots of shampoo that I like and... Oh... Wow! A new tooth brush." He walked over to the table, pulled out the slinky and watched it as it slinks from the table to the chair, but it's a big drop and it flipped off the chair. "Can I walk over to the stairway?"

Sandy nodded, "Yes you can." She stood holding onto Woody, and watched her son showing happiness. Sandy smiled with contentment.

Sandy was rooting around to find a seat so that she didn't fall if she got light headed. Woody walked to the first long table in the cafeteria and pulled out a chair at the head of the table. "We can sit here I believe, can't we? Aren't we here to eat?"

David looked at Woody. "I'm glad you came. I love hot dogs."

Woody said, "Me too."

Sandy said, "Me too. With lots of mustard."

David scrunched up his nose. "No mustard... Ewww..."

After they ate David wanted to try his slinky out on the steps again. Sandy smiled and said, "Of course."

As the two sat quietly through the jibber jabber of the busy cafeteria Jane looked at Woody. "I have something I want to tell you Woody."

He looked over at her. "What's that?"

"It starts out how I met Ernesto. He came into Louie's Bar where I worked every day. I hardly knew him; just that he was nice and left big tips. It happened so quickly that I didn't even realize what I was doing. Instead of Jane dropping me off at home, he would. He fell for me. I was just tired of being broke all the time. I never really loved him."

Woody stared at Sandy. He smiled. "It's the past. I've gotten through it. We're friends now, right?"

Sandy grabbed his hand and held it tightly. She was holding it way too tight. "I'm sorry for what I did. But there is more to the story."

Woody looked at her wondering what more could there be. That was all there was. Suddenly she let go of his hand and fell down off the chair with a severe seizure. Woody looked over at Mrs. Lee. She had been watching them and jumped up. She knew there was a doctor that was visiting one of his relatives at the orphanage. She yelled for him, "Dr. Townes!" A man from an adjacent table came running.

Woody stepped back holding David's hand. "Let's go over to the steps and wait for Mrs. Lee to tell us everything is okay." David began to cry and Woody sat on the step and held him close. "It's going to be okay. I promise." The seizure lasted the longest three minutes that Woody had ever experienced. He had never seen a seizure before. He worried that Sandy was getting closer to the end.

When Sandy came out of the seizure she was lying on an examination bed in the dispensary. Dr. Townes said very confidently, "You're going to be okay Mrs. Dooley. Your husband is going to take you home now. We were going to call an ambulance but you revived quickly and Mr. Dooley said you were going home to bed. Which by the way I believe would be a very good idea."

CHAPTER 26 The Deal

Joe Palermo and Michael Gaines, aka Mickey, were talking with Whitey at a table in a cold grey conference room in the federal prison. They were discussing how Whitey would be expected to pay one hundred fifty eight thousand dollars plus fines of up to sixty thousand dollars.

"I told my ex-wife I was going to buy her a home and I'm not going back on my word."

"Your ex-wife will have to wait George." Mickey snapped. "This is not joke. What if you sell the junkyard and move to a new location? Buy a large property and put your ex-wife there. Build yourself a beautiful house and have more land."

Whitey laughed cynically.

Joe shook his head. "You've got a slew of kids. I like her. Miriam that is. She's raising eight of your kids."

"Why don't I put My wife and Miriam next door to each other and make them deliriously happy?" Whitey looked at Joe. "You know Miriam. She'll squeeze the life out of Alice. They hate each other."

Joe shook his head. "Well, I didn't mean put them side by side. But you know what I mean." They all laugh.

Mickey stopped the laughter. "Look. We can work with IRS so that you can pay it off in one year. They would be thrilled. They suspect you have a lot of that cash stashed away, but they'd rather you just paid up then prosecute you. You will be home. But you must not fool around with them or you'll be back in the slammer. You have to start paying your taxes." Mickey stared with serious concern. "I have an accountant, Maury Green, that has already drawn up a payment schedule. I know you've never had a checking account. But your business needs one now more than ever. You have to charge taxes when you sell anything. That's how life is George. Who cares if you have to charge four cents more on a dollar? I'll bet there are pennies all over the grounds of the junkyard. Right now I'll bet those guards have four pennies in their pockets. I have pennies in my pockets. You can laugh but this is your life. Don't mess it up anymore."

Whitey just continued to laugh.

It was the end of September and all the kids were back at school. Georgie was in Europe. Miriam had found a job that was within walking distance at a local delicatessen. It was a mile away; her doctor wanted her to do some kind of exercise anyway. The only problem was there were no sidewalks and the road to the deli was narrow. It was Monday and she was starting Wednesday. She decided to walk up to the deli and find out what her schedule was. She wanted to be home when the kids arrived from school. As she was leaving the phone rang. It was Alice.

"Mir, how are you holding up?"

She answered impatiently, "Why are you calling Alice?"

"Oh... I was worried about you and the kids."

"Umhum... If you're wanting money, I'm flat broke. You'll have to get it from your mommy."

"Miriam, be a grown up. I'm wanting to go downtown to see George and I was wondering if you could give me a ride. I need milk for the baby and I want to see what's going on."

"I have to go on an errand. I will pick up milk for your child but... Look, Alice, you made your bed. Don't ever ask me for anything again. You need to get a driver's license. Or take a bus like other people do. I'll send Billy over with the milk when he gets home from school. You should know that George is coming home tomorrow. Why don't you know that? For Goodness sake." Miriam hung up.

Jane was singing in the bath tub. Sandy was laughing. She was still in bed but she followed some of the words to the song. "... Darling you...ooo send me... You...ooo send me... You...ooo send me... Honest you do... Honest you do... Oh, oh, oh..."

Sandy called to Jane in the bathroom. "Was that song by Sam Cook?"

Jane, with a towel wrapped around her, opened the door and laughed, "I think so. I love that song."

"You must have had a good time last night," Sandy said with happiness in her voice.

"Yes, I sure did." Jane looked over at Sandy who appeared anxious to hear the details. "The only problem is he's like around twenty nine. The guy is sweet but I think there is something going on in his life that he is hesitating to talk about. Which... I don't care! But I do know he's a good kisser." They both laughed. Jane put her robe on and began towel drying her hair.

Sandy took her pills without coaxing from Jane. She looked over at Jane and said, "I had a seizure last night in front of David and Woody."

"I was afraid that would happen. But look, it happened and everybody's alright and life goes on. Right?"

Sandy nodded. "Your right. That was scary for David. But he was fine when we left. Other than that..." She looked out the window. "It was all okay, but I didn't tell Woody about David yet."

Jane turned around dressed in a fresh clean pair of dungarees and clean sweat shirt. "I'm going outside for awhile to water my plants and check the birdfeeders and the cat's dishes. But when I get back in I'll make a big breakfast for us."

Sandy looked a bit sad. "I'm just going to have my corn flakes later on when I feel hungry. So nothing for me yet, thanks."

"The newspaper has a huge front page article on George King's incarceration," Jane said. She always put the paper on Sandy's night table. Sandy read it, *George King will be released from federal prison today after paying fines and half of the back taxes amounting to over one hundred and forty thousand dollars.*

Sandy called Woody on the phone but there was no answer. She looked at her wedding ring that she kept on the night table in a small angel dish. Sandy talked out loud while looking at her ring. "I'll love you forever."

Joe Palermo pulled up Whitey's driveway in his big Cadillac. Alice was sitting on the porch that was on the second story, waiting. She stood up and looked over the wrought iron rail that enclosed the porch. Joe got out, walked around and stood by the passenger side of the car. Alice waved and said, "Hi Joe. Is he with you?" She chuckled.

Joe looked up at Alice. "Good morning Mrs. King. He is. I brought him home to you safe and sound." Joe looked at the car's passenger side door. There was no activity. He stood there and waited, but nothing. "Maybe he is waiting for me to let him out?"

"You should have arranged for a chauffeur. Oh, he probably doesn't know where the handle is." They both laughed.

Joe reached down and opened the door. Whitey hollered, "What the hell kind a car is this? Where's the damn handle? I couldn't find that skinny little handle." They all laughed.

Joe said, "You certainly helped me buy this car George. It's a Cadillac. An Eldorado. One of the best."

Alice had made her way down the steps. "It's beautiful Joe. We should buy one George." She gave Whitey a kiss.

Whitey looked at her. "After this we can't afford jelly beans."

Alice asked Whitey, "Do you need help with your suitcase?"

Whitey looked into his wife's eyes. "Alice, I went to Jail. Not some fancy hotel. I don't have anything but the clothes on my back." They chuckled.

Alice asked Joe, "Would you like to come in for a bite?"

Joe glanced at Alice, said nothing, and returned his attention to Whitey. He shook Whitey's hand and with Sincerity said, "You did good today. Now, be sure to call when you have any questions."

Whitey laughed and said, "I have only one left."

Joe looked at him questionably.

"You know, what I'm going to ask, don't you?" Whitey said and walked away. "Just send me a bill. I'll see ya later."

Joe got in his car and backed out quickly.

At three o'clock in the afternoon across the street at the junkyard the kids walked into their house after school.

Billy said, "Dad's home."

Jimmy asked, "How do you know?"

Billy said, "Because I saw Alice yesterday when I had to take her that quart of milk. She told me everything."

Miriam looked over at Billy. "You shouldn't be talking to her."

Billy looked up at his mother. "Why?"

Miriam walked away and said, "Because I said so! Now do your homework."

Woody knocked on Miriam's door. "Hey, hi Mir. Can I ask one of the boys to watch the yard while I go see Whitey?"

Miriam told Jimmy to go because Billy had so much school work. Jimmy said he didn't have any.

Woody walked up the long flight of steps to Whitey's house. His leg was sore and he had been working quite a bit at the yard. Alice answered the front door. "He's sleeping Woody. He'll be over tomorrow. I'll tell him you were here."

Woody nodded and turned to go back down the steps but his bad leg gave out and he fell. He tumbled down several steps. Alice came running down the steps to where Woody was lying. "Woody, are you okay?" He didn't answer at first.

She immediately called Miriam. Miriam answered, "Hello. Oh it's you again! Why do you keep calling me? ...Woody? ...Oh my!" Miriam's tune changed when she realized the seriousness of the call. "I'll send Billy right over."

Billy helped Alice walk Woody over to an outside bench near the entrance of the stairway. Woody managed to sit on the bench with their help. He smiled at them. "You two are the best! Thanks. I'm fine guys. I have a crippled leg that works some of the time. It's just a bit weak. I'll be just fine. Billy and I are going to walk nice and slow across the street and I want to thank you for your help Alice. Tell George I just came to say hello... Goodbye."

Alice watched as they slowly crossed the old gravel road to the yard. Billy was shorter than Woody but he was strong. He acted as a support for walking him across the street to Miriam's porch. Billy helped Woody prop himself up on a comfortable chair.

Miriam sat outside with Woody on the porch. They drank lemonade and Miriam went inside and made him Campbell's Tomato Soup and a grilled cheese sandwich. They chatted for an hour and a half. He enjoyed Miriam's company. He found out she was starting a new job at the delicatessen the next day and was working from eight a.m. to three p.m. Also, she said she might be bringing home some delicious sandwiches from the deli to surprise the kids. She told Woody not to make dinner because a cheese steak sandwich was coming his way. Miriam was happy and delighted to see Woody was not seriously injured. They had a great conversation.

They laughed about Whitey not knowing anything about her working at the deli he frequents. She said she was just going to surprise him. She was happy that the kids wouldn't have to be alone since she would be home before the bus arrived.

Billy locked up for Woody. As Woody limped home he felt lucky to have such a caring family no matter how convoluted they were.

When he limped to his new home smudge was waiting for him on his front porch. She rubbed up against his leg asking for a pet and bowl of milk. Woody went in and brought the bowl out and sat with the kitten to watch her drink the last drop. "There my friend. The phone is ringing. I'll see you later."

The caller was Sandy. "Hi there. How are you doing?"

Woody said, "Fine now that you called. I was just thinking about you and hoping all is well in your part of the world."

CHAPTER 27 The Rape

Michael arrived at Jane's house at five thirty, early for their date. Jane wasn't expecting him for an hour since he told her he lived thirty minutes away and might be late.

Sandy decided to entertain Michael until Jane was finished getting ready. She walked out and formally introduces herself. "Hi Michael. I've heard so much about you."

"All good I hope. I'm just enjoying the view."

Sandy smiled and took a deep breath. "I didn't realize when I moved here that I would be so mesmerized by it. It reminds me of postcard pictures."

Jane's hair was still wet and she didn't have a hair dryer. She could see Sandy enjoying his company. Michael was taking Jane to visit a cabin his family has had for many years in the Pocono Mountains.

Jane saw him sitting outside at the picnic table with Sandy. She was surprised to see Michael drinking a beer. She poked her head out and said, "Give me ten more minutes." Worrying he was starting to drink a bit early, she called out, "I have lemonade if you get thirsty."

Michael nodded and walked to his truck. He looked over at Sandy, "You want a beer?"

Sandy nodded and laughed. "I probably shouldn't but..."

Jane was finally ready and came outside to join them. She was dressed in cute corduroy pants with a flannel shirt to match and pigtails. She could see many empty beer bottles lined up on the picnic table. The smell of beer permeated the air, with a slight scent of vomit. She stood near the table and looked at the two of them. "What in the world? Sandy, are you drinking?"

Sandy giggled and nodded.

Michael looked over at Jane. "I'll clean this up." Michael and Sandy both started flailing a bit with the bottles. Two break. Jane ran in the house and brought out a large paper bag. She started cleaning up the mess. "You're not supposed to drink Sandy."

Sandy shook her head. "I only had a couple... Maybe three."

Michael said, "My fault. I had no idea she wasn't supposed to drink. Anyway she only had two or three beers."

Sandy walked into the house giggling like a naughty school girl. She turned and waved to Michael. With a little buzz on Michael said, "Good talking to ya fun lady." Michael waved to Sandy and smiled.

With concern in her voice, Jane called, "Sandy... Sandy." She came back to ask what Jane wanted. "Is Woody coming by today?"

"Yep, he sure is."

Jane looked into Michael's eyes. "Are you okay to drive?"

He nodded. "Of course, I feel so fine. I couldn't feel much better." He kissed her on her cheek. "I love your pigtails." Jane shyly smiled and got in the truck. They left.

Woody arrived about a half hour after Jane and Michael had left. Sandy was sleeping. He warmed up some day old spaghetti and sat down at the small round table in the kitchen. His leg was still aching from the fall. Sandy woke up to the aroma of an Italian restaurant.

"Hi stranger," Sandy said and walked over to give Woody a kiss. She had a strong smell of beer on her. "I see you found the spaghetti leftovers."

He laughed. "This stuff is delicious."

Sandy served a spoonful of spaghetti into a small bowl and joined Woody. He got up to get two napkins and staggered to his seat. Sandy asked Woody with concern, "Are you okay?"

"I fell down some steps at Whitey's house yesterday and I'm still achy. This spaghetti is helping me forget about it."

"I think you need someone to help you forget about it."

Woody smiled and nodded. He asked, "Where is Jane?"

Sandy said, "Jane went to the mountains with Michael."

Woody looked over at Sandy suspiciously, "She doesn't know him very well."

"He's cute. He probably wants to take advantage of her. And she probably won't mind. I don't know... She's a big girl. She can take care of herself," she commented impatiently.

After Woody finished his dinner Sandy washed the few dishes and walked Woody out to the picnic table. The weather was particularly warm and relaxing. They sat outside. Sandy put her head on Woody's shoulder. "Woody I have something I want to tell you and I hope it makes you happy. It's been on my mind for a long time. I need you to understand. I..." The phone started ringing. "It's important and you need to know. Just a minute... I'm going to answer the phone first." She ran back to the house. "Hello... Hello... Hello... Who is this?"

The person on the other end said, "Sandy, it's Jane. I'm talking quiet so Michael doesn't hear me. I'm in some tiny town in the mountains. I need Woody to come and get me."

"What? Why? I thought you liked Michael."

"Well, he's trying to rape me. I told him no and he won't take no for an answer. He slapped me and he's drunk. I don't want to be anywhere near him. He's drunk and treating me horribly! He's a monster!! I want to go home..." She began sobbing.

Sandy blurted out, "Jane was raped by Michael. He's drunk. He's a monster."

Woody grabbed the phone. Let me talk to Jane. "Jane, this is Woody. Where are you?"

Jane hurriedly said, "His cabin is about five minutes away. But he wanted to buy beer. We stopped so he could get gas. His cabin is on Pine Cone Lane. That's all I know. Wait... I'm right outside of Easton. It's near a church that has a cupola with a bell in it. It's right near an exit off the turnpike at the Sinclair gas station. Woody, he just got out of jail!"

Woody thought to himself that he knew the exit she was referring to. In fact, he was pretty sure he knew the gas station they were at because there was only one there that sells beer. "Did you call the police?"

"No. Here he comes. He looks mad." Click... The phone went dead.

"Jane... Jane! She hung up. "We're calling the police and I will be back when I find her or the police do. Don't worry." Woody limped to his truck with Sandy following behind. "I can't take you with me. Too dangerous! You call the police, Sandy. Go in the house. If Jane calls tell her the police were called and I'm on my way."

"Woody, I'm worried."

He rolled his window down. "I'll call when I find her."

Woody's truck spun back down the driveway and out of sight.

Chilled by the evening air, Jane wrapped her sweater around her shoulders and walked back to the check-out area of the gas station where Michael was waiting for her. She returned a key for the ladies room to the cashier. "Thank you."

Michael asked Jane, "What took you so long?"

Jane said sadly, "I went to the bathroom and..." She started to get angry and continued, "My face is swollen and turning red where you hit me. I was checking to see if you broke my nose. It was bleeding. You tore my corduroy pants also." She looked at Michael imploringly. "I wish you'd just drive me home and call it a night. I don't want to see your cabin now."

Staring at Jane with frustration he growled, "Who were you talking to?"

Jane replied that she was talking to Sandy. Michael opened his bottle of beer with an imposing looking hunting knife he carried in a sheath on his belt. Jane had never seen anyone do that before. Her uncle had a knife like that he'd use to skin rabbits. She thought he had it from when he was a Marine in the war.

Michael shook his head. "What'd you tell her?"

Jane responded with annoyance in her tone, "I didn't tell her anything. I just asked her if she was feeling okay. You know she has seizures. She's sick you know."

Pompously he said, "Is that so? Well, she didn't look too sick to me. She slugged down that beer like she was a real back woodsy kinda girl. The kind I kinda like." He swigged down a beer like it was nothing. "Beer never hurt nobody. It'll put hair on your chest." He drunkenly said, "Get in the truck. I'm going to show you my cabin. And some other stuff. We're not far now."

Jane struggled to get back in the truck while unobtrusively scoping out the area. She noticed a man jump in his truck and drive off. She looked around at the parking lot of the gas station but hadn't seen anyone else nearby. After getting back in the truck she began to feel brave. With a mean look she said, "You know, it worries me that you're drinking and driving, Michael. You were swerving all over the place."

He responded forcefully, "Hogwash."

A few minutes later they pulled up to the cabin. It was pitch black; visibility was down to a few yards. Jane was afraid of what might come next.

When he got out of the truck he barked at her, "Stay put." He then wobbled a bit and slipped on the path toward the door. She couldn't see where he was. She desperately wanted to get out of the truck, but on second thought she decided she would switch to quietly following his demands. She had no idea where she was. She asked herself, *What in God's name are you going to do Jane?* Everything around her was extremely dark and quiet. She was beginning to feel panicked. The thumping of her heart was the only sound that could be heard... Until the idiot dropped his keys. She started to listen carefully and soon heard the jiggling of the keys again. She got out of the truck leaving the door unlatched. Her eyes began to adjust to the darkness. She focused on the front porch. Through the partially open door she could see something moving inside the house. She realized it was Michael's shadow. She was filled with fear of what he was going to do to her.

Who was this ruthless wild animal?

She remembered the ride... Michael pulling over and holding her down. He ripped the zipper completely off her favorite corduroy pants. His strength overpowered her and she couldn't move. She remembered pushing him and screaming although there was no one there to hear. The only landscape around her were the trees and unpopulated mountains. He reached up with one hand and pulled her bra off on the first try. He didn't kiss her, although his foul smelling mouth covered hers and his beery saliva slathered her cheek. Then he bit her! The pain was excruciating. She screamed as loud as she could. He yelled at her, "Stop fighting bitch! You know you want it." She remembered screaming and the shock of being pummeled with his big fist. Her flannel shirt was missing buttons and ripped wide open. Blood was dripping down past her chin onto her breast that was now exposed. He glared at her like a monster. "You bitch!"

Michael walked over to where Jane was standing. "Let's go. You just need a drink."

"I just want to go home, Michael. You hurt me and I'm not feeling well."

Michael grabbed Jane's arm and pulled her along the path that led to the small cabin. He dragged her across the porch and into the cabin where he released her. She quickly walked straight back to a bathroom. Michael went back out to the truck.

Could she escape? She peeked out of the bathroom and could see the door was wide open and Michael was nowhere to be seen. She buttoned her shirt with the two remaining buttons. Her trouser's zipper was broken but the snap worked and held the pants closed satisfactorily. She felt a sense of wanting to get free of this man that had no respect for women. He bit her! She looked in the mirror and saw her cheek was red and swollen. Her nose was also swollen. Jane washed her face with a wash cloth that was sitting on the sink.

She wondered if her purse was still in the truck. Could there be a phone in this place. She was determined to escape. Maybe she could watch him drink himself into a stupor. She realized her mistake in trusting a man that no one knew anything about. She walked out of the bathroom with an agenda... Figuring how to get out of this mess.

Dusk turned into a very dark night pretty quickly with a new moon and mountains looming all around. Woody was heading north where temperatures drop substantially every evening. He was feeling chilly already so he closed his driver's side window. His heater wasn't working and its becoming clear he was in for a cold ride. where he was going it could easily drop ten more degrees.

The Pennsylvania Turnpike was slow tonight due to road work on one of the two lanes heading north. Most visitors heading to the Poconos on a Saturday evening were already at their destination. He was close now because from his vantage point he could see an advertisement for the Sinclair gas station as *Having everything one might need for enjoying a fun time in the mountains.* Poor Jane he thought. You're not having much fun. Woody wondered why Jane would make such a bad decision and venture all the way to the Pocono

Mountains on a second date. Suddenly he realized he'd missed his exit. When you miss your exit on the turnpike you're like a gerbil on a wheel. It seems impossible to find your way back.

Jane Rathgeb had never been married, but she lived with a man for ten years. She loved Dick Carter and although she was not able to have children, she wanted more than just becoming a habit with him. She wanted marriage, the whole kit and caboodle. Jane wanted to feel like the man she loved was part of her family. He would be all she needed. Dick hadn't seemed to want the same thing. He hadn't seemed to know what he wanted. At first their relationship was perfect. They spent most of their spare time together, riding their bikes, cruising second hand shops and antique shops. They would both share their hobbies with each other, like collecting bottles and building kites.

Dick had a degree in History. He worked at a book binding company for most of his life. This may have been the fodder he needed for writing his own book. His dream was to complete a book that he had started. In ten years Jane could only remember two chapters that were almost completed. He would get in a writing frenzy. A chapter would be well written and the next week he would rip up the well written chapter and write something that didn't make any sense to her. Then for weeks he would not write anything. He claimed writer's block. He had four different versions of the same story and trashed them all. The truth of the matter was he never really finished anything he started. He lost his interest in camping, something the two of them enjoyed together. He seemed to lose his desire for everything they did together. As his interest in Jane began to fray she realized their relationship was spent. They eventually went their separate ways.

Dick was on Jane's mind at this moment. She remembered the musty smell and the one room cabin that felt familiar. She wanted to go back in time because her memory was of someone that loved her once and wanted to get away with her and enjoy nature and the great outdoors. She was now feeling scared for her life and thought that no one would find her.

Jane could see a clock on the other side of the room, but the flimsy light Michael turned on was too dim to see the time. It appeared to be eight p.m. but she realized that it probably was off by an hour. It must be nine. Where was Woody and would he be able to find his way out here in the dark wilderness?

As soon as she left the bathroom, Michael grabbed hold of her upper arm restraining her again. Her arm hurt with the tight vice grip he had on it. He attempted to unbutton her shirt again. He was trying to undress her but in his drunken state he just stared at her in a stupor.

The stinky cabin was dark. It was all one big room. There was a table in the middle of the room with six chairs. There were bunk beds next to the windows on both the left and right sides of the room. Next to another window was a single bed. There was also a curtain that separated off an area that had a double bed draped in a rustic animal print bedspread. It was like a room of beds!

Michael roughly set Jane on the animal print bed and pushed off his thick leather boots. He was laughing at Jane. "I want you to see my pretty acorn tree out front. I know you love trees. The leaves are red. Come on Janey." He was holding her arm tighter.

She pulled away. "Owww... That hurts." Michael loosened his grip.

Michael said, slurring his words, "Look... You've wanted me for a long time." He attempted to kiss her on the mouth but she moved and the kiss landed on her head. "We are good together," he mumbled and moved his face closer to her's. "I'm sorry I lost my temper back there. Let's just make up and..." He kissed her shoulder. She tried to push him off.

"No, Michael. I don't feel well. Haven't you tormented me enough? I'm in pain and scared."

They were sitting on the spotted animal print bed. Michael pulled Jane back down onto the bed. She resisted and maneuvered her body to be stiff and rigid. She screamed, "Get away from me!"

He pulled his knife out of its sheath. "Shut up bitch." Michael held the knife in a threatening manner over her face. "This is not a joke."

Jane looked away from the knife. Her body was shaking and she realized that he meant business. She tightly closed her eyes and started pleading, "Please don't hurt me Michael... Michael... Please don't do anything crazy." She pushed his heavy body away from her with a strong shove. He dropped the knife onto the floor. His drunken flailing got the best of him and he lost his balance. He found himself lying next to Jane on the bed. He knelt, grabbed both of her arms and pushed them up and over her head. He then attempted to unzip his dungarees. The snap was all he was able to maneuver.

"You bitch!" He laid on top of her, holding her down with his body. "Bitch... Bitch!"

Jane screamed as Michael pulled her shirt off. All the buttons burst and her breasts were fully exposed. She was crying. She grabbed at the remains of the torn up shirt spread out next to her and attempted to cover her bare breasts. "No... No... Michael, please."

He ripped her pants but he couldn't get them off. She hit Michael in the face, shocking him. With both his hands he grabbed at Jane's neck and began squeezing. Jane couldn't scream. Her legs were kicking and her knee was able to hit the jackpot. Michael let go. "Damn you!"

Jane screamed, "Help... Somebody help me!"

Michael stood up holding his privates and grimacing in pain. He had completely let go of Jane. She attempted to get up. He pushed her back onto the bed snarling, "Stay still, bitch!"

A car's headlights appeared next to his truck. He staggered to the door barefoot and could see someone opening the driver's side door.

Michael opened the front door and yelled, "Hi... Can I help you?"

The person had climbed out of the vehicle and was standing on the path. The passenger opened his door and followed closely behind.

The man in the lead said with a commanding tone in his voice, "I'm looking for a girl named Jane Rathgeb." He continued walking up the path toward the front of the cabin.

Michael began heading toward the man preventing him from walking any further. "Nobody by that name here," he said.

"My name is Sheriff Stanley Clifton..."

Jane screamed, "I'm Jane Rathgeb! Help... Help... Help!"

The man began again speaking rapidly while drawing his weapon at the same time, "My name is Sheriff Stanley Clifton... I can hear someone in distress in your cabin... Freeze! You're under arrest."

Michael attempted to run barefoot toward his truck. Sherriff Clifton's senses went on high alert. He pointed his weapon at Michael. His finger went inside the guard and wrapped around the trigger. Michael stumbled and yelled, "Owww, I stepped on something sharp. Owww..." The sheriff's deputy, Larry Clifton, moved quickly to subdue then cuff him. He started leading Michael toward the police cruiser. Michael attempted to hop on one foot. He cried, "My foot is bleeding."

"Awww... You stepped on one of those acorns from that big tree in front."

Jane was crumpled on the stale smelling animal print bedspread. She was gripped with fear that Michael wasn't finished with her. She laid motionless.

Sheriff Clifton entered the cabin and walked over to her. "Are you okay young lady?" He took his jacket off and dropped it across her partially naked body. "Don't worry about that asshole. He's handcuffed in my car. He's not going anywhere. We'll call your home and let them know your safe, then we'll get you to the hospital."

Jane pouted and begged the Sheriff, "First... There is a sweater in the front seat of that truck out there. Also my pocket book is there..."

Sheriff Clifton said calmly, "I'll get everything of yours... Hold on."

He headed out to the truck then returned in a couple of minutes. He handed her the sweater and set her pocket book next to her. He said, "I'll give you some privacy and go out on the front porch. Holler at me if you need anything."

He started to turn to leave, but paused. Something on the floor near the bed caught his eye. He bent down to retrieve it and exclaimed, "Whoeee! That's some wicked looking K-Bar."

Jane said, "That's Michael's knife! He held it to my face..." and she began to sob.

The sheriff whistled quietly and said to himself, "That'll put some icing on this cake."

Jane sat up shielding her naked breasts with the jacket while she quite efficiently put the sweater on and buttoned from top to bottom. Jane looked around for the Sheriff, then called, "I'm dressed."

Sheriff Clifton came back into the cabin, slipped his jacket back on and told Jane he would meet her at the hospital after he took the asshole to jail. Jane assumed he was talking about Michael. The sheriff walked over to the window and looked out. He walked back to her and said, "They're here for you... The ambulance that is."

A man and a woman came in carrying a stretcher. Jane got up with their help. "I'm okay, I assure you. Why do I have to go to the hospital?"

The man replied patronizingly, "Well... You have a swollen face and a black eye. And anything else that's wrong will be noted. We don't want that guy to do this to anyone else."

They helped ease Jane unto the stretcher and carried her out to the ambulance. They carefully loaded Jane and the stretcher through the open back doors. The ambulance took off. Jane cried softly. They pulled up to the hospital quite quickly. The back doors opened and Jane, on the stretcher, was slowly lifted out. She found herself in an emergency ward with a curtain surrounding her.

She was being examined by a kind nurse with a pin on her collar that said her name was Millie. The nurse said, "We're going to put you in a gown and check you over. Did the perpetrator penetrate you Jane?"

"No! He was drunk and didn't get past second base. He squeezed my neck though and my throat is very sore. I couldn't breathe for a while. I kneed him pretty good... I think I hurt him."

The nurse looked at her with a slight smile. "I can see quite a bit of redness there." She felt all around her neck. As she was examining her she said, "Sheriff Clifton said you wanted someone to call your friend."

Jane nodded and told the nurse the telephone number.

Millie dialed Sandy's number. Sandy answered and Millie related all that had happened. Sandy replied, "Thank you for letting me know. What hospital is she at?"

"Regional General."

"Okay, thank you, someone will be there sometime soon... I hope."

Woody finally found his way back to the Sinclair gas station. He found a phone booth and called Sandy. She gave him the name of the Hospital. Luckily, it was only ten minutes away from where he was and he didn't have to get back on the turnpike and possibly miss his exit again!

Woody filled his truck up with gas and took off toward the hospital. He began to worry more than a friend would normally worry. His feelings for Jane were strong and he realized they were more than just friendly. Ten minutes later Woody pulled up to the emergency room parking lot.

Woody was at the front desk of the emergency room asking about his friend Jane. For some reason he couldn't remember her last name. "It's a funny last name. It starts with an 'R'. I can't remember... Damn it!"

The young female hospital representative listened to Woody and replied, "Please wait here sir." She then walked from the ER desk to Jane's room. "There is a man out in the waiting room asking about a woman by the name of Jane, but he doesn't know your last name. His name is Woody Dooley. Do you know him?"

Jane smiled "Oh, that's my girlfriend's husband. Please tell him I'm okay and I'll see him when they release me." She looked at Millie and asked, "Can I go yet?"

"Not yet... But I'm sure it will be soon. The doctor and a detective want to speak with you first and then you can go."

...an hour and a half later...

Jane and Woody walked to his truck. No words were spoken. Woody, limping along, was pretty dead on his feet, but he still attempted to help Jane into the truck. She looked at him and cried, "Woody, he tried to rape me." He turned to her and took her in his arms. They stand by the truck and hold each other tenderly and with care for what seemed like an eternity. Neither of them wanted to be parted from the other again.

A pea soup fog had set in and Woody found his way back to the highway on a wing and a prayer. The remainder of the trip was easy because he remembered the route like it was yesterday. The Hope House had taken the school aged children for a hiking picnic that lasted all day. It was memorable because it was so much fun despite his bum leg and he vowed to do it again someday. He looked over at Jane. She had fallen fast asleep.

CHAPTER 28 The Dooleys

It was two days later and Woody had extra morning chores. It was Monday and the boys who normally feed the dogs had already left for the bus. Woody was feeding Zeus and Sampson. He saw Sampson panting heavily and not eating. He petted him and noticed he felt warm, like he had a fever. He continued on with his chores but decided that before he opened the yard he should contact the local vet and ask if he should bring Sampson on in for a checkup.

It was now eight a.m. and Whitey, like clockwork, arrived and was already examining what Woody had accomplished. He asked why the yard wasn't open. Today he seemed to be nit picking and in a finicky mood.

Woody explained to Whitey about Sampson looking sick. Whitey took a look at Sampson and laughed. "He's just not hungry. He'll be fine, Woody. Now get those cars in the back lot ready to go. I'm looking at a new property with a lot more acreage. We've run outta room."

Whitey yelled to Woody, "I'm going to breakfast with my two scrappers, Mo and Curly!"

Woody asked, "What's their real names?"

Whitey laughed, "Who knows. I never asked them. They just bring me what I want and that's how we do business. Last week they brought me three cars for twenty bucks. And I just sold one of them for fifty."

The scrappers pulled up and left their banged up grey Ford along side of the garage and walked around both looking at an old yellow taxi cab that was near the garage. Mo examined the car inside and out. He was about five feet, with thin wispy brown hair and the most ridiculous mustache anyone ever grew. No beard, just a long bothersome looking mustache Fu Manchu style. He signaled to the other guy. Curly lifted the hood. He was average height but on the chunky side. He looked interested and stared at the engine of the cab. His hair was black and curly. He had a full beard and mustache.

Woody yelled, "A hundred bucks."

They both started laughing and shaking their heads and walked over to Whitey and piled in his tow truck.

Whitey headed to the diner with the guys who bring him a goodly amount of business. They all decided to swing around and make a quick stop to purchase tires just up the pike a couple miles at Joe's Tires. They all jumped out. Woody noticed two people walking very slowly with what looked like a baby carriage full of paper bags, clothes and even a birdcage balanced on top.

The man pushing the carriage was walking too fast for the woman. "Clyde, slow down."

Whitey was saddened. He couldn't believe what he was seeing. Mo said, "I've seen them almost every day this past month. There's a flop house about a mile up the road. I think they must either live there or stay there sometimes."

The sad looking couple sat on one of Joe's tires. The woman seemed to be exhausted. She took a floppy shoe off and began rubbing one of her feet.

Whitey said, "That's a shame."

Joe hollered, "Get out of here!" He walked over to the elderly couple. "How many times have I told you. This ain't a park!"

The couple slowly got up and continued their slow walk up the hill past Joe's Tires. The woman seemed to be crying.

Curly checked out the tires. He asked the guy running the sale. "How much? We'll buy all for the right price. How about two fifty?"

Joe said, "Nah, won't make any money on that."

"Two seventy five?"

Joe looked at the three of them and said, "Three hundred is the best I can do."

Curly looked at Whitey who shook his head.

Joe said, "Read the sign... The best tires in town. Three hundred..."

Whitey said, "Give him two sixty and that's it! He's a real jerk."

The guy screamed, "What's wrong with you? What are you, highwaymen? I gave you a deal that you won't see anywhere else."

Whitey said, "Let's go." Curly stared at him for a minute.

Joe yelled, "Damn it!" He walked around in a circle. "Ok, you guys You robbed me."

Whitey headed to Big Stop Diner. The truck cab was full of laughter. When he and the scrappers step inside Big Stop, Nancy, their favorite waitress, took them to one of her tables since the hostess wasn't in yet.

She patted Whitey on his shoulder and said, "Same booth okay?"

Whitey nodded. He continued standing while he chatted with her. "Hey Nancy, have you ever seen that couple that wheels a baby buggy around with all that junk in it?"

She laughed and shook her head. "So sad, aren't they? Who would have thought they would have lost all that money," Nancy continued, "They're the Dooley's. They almost owned Westminster at one time. I don't really know much. Except I think they were rich once."

Whitey showed a serious interest and asked, "What's her name?" He stayed glued to everything Nancy was babbling. He asked again, "Nancy, what are their names?"

She said, "I really don't remember Whitey. I think they had a child that died. There was some big scandal. Let me go get you guys some coffee and you want the same old?" He nodded. "How about your friends?"

Mo said, "I'll have what he's having," and Curly said, "I'll have the same but with bacon instead of scrapple." Nancy took off in a snap.

Curly smirked, "That couple comes here a lot and Burt gives them old bread and egg sandwiches. They eat okay. Better than some people I know. That woman though... Whoa... *She's* not doing so good. I've seen her lie down right on the side of the road. Flat out. People have stopped to help her but she just says she has to rest and doesn't get up."

Mo said, "We're gonna split the tires?"

Whitey laughed, "I'll take half."

Curly whined, "Man alive. You're a tough one."

Whitey laughed. "We gotta deal?"

Mo nodded. Curley looked at him and say's, "Okay... Man."

Whitey looked at both of them and smiled, "Look... You guys made out. You can make a killing on that sale."

Jim, the electrician they sometimes used, was in the next booth. He called over, "Whitey... Hi. How's Woody?"

Whitey nodded his head, he waved his hand in a positive manner and laughed. "My brother's getting popular these days. He didn't ask about me."

Nancy brought everyone the whole caboodle. Coffees, food and the checks. Today Nancy's being extremely efficient. She also brought Whitey a newspaper.

She walked over to Whitey and said, "Do you want me to take all three checks?"

Whitey said, "Of course," and looked at his buddies. They smiled real big Cheshire Cat smiles. He said, "One check will do it Nancy." He handed her a folded bill and said, "That's yours." He paid for the scrappers. They continue their silly smile. They all left.

October in Bucks County Pennsylvania had typically been the month of the harvest. Pumpkins, gourds, and indian corn could be found at all roadside markets. Some shops offer hay rides for the kids and adults. Popular jellies and apple butter among some of the favorites. A small paper cup of delicious apple cider was offered at the better shops. It was important to find the very sweetest apples for customers to try out. Apples were one of the better crops around and the sweetest type wins. The selling feature of their year-end apple crop, apple cider, was a perfect way to market their apples. Saturday and Sunday these shops were packed with customers. They sometimes even carried baked goods from the local Amish families. Cinnamon buns were among the most popular items on the week-ends.

Sandy awoke with a hankering for cinnamon buns. She wanted to buy something that would make Jane smile. Jane was cocooned in her bed, with her blanket hiding any indication that she was a person. Even her face was hidden.

The phone was already ringing. Who in the world would call before eight a.m. on a Sunday morning? It was Woody. He wanted to stop by and check on everyone and asked if Sandy wanted anything at the store. "As a matter of fact I was just hankering for cinnamon buns," Sandy replied with excitement. "I'll make the coffee if you bring the buns."

Woody responded, "I would be happy to fulfill your wishes madame. How's Jane doing?"

Sandy said, "Not too good. That just might cheer her up though. She was really beat up."

Woody didn't say much except, "I'll see you in a little while."

They ended the phone conversation and Woody stepped outside to see his buddy Smudge who was normally waiting on the front porch near the newspaper. Today the paper was on the porch but no Smudge. Woody stepped outside and called him... Nothing. No sign of his favorite kitten. He smiled. "He must be mousing around," he thought. "That's my brave warrior smudge."

Woody walked outside and over to the large can to feed the dogs. He noticed Zeus was not running around. He was just lying on the porch where the kids usually greet him before he was fed. Woody reached in the deep galvanized trash can and filled a bucket of dry kibbles to put in their bowls. He held onto Zeus's collar and led him to his own pen. And there was Sampson lying in the adjacent pen, dead as a door nail. Woody couldn't believe it. Sampson was turning into such a sweet dog. Zeus showed no interest in going in his pen. Woody had to force him in. Normally the two dogs were excited about breakfast. Today Zeus showed no interest. He was sadly upset. He began to cry... Not bark... Not growl... But whine, like a child. He was crying, Woody believed. He looked all around the junkyard for any sign of what may have caused the death of this great dog. That was when he spotted little Smudge under an old Buick near the dog's pen. He was also dead. There was an intact wrapper next to the car. It was labeled *Rat Poison*. Woody realized giving a chore like putting out rat poison to one of the kids was a big mistake. Billy or Jimmy shouldn't have been given that job.

Woody cried quite sorrowfully. He remembered telling Whitey that he felt Sampson needed to go to the vet and just two days later he was dead. Now he was wondering if Zeus needed to see a Vet. The yard was closed on Sunday and the veterinarian was most likely closed also.

He headed over to inform Miriam. He knew that the kids were sent to church on Sunday. Knocking on Miriam's door was unusual on a Sunday. Woody had already elected to manage the dogs every morning during school days and Sundays. Saturdays the boys had their work cut out for them at the yard. They had plenty of chores on Saturday. But church was the main event on Sunday. Woody realized that they might be bathing. Sissy answered the door. "Hi Woody. Mommy's scrubbing Dee Dee. She said if it's important to let her know."

"Tell her that Samson was found dead and the little kitten with a black smudge on his face was also found dead. I will bury them both. I don't want them to put the rat poison out around the cars anymore. The animals were able to reach it and apparently they like the taste."

Sissy didn't say goodbye or anything. She just closed the door. Woody could clearly hear her screaming the words, "Mommy... Mommy... Sampson's dead!"

Woody trekked back to the dog pens. Zeus still had not touched his food. His body was facing the opposite side of the pen, almost as if he was frightened. Woody talked to him, "It's okay buddy. I'll bury your brother. You poor boy. I know you loved him."

Woody pulled the dead dog by his back legs over to the trash pile. Rigor had started to set in so he couldn't manipulate the body into the hole. The hole had to be deep and wide. The dog must be close to a hundred pounds. After finding the pick ax and a shovel he began the arduous task of burying him. Tears streamed down his face. He would miss that amazing dog.

Whitey came trailing down the driveway with two of his boys toward the burn pile and Woody. As he approached he yelled, "Damn it! You were right... Sorry. I didn't make the right decision. I should have listened to you. He was a great dog. Oh my God! Billy, you and Jimmy go to church now."

Both boys were crying and ran into their house. Whitey picked up the shovel while Woody planned out the shape of the hole and decided where they needed to scalp out the turf. Once the hole was deep enough they both pushed the dog into the hole and quickly began covering Sampson with the loose dirt. Whitey said, "Goodbye my friend." He was crying hard and shaking his head. "... I'm so sorry."

Woody said to Whitey, "He probably couldn't be saved anyway. Don't kick yourself anymore."

All the kids except Bobby piled into a car that Whitey had given Miriam to drive around town in. They rolled their windows down stuck their heads out the window blurting bits of sad wishes and condolences, since Mommy wouldn't let them join Pop and visit with the dog.

"Pop," Nancy hollered. "Tell Sampson I love him."

Sissy and Carol yelled, "We love you Sampson."

Bobby ran up to the hole. "I love you Sampson." Miriam yelled, get back here!"

Dee Dee began to leave the car but Miriam grabbed her by the arm. "Say goodbye from here."

"Good bye. I love you Sampson." Dee Dee looked mad. "I wanted to see Sampson."

Miriam snapped at her daughter, "Get in the car. You'll be late for church. Sampson knew you loved him." Miriam, with a tear in her eye, got into her car, waved and drove away.

Whitey could see the dead kitten and the package of rat food that Billy had put next to the Buick. "No more rat poison until we can figure out how to keep the animals from finding it. If rats can find it than cats and dogs can find it too."

Woody said, "I'll take care of the cat, Whitey."

Whitey looked at his brother who was still crying. He nodded his head.

Woody limped next to the shed carrying Smudge in a greasy towel he found next to the Buick. "I'll bury you separately. After all, you were my baby. You deserve a proper burial," he said quietly with a tear in his eye. He found a mound of dirt the builders had left and where Woody first met Smudge. Woody dug deep. He picked up a single chrysanthemum that Woody found near Miriam's house. He put the flower on top of what was according to Woody the Smudge mound. "Good bye little tiger."

Jane woke up from a very deep sleep. She found Sandy sitting outside under the maple tree. She opened the door. "Good Morning. Do you need coffee?" Sandy held her cup up.

She said, "That eye looks so sore."

Jane said, "It is."

Sandy was headache free right now. She was wrapped in a blanket sitting at the picnic table with her coffee. She was seemingly as happy as a June Bug. If it wasn't so darn cold it would be perfect. Jane returned dressed in her bunny rabbit pink robe. She made her way barefoot across the wet grass to the picnic table and poured Sandy's coffee.

"Good morning, Sandy, I figured you needed a warm up. What a night! I had a nightmare that the Sheriff didn't come and Michael cut me up with that sharp knife he put up against my face. I think I'm going crazy Sandy!" She put the percolator on the picnic table.

Sandy shook her head. "Just relax and enjoy the scenery. Don't even think about it. My headache was throbbing this morning but for some reason when I sit out here it goes away. So here I am, waiting for the love of my life."

Jane looked at Sandy. "Is Woody coming?"

Sandy smiled. "He said he was, but that was two hours ago. I don't know what's taking him so long. He's bringing a special treat for us he said."

Jane pulled her hair back. "I look a wreck. Let me run in for a sec. I'll be right back."

Sandy smiled. "You look fine Jane. Anyway, here he comes up the driveway." Jane sat back down.

Woody pulled up the driveway and got out of his truck. He was carrying a box that looked and smelled suspiciously delicious.

Sandy said, "Good morning, and what do you have here?"

"Cinnamon buns for two of the best girls I know."

"What took you so long?"

"I had to bury a dog and a cat that died from rat poison at the yard."

"Oh no," Sandy replied with sadness in her voice. "Such a shame."

Jane said, "My condolences, and thank you for thinking of us."

Woody stared at Jane and shook his head. "You poor girl... That eye... Too much darkness." He could see her eye was very black and blue and her neck still showed red finger marks. They were an indication of the sheer terror she must have gone through. "Maybe cinnamon buns were a good idea after all." Woody looked around at Sandy and then Jane. "I could use some coffee. Is it hot? It's empty. I don't mind making some." He carried the percolator toward the door and began walking into the house.

Jane moved quicker, stepped in front of him. They met halfway. She began to take the coffee pot from his hand. He placed his other hand over hers and held it, keeping it there for several seconds.

Woody located the ground coffee in the cupboard. As he started to scoop the grounds into the percolator's filter, Jane moved in to help. Their hands touched again. She heaped one more tablespoon than usual. She then filled the percolator with water and set it on the stove. They both returned with the hot prepared coffee. Woody poured some into Sandy's cup first and then into Jane's cup, and finally he poured himself his first cup of coffee of the day.

Jane said to Sandy, "I remembered napkins." Woody smiled.

Sandy took her first cinnamon bun. Looking depressed, she put it on a napkin. It seemed she had suddenly lost interest.

Woody ate at least two buns and drank two cups of coffee. Jane was working on her second bun. She asked Sandy why she hadn't touched any. Sandy said, "For some reason I've lost my appetite."

Woody moved close to Sandy and attempted to feed her a bite. She smiled and then finished the rest.

Sandy said, "Thanks guys for all the hospitality."

Woody said, "Thanks for everything the two of you do for me."

Jane looked at him and said, "No... Thank *you*."

They tackle the cinnamon buns, ravaging every last one. Their conversation was about the poor dog and what he meant to Whitey. Woody mentioned how sweet Smudge was and the closely bonded relationship he had with the cat. They also talked about the temperature changing. They were not looking forward to snow and the winter months. They did not speak a word about last night's drama. There was no mention of the terror that Jane went through.

"They were so delicious Woody. Thank you," Jane said and walked toward the door that led into the kitchen. "I'll be back. I want to get a shower."

Sandy moved closer to Woody and kissed him. "You are so sweet to have done that. Thank you."

Woody stretched and walked over to stare at the view. "Would you like me to take you to see David this week?"

"Yes, Woody. I would like that very much."

"So I will probably not stop by too much this week because Miriam is moving and I promised to help her. But I will stop back when you feel it's a good time... Friday?"

"Yes. Have dinner with David and me at six. He would love that."

Woody nodded his head and started to leave. "Tell Jane good-bye for me."

Sandy stared at Woody. He didn't kiss her goodbye. She was perplexed as to why he left so suddenly and without much explanation. She assumed that maybe he was sad about the dog and kitten. She thought, something's missing that she couldn't nail down.

Jane came outside completely clean and her lips were lined in a lovely shade of reddish pink. Her hair was brushed and wavy hiding some of her black eye. "Where's Woody?"

Sandy was heading back to the house. She noticed Jane's makeup. "You look nice Jane. Woody had to go and help someone who is moving into a new house." In passing, she looked at Jane. "He already left. Wasn't it nice he brought those delicious cinnamon buns just for us today?"

Jane, looking, sad said, "Oh yes. Very nice."

Jane ran back in the house and grabbed her pocket book and keys. She quickly left, "I'll be right back."

Sandy stood with her mouth open. "Whaaa...Jane?"

She hurriedly climbed in her car, started it and drove out of the long drive backwards dangerously fast onto the busy road. Jane was on the run to catch up with Woody. She took the route she believed he would take, but she didn't find him until she actually got to his house. She parked her car on the road and ran up to his door. She knocked almost frantically.

Woody opened the door. They stared at each other. Jane was panting from her chase. He, still with keys in his hand, looked at her. He invited her in. Without warning they fall into an embrace and kissed for what seemed like forever.

"Jane... Jane... Jane! I don't know what to say, but I'm glad you're here. We don't have to talk. We can just sit and drink another cup of coffee, if you'd like. Actually... That's all I have in the house." He chuckled. "But..."

"That would be great." Jane said, "That would be just fine," she said almost apologetically. "I just want to sit with you and feel safe."

Woody made them both a cup of coffee and they sat side by side without speaking for a long, comfortable amount of time.

CHAPTER 29 The Meatloaf

Woody held both of Jane's hands. "Look, Jane. I feel very attracted to you. I actually think I love you. That scares the hell out of me. I feel like you are what my life needs right now. But you, like me, are vulnerable. Just because I helped you from the big bad wolf yesterday doesn't make me a hero.

You had a horrific experience, but you're so special he didn't win. He's in jail... And your safe. Your here in my arms."

Jane began crying. "I love... Love... Love you."

Woody slowly brushed his hand over Jane's face. He pulled his hanky out of his pocket wiped her tears. "Shhh... Shhh... Sweet, sweet Jane. We have to be very careful when it involves Sandy. As strongly as I feel about you Sandy is still my wife and I believe I am helping in keeping her going. She thinks she loves me. Maybe she does. I still care for her, but I could never truly love her the way I felt before she left me. That's gone! So look..." They were both crying. "We can't do this." Woody stood up. "Let's just go about our business and take care of Sandy and her son, David. Let's make sure she gets to see him as often as she can. We'll see each other. And I'll help in any way including financially with some of the bills that I'm sure are accumulating. I'm taking Sandy to visit David this Friday. That will bring her spirits up."

Sandy nodded. "Good! I'm going home now. Thank you for being you Woody. I love you."

Woody held Jane close. He examined her neck and gently kissed the welt. "Take care of yourself Jane." He stared at her black eye. "He's lucky to be in jail. I can't stand men who beat up women."

Jane began to leave, pointing at a mound she noticed on the ground she looked back at Woody and said, "Is that Smudge?"

Woody nodded and Jane stopped for a moment looking at the mound. She then walked to her car and threw Woody a kiss and left.

An hour later Jane pulled up her driveway. Sandy was sitting in the living room reading the paper.

"Jane. Where were you?"

Jane set a bag on the table. She looked at Sandy. Her lipstick was a bit smeared. "Driving and clearing my head."

Sandy suppressed the urge to mention the smeared lipstick. "Well, is it clear yet? Because I was hoping you picked up some burger and ground pork to make that meatloaf we talked about."

"I did." Jane reached in the refrigerator and pulled out eggs, onion, celery and catsup. And from the pantry she added breadcrumbs and a Lipton Soup packet and of course salt and pepper. Jane washed her hands and got right into this dish. It entailed a lot of mixing; getting down and dirty with an addition of some love. This was definitely Sandy's favorite.

Sandy said, "Jane, this is your best kept secret. If it gets out how am I going to survive?" They laughed.

At five o'clock Jane removed the meatloaf from the oven. "It's perfect! I can tell just by looking at it," Sandy said.

An hour later the two were back outside. The temperature had warmed up to sixty eight degrees and their bellies were full.

"Jane. Don't think I'm crazy, but I had a funny feeling today that you drove after Woody. That you are in love with him."

Jane looked at Sandy. "That man is your true blue. You're talking silly now. I think the meat loaf went to your head." They both laughed and Jane gave Sandy a big hug.

Sandy looked at Jane. "You do look pretty funny with that black eye. Let's go in the house and see if we can finish off that ice cream in the freezer."

Jane said, "How can we eat another thing?"

Sandy laughed and responded, "I'll show you."

At six p.m. Whitey was sitting in Woody's kitchen with Zeus on a leash by his side. "I don't know what to do with Zeus. All he did today was whine and bark and whine. He must be grieving."

Woody had a tear in his eye. "Yes, Whitey, he's upset. His partner in crime is gone. He's lonely. I know how that is... I get lonely. Think about it. I have no one."

Whitey looked at Woody. "You know you have us."

"I know. Thanks for everything. I do feel you are family. But my wife, who is dying of cancer, is all I have and she's not living with me."

"Why not? You said you still care for her." Whitey shook his head.

"But it's not the same, Whitey. I used to cherish her and I thought she had the same feelings for me. But one man comes along and Puff! Gone, she was otta here."

"I remember that day. I'd a knocked that guy out for what he did to you. He even had the balls to slash your tire. Woody, she got what she deserved. He left her after she had his baby."

"I've been thinking about that too."

"Woody, I almost forgot to ask... Are you helping Miriam tomorrow? She seems to think you're going to help her clean out the house."

Woody nodded. "Whatever she needs. I'll be there."

Whitey said, "I'll open the yard while you take her kitchen set to the house. You know where it is?"

"Yep. I'll help her... Up until noon. I'm taking Zeus to the vet's Whitey. He looks sick, but he could be just sad about his brother. I'll find out tomorrow."

"Woody, don't take this like I'm getting all soft and all, but I don't really know what I would have done without you. I'm so damn proud that you're my brother."

Woody looked at Whitey. "You're so proud you forgot to pay me Friday." They both laugh.

CHAPTER 30 The Move

Smells of death and conifer trees had the nuance of the deep forest. Today Miriam was standing in her back yard under a beautiful tall eastern hemlock tree in Westminster. Her children grew up loving this tree and made Christmas decorations like ornaments and pine cone wreaths from it. She would be gone soon but the tree would remain. Who would love this tree like Miriam and her family? The tree the cats used to climb and the kids played hide and seek behind. It shaded her house that they loved it, as plain and simple as it was. She was teary eyed over a tree. Woody spotted Miriam talking aloud. She said, "Thank you," with her hand rubbing the tree.

"Good morning Miriam. You're going to miss that great tree, aren't you?"

Miriam nodded. "I really am." She looked up at the waving branches and gave it one last pat. "I used to clap my rugs on that tree. Some things that you're used to, when they change, your whole life changes. I can only hope it's for the best.

"No time for coffee?" Miriam looked at Woody with a pleading question in her eyes.

"No... Thanks Mir. I had two cups. My limit."

"I am going to miss you Mir... And the kids. It won't be the same."

"Don't worry. The kids will be here every day after school. Oh, and all day Saturday. You'll probably see them more often than you do now. I'm afraid you'll see my fat ass often until he deeds the new house into my name. You know he paid cash for it. Can you picture him counting out all that money in twenty dollar bills. That real estate agent, I think her name is Mary, she must have had a conniption fit. She made a good commission though so..."

"Mir... a... I've gotta go. If you don't mind I'm going to swing my truck around to the front porch here. I'll be right back." Woody limped quickly back toward his house.

Miriam had already carried all six chairs out onto the driveway. She had two more chairs but they've been broken for many years. She didn't want to bring them because they'll never be repaired. She said that someday she may be back to pick them up and fix them herself. Miriam and Woody worked well together. Neither backed down in using their brute strength. The truck was filled in a short period of time.

The two of them drove the three blocks away to Miriam's new house. It was a two story that needed to be painted. It was a typical stucco that had the upstairs converted into an efficiency apartment. Whitey bought it after it had been on the market for six months. He was able to finagle the price down with a full cash offer. The house had better plumbing and an extra bedroom now that the kids were growing up. It had a newer washing machine in the kitchen and a stove with all four burners working. The back yard was at least an acre and had many great trees just waiting to be climbed. There was a bus stop right in front of the house. It was set next to a gas station with a small convenience store that sold groceries. There was a sun porch attached that the kids were looking forward to using for games. It had a catch all garage where the kids could store their bikes.

At noon Woody led Zeus out of the busy vet's office. Zeus, who normally would be difficult to handle, was almost lethargic. The prognosis was poor at best. How was he going to tell the kids that their favorite dog in the world was probably going to die?

Woody moved his truck slowly down the junkyard driveway. Whitey was greeting him at the office. He waved Woody to stop. As Woody opened his door the dog tried but he couldn't jump down. "He's not doing too well, Whitey."

"What the hell?" He lifted Zeus out of the truck and his dead weight caused Whitey to fall back with the dog in his arms. He got up looking down at his dog. "What happened Zeus? Don't you dare die."

"The dog is very sick," Woody said. "They can't do anything for him. That rat poison is lethal, Whitey. He's probably dying. The vet said watch him and if we're lucky he'll pull through. Make sure he has plenty of water. But most dogs die because by now the poison has affected his organs."

"No... No... This can't be happening. It's my fault. I should have listened to you." Whitey started crying and holding the dog in a helpless manner. "Zeus, I'm sorry. I didn't know you were sick my friend. Let's keep him warm. The temperature is going down to freezing tonight."

Woody said, "He can stay with me. I'll watch him tonight."

Billy was home from school early because he had to go to driver's education in a few minutes. "What's wrong with Zeus?"

Whitey said, "We don't know if he's going to make it, Billy. He ate the rat poison too. Maybe not as much. He's going to stay with Woody tonight."

Billy knelt down and held Zeus in his arms. Whitey turned and started to cry.

A big white Chevy pulled up. The man rolled down his window and asked if Billy King lived here. Whitey turned and sobbed, "Who are you?"

"I'm Gerald Thomas with drivers ed." He pointed to the sign on his door.

Billy got up and wiped his tears. "That's me. I have my permit in my pocket." He waved. "Bye Dad... Bye Woody... Bye Zeus."

Whitey asked when he would return. Mr. Thomas said in one hour. Billy was in the driver's seat and made a perfect u-turn and drove away like he had been driving for years.

Whitey and Woody put Zeus back into the truck and they left to go to his house.

Woody asked, "Are you going to leave the yard open?"

Whitey looked at him and said rather sharply, "This is an emergency."

Woody pulled up to his house and they both carried Zeus into the house and lay him on the floor in Woody's bedroom.

"Thanks brother. Let me know if you need anything." Whitey left. Under his breadth he could be heard talking to himself, "You stupid ass, George."

CHAPTER 31 Clyde

Woody woke up early. He checked on Zeus beside his bed. He reached down and felt him. He was breathing and felt warm and comfortable laying on a woolen blanket that Woody used for cold nights. "Zeus," he called.

The dog's ears perked up. He picked up his head and stood fully erect, a bit wobbly but on all fours. It was not daylight yet but the moon shine was all Woody needed to find his chair where he draped his dungarees at night. He slipped them on and found his flannel shirt that had fallen on the floor. He dressed in yesterday's complete attire. He would probably change his clothes in a couple days but for now he was interested in a *get up and go* attire.

"Let's go my buddy." He walked into the Kitchen and found his slip on work boots. The dog was now anxious to go out. The grass had a layer of frost; a tell tale sign that he needed his coat. He grabbed his coat that was resting on a kitchen chair. He clipped the leash on Zeus and walked the dog across his backyard. Zeus was walking fast; he had an agenda. Woody had to hurry to keep up. The dog squatted and made a soft but well formed duty call.

Zeus pulled Woody toward Sampson's burial site. "Your friend is watching over you Zeus. He's making sure you're doing okay." Woody led Zeus the opposite direction toward Miriam's front porch. Woody grabbed the bucket and carried the dog food to Zeus's pen. He releases Zeus to his familiar home. Zeus began a slow change. He was eating with definite enthusiasm and he seemed to be content. Woody watched him crunch each bite. He only ate half of what he would normally eat but Woody believed he was slowly recovering.

The King children were walking on the road next to the junkyard toward their old school bus stop. Billy saw Woody and called, "Woody... Woody... How is Zeus?"

Woody held his hand up. "Go back to the bus stop. Zeus is healing well. Go to school."

Billy was standing next to Zeus's pen. "He's going to be okay, isn't he Woody?"

Woody hugged Billy. "Yes, I believe so."

Billy ran back to the bus stop corralling the kids that were heading toward the dog pens. Billy hollered, "Zeus is okay. Now look... Here comes the bus." They all ran back to the bus stop. Woody waved to the kids.

Whitey had opened the yard. He was sitting in the dark dingy office using a magnifying glass to read a letter he had received from the real-estate broker who took care of the sale of Miriam's new house.

"Hi Whitey. Zeus is feeling much better than yesterday. I'll keep checking on him from time to time, but he should be fine."

"Good... Great! Woody, there's coffee. I made it strong. Miriam wanted me to thank you for yesterday. She just left. She was here to try and convince me she needed a car. I gave her the Buick. She is looking for a second job. She said you did everything. You even put up shades in the bedrooms. They don't make people like you anymore. You take after your father."

While Whitey was talking Woody noticed out of the corner of his eye a man sitting on a small stack of tires in a dark area of the garage drinking coffee. "Who in the world is this?" He pointed to the strange looking very old man.

Whitey started a hefty, hearty laugh. "That guy is Clyde. His last name is Dooley, like yours. Maybe you two are related." He laughed again.

Clyde held his hand up and said, "Hello young man. Your brother has told me everything about you. He has an enormous amount of respect for you."

"Look, Woody... I put Clyde and his wife In Miriam's old house. He's going to help keep an eye on the yard. He had no place to go. He and Muriel had been homeless for some time now. No relatives to help them out. So I gave Clyde a job. He has to answer the phone and open and close the yard. He is quite capable of doing that. Muriel has some difficulty managing the stones on the driveway. I saw her fall yesterday."

Woody stood listening and taking in the meat of the story. It was quite surprising that Whitey would do such a thing.

"Their name is Dooley? Hmmm... You surprise me everyday Whitey," Woody said with sincerity.

Clyde said, "Muriel is sleeping right now. She's lying on that mattress that is on the floor in the big room... The dining room."

Whitey speculated, "I think that's a mattress that Miriam left. It was getting too old. Anyway, she bought a new one. I gave them a heavy blanket too."

Woody was finding it a bit unusual that Whitey would do that for two strangers. "Okay. What can I do to help?"

"I already called a plumber. John, that worked on your house. He's coming over to look at the toilet and make it workable." Woody nodded. Whitey continued, "You're going to be involved though. They need a place to sleep, eat and go to the bathroom. It would be a good idea that they have a small block of ice. When the ice man comes by make sure they get a block. Also, the coal man will be bringing coal because Miriam didn't cancel her order when she left. But the nights are getting pretty cold and they will be needing it soon enough."

Clyde walked over to Whitey and hugged him. "You are amazing."

He belly laughed and said, "Well, first we're going to get you two new sets of clothes." He looked over at Woody and held his nose. "And anything else that you might need to get by. In the mean time Woody is going shopping to buy food for you two and that's that. Everything will be fine."

Clyde sat back down and began bawling. "I knew there would be a treasure for Muriel and me. I thought I would find it when Muriel and I died. In heaven. God Bless you. I think we found it. We found our treasure in a junkyard."

Muriel was having trouble navigating the stony driveway. She tripped and fell. She was having more difficulty getting up.

Whitey saw her before Clyde did. "What are you doing Muriel?" He darted over to her. She was lying down. He lifted her up and walked her back to the front porch. He placed her on a large container that was used for dog food. "Now sit there. Those stones are hard to navigate even for me."

She looked up at Whitey. "You are such a blessing. I'm not allowed to stay here too long. I have to keep moving."

He said, "What? You are allowed to stay here for as long as you want. You don't have to move one bit." Whitey had to hold back a laugh; He had such a childish sense of humor.

"They are letting you stay in that house you were sleeping in. So why not just go back in the house and stay put, sit in that comfortable chair they said you can sit on and look out the window for a while... Or how about a book? Miriam left some of her books in one of the boxes in the dining room."

She smiled, "I can't see very well anymore. I lost my glasses so many years ago... I don't know where."

"A nice man will be coming to fix the plumbing problems today." He laughed. then quickly stopped himself.

Muriel said, "That's very nice of him." She walked back out on the stones.

Whitey couldn't believe it. "Muriel... No."

She fell a second time. She looked up at Whitey and smiled. Then without warning she started bawling.

Clyde walked over to Whitey and Muriel. Whitey was much taller than Clyde. He put his arm around his shoulder and quietly said, "She fell on the stones, twice. Is she alright, do you think?"

Clyde bent down and cradled her momentarily. He gave her a kiss. He and Whitey pulled her to an upright position. Clyde then led Muriel by the arm back into the house.

Woody walked over to Whitey. He asked, "Everything okay?"

"No, but we'll talk. We had a slight problem with Muriel. But Clyde is so diplomatic about everything... Stopped me in my tracks. He makes Muriel look quite normal. Let's move to the office for a rundown on what has to be done. She must be losing her mind. She thought she's still on the street. I think she'll need a new coat for the winter months. She doesn't even have buttons on that coat of hers. Her shoes flop off her feet when she hits a stone. And one of the shoes doesn't even have a heel. She'll need new shoes. I have a plan to make sure the coal stove is functional for them. Miriam said it's pretty full and we just have to get it running. That should be completed before the next cold spell. They should have access to the taped, broken ice box and a two burner stove. They were already using the washing machine. They've officially made themselves at home which is perfectly fine. Muriel might need to see a doctor soon. She rambles and speaks with confusion, and can't see."

Miriam stopped by and almost had a heart attack. No one had told her about the couple. When she opened the unlocked door of the house the couple smiled and asked if she would like a beverage. Clyde was sitting on a once broken chair that someone had since repaired. She apologized for entering without knocking but said she was looking for her broom. Muriel, who was sitting on a comfortable car seat from an old junker, pointed toward the kitchen. She got up to lead Miriam to the broom.

"Okay, thank you. Have you seen George?"

Clyde answered, "You mean Whitey?" Miriam nodded. "I think Whitey is working with a contractor in the office. They are going to fix up this house for Muriel and me."

Miriam miles and said, "Nice." She stared at where he was pointing at the bathroom and asked, "They're going to fix the toilet?"

Clyde said, "Yes ma'am. Isn't that wonderful?"

Miriam tightly closed her lips. "What? Oh that is so very nice of that man." She found it difficult to ask anything else.

Clyde said, "Did Muriel find you the broom?"

Miriam nodded. "Thank you. Good bye."

As Miriam began to leave, Clyde asked, "Are you borrowing that broom?"

Miriam answered him in an matter of fact way, "Yes, I guess I am."

He said, "Alright then. I think Muriel already swept. So keep it as long as you need it."

Miriam said, "Okey-dokey... Bye."

Woody saw Miriam leaving and waved her down. Miriam walked toward Woody shaking her head.

Woody said, "You know Zeus is okay now. He still isn't his old self, but if my prediction is right he'll be fine."

"That's a blessing. Thanks for everything Woody. I have one more thing to ask of you, but I know how busy you must be... With these vagrants." She pointed to the house. "They're living in my old house. the toilet has been broken for God knows how many years. George is going to fix it today? They just moved in without any notice and he's fixing the toilet that the kids and I have needed to be repaired all those years, and today he decides to fix it?"

Woody looked down with a smile and said, "Yes, they were found on the street in poor health. I think everything is piling up on him, and he's trying to do the right thing. Everything is getting to him now."

Miriam, feeling defeated said, "Okay. Where did he find them?"

He shook his head. "I really don't know all the facts Mir... They're harmless. He sometimes had a good heart. you know your ex. I think he found them wandering somewhere in Willow Grove walking with a carriage full of stuff. They need some help because I think it's going to be cold tonight. He said he saw them the other day in the same spot and thought they might need a helping hand. Well you know him. He heard their whole life story. I think it's a sad one so, here they are."

Miriam said, "I guess I could bring over some food. Anyway I have a problem. Would you help me set up the kids bunk beds?"

He said, "Sure. I'll be over after work."

Miriam said apologetically, "I'm sorry I can't be more helpful. You know I won't be there until six. You'll already have the beds done by then." She looked over at her house. "I can't believe he's fixing up the toilet for strangers. I thought he was planning on tearing that house down."

"He was planning on tearing it down. But he may use it for storing tires. Things he wants to keep sheltered. He tells me they have the same last name, Dooley." He said, "Maybe we're related." Woody laughed. "Whitey gets all sentimental about homeless folks."

Miriam nodded her head. "They have the same last name? Huh... Thanks Woody. I have to go to my second job. It's at the hosiery store in Willow Grove. So I'll talk to you later. If you see Billy will you ask him to go right home? Because tonight I won't be home until six or after."

As she began driving off, Woody hollered, "I'll take care of the bunk beds." Miriam beeped her horn.

That afternoon Miriam's kids all gathered around the old house. Woody stopped them from going inside. They gravitated down the path to the dog pens and tried to pet Zeus. Woody saw them and held his hand up. Jimmy separated from his brothers and sisters and headed down toward the house. Cassie followed.

Woody said, "No one is to go inside the house."

Cassie asked, "Why can't we go inside?"

Billy was standing by the dog pen. He said, "Look, there is someone in there. Look... They're staring out the window at us." Two gray haired elderly folks were smiling from the kitchen window. The woman waved.

Woody led all of them over to the office where Whitey was reading his mail.

Jimmy asked, "Can we go inside our old house pop? Who are those people?"

Whitey blurted out, "No! What do you need in that house? You have a new house. Why don't you get off the bus at the bus stop in front of your new house?"

Nancy said sadly, "Because we miss the old house and nobody's home there."

"Billy's in charge and you have to do homework anyway. Right?"

Jimmy said, "I don't have none."

Cassie responded to Jimmy, "It's, 'I don't have any'."

Jimmy snapped back, "Either do I."

Cassie said "It's, 'neither do I'."

Jimmy looked at his father. "See, nobody has homework."

Whitey laughed another of his ubiquitous full on belly laughs. "Now, git..! All of you."

Sissy turned toward Woody and asked, "Is Zeus going to be okay?"

Woody answered, "Yes, he's fine... Just fine. He'll be in good shape by tomorrow."

Nancy, Sissy and Cassie all hugged each other. "Hooray." Bobby and Dee Dee hugged each other and jumped up and down.

The girls all ran over and gave Pop a big kiss. The boys had already sprinted toward their new house; they don't wait for anyone.

Billy was searching for his key. He realized he might have left it in the jacket pocket he was wearing and maybe left in the office at the junkyard. He sent Jimmy back to see if he left it there. Jimmy came running back ten minutes later with the jacket and key.

"I saw the man that lives in our old house. His name is Clyde. His wife was sitting on the porch. They're *real* old. He wanted to know why I was running on the driveway. I said because that's how I get to the key. He looked confused and said 'Oh, okay. So what's your name?' I said 'Boogie Man.' Nobody else was there. So I took the jacket and ran past him and he just scratched his head and watched me. He waved and said 'God bless you, Boogie Man!'." Billy laughed.

They opened the door and went straight to the wonderful working refrigerator, then to the peanut butter and jelly that was left all over the once clean table. Remnants of seven healthy happy kids that had just come home from school to their new house.

CHAPTER 32 Critical

Woody walked through Miriam's new house. The thick smells of Pine-Sol and Clorox were strong and gripped his nose making it itch, but in a clean way. Billy and Jimmy were ready and willing to help Woody right from the start. They gathered all the tools Woody instructed them to; tools that he needed to erect the bunk beds. The boys were especially excited. They never had bunk beds before. They were tired of sleeping on a mattress on the floor for most of their young lives.

This was Woody's last dangling chore that was left on Miriam's to-do list. He admired her for the enthusiasm she had for her kids. But at the same time he was beginning to think he was now working a second job. She always seemed to be finding one more job. It was like 'would you mind one more thing, Woody?' He finished assembling the bunk beds, then as he left the house and headed home he remembered a comment from Billy that made him smile. *Thanks Woody. We get to sleep in a real bed tonight.* Billy and Jimmy gave Woody a tight hug.

As Woody opened the door to his quaint house he felt a sense of contentment. His new abode still had that smell of freshness. The dog that spent the night did not affect the newness scent of his home. The smell of fresh paint and new lumber gave the promise that this house was a keeper. He looked around; this would be his home forever.

He recognized he was surrounded by people that loved him. He would always feel loved by the people who stuck with him; especially Whitey. Sandy popped into his mind. She once made him feel whole and loved but now he realized he could feel whole and loved with or without her.

He looked at a picture he had in his wallet of Sandy and himself when his hair wasn't so grey. It was a picture of the two of them when they were deliriously happy. He with a mustache and Sandy in a sexy two piece short outfit at an amusement park. They were young and in love. It showed in the picture that he had never been so happy.

Woody rooted through his refrigerator and found lunchmeat and pickles. He still had bread, so he made himself a sandwich and grabbed a glass of milk. It was not much of a dinner but it made him feel satiated.

He walked out to the dog pens to bring Zeus back in to sleep where he could keep an eye on him for one more night. Woody found Zeus sleeping. The dog woke and jumped straight up and down, he was so excited to see his new roommate.

"Hello my friend. We're going to bunk together one more night." He leashed him and brought him back to the house. This is the last night Zeus. We are going to be best friends." Zeus followed Woody through the house exhibiting 'wagging tail' friendly behavior. Woody petted him and said, "Who's the best boy?" This made his whole body wag. "It's getting late. I'm going to make a phone call... Be a good boy."

He dialed Sandy. The phone rang once. Jane answered, "Hi. I'm glad you called. She had a lousy day today. She had a seizure at noon and has been sleeping ever since. She hasn't been suffering much with those classic headaches, but she was in somewhat of a strange mood."

"Thanks for letting me know Jane. How are you doing?"

Jane paused for a moment. "I'm okay. Hanging in there."

There was a long silence on the phone. Woody asked, "Are you really okay?"

Jane said with tears in her eyes, "Um hum," keeping her feelings deep inside her.

There was more silence. Woody didn't know what to say. "Okay Jane. Have a good night."

Jane, in desperation, said, "Are you okay?" Whew, she thought, she had prolonged the call.

Woody replied, "Yes Jane. I'm fine. Good night." He hung up.

When Jane hung up she sat at her kitchen chair and sipped a glass of water she had been drinking for the past hour. She daydreamed of that magical kiss she and Woody had the other day. How she missed him. She suddenly snapped out of her trance and prayed. *Oh my God. Why, why? Dear God please help me not go there. I'll always love him, but I know my limits.*

Woody was getting ready to have a good night's sleep. He was pretty bushed and sleep was a much needed gift.

Very faintly he heard a *tap tap* on his door. Woody looked out his door window and he could see it was Clyde's wife Muriel.

"Yes, Muriel, what can I do for you?"

She said, "I just wanted to thank you. You put that bag of potatoes and other groceries at the door, right?" Bark... Bark... Ruff... Ruff... Snarl! Suddenly, Zeus came running to the door with a big tuft of hair on his neck standing straight up and his teeth showing. He growled and barked loudly. Muriel backed away. "Okay, thank you, good bye."

Woody pulled on Zeus's collar with a tight grip. He then petted him. "You're back to your old self I guess. Now let's go to bed. I know... I know... it's early." The two walked back to the bedroom and Zeus sighed a deep breathy breath as if to say 'This is a hard job, watching your place!' and laid back down.

At eight o'clock at night back in Grand View, Sandy got up hungry. She found her way to the refrigerator. Jane met her there. "Good evening Sandy. Do you want me to warm some meatloaf?"

Sandy lifted the milk and smiled. "Yes, please, I'm very hungry. I heard you talking to somebody about an hour ago. Was it Woody?"

Jane turned and looked at her. "Yes, it was Woody. He wanted an update on how you were doing. I thought you were asleep. I said you had a rough morning... That's all. He said he would call tomorrow."

"Okay... Tomorrow... If for some reason I happen to be sleeping and he calls, will you wake me?"

Jane looked over at Sandy as she sliced the meatloaf and put it in her toaster oven. "I will wake you the next time he calls if you're asleep. Anyway, how are you feeling Sandy?"

Sandy said lazily, "Oh, not too bad. My body feels like it's suffering from one big charley horse. All my muscles are so sore. It's hard to explain. Now my headache is back. So I took something for it."

Jane shook her head. "I can't imagine. Anyway I didn't eat yet either so I'm joining you. I'm making a meatloaf sandwich."

Sandy looked at the sandwich and said, "Looks good, me too."

They both had a delicious meatloaf sandwich and topped it off with a tall glass of milk. Suddenly, out of nowhere Sandy got up and moaned, "Ohhh... It's coming." She made it to the sink and vomits her whole dinner. "I'm sooo... Sorry."

Sandy ran back to her bedroom and Jane could hear a serious bellowing sound coming from the bathroom. She ran to the bathroom door and called, "Sandy can I help you?"

With heavy anguish Sandy said, "No... No... No one can help me."

Jane woke early. She could see from her window the maple tree's branches as they tossed around in the wind. They waved at her, as if to say, "I'm still here my friend... You can do this."

As Jane stood up and stretched she felt a charley horse stab at her big toe. She whispered, "Owww." She turned toward Sandy worried she might have disturbed her. Luckily, she had not even flinched. Her blanket had fallen to the floor. The percolating, gurgling sounds that this five foot pint size girl could belt out were monumental. Jane thought only large men could create such growling bursts when their asleep. Almost like she knew Jane was staring, Sandy rolled to her side. Her crunched position changed her look to appear scared, and her snore changed to a bubble popping snap sound that reminded Jane of the first night they were roommates. Sandy snored so loud Jane had to put her radio on so she could fall asleep. Jane glanced down at her toe and pushed it against the bedpost. She attempted to force the pain away. The muscle cramp in her toe was now subsiding. She hopped over to the chair where she grabbed a warm blanket. Jane quietly hopped back over to Sandy and draped the blanket over her body. She pulled up Sandy's exposed arms and covered them. Jane looked at her friend who she had known for twenty five years and wondered if this was the beginning of her end.

Jane slipped into her warm bunny rabbit robe and quietly closed the bedroom door. She headed to the kitchen. Coffee was calling her name. Today Jane had a funeral at two p.m. and she was expected to make sure that the funeral director, Paul Wiley, had access to the burial site. She phoned Bucky, one of the diggers, and gave him Paul Wiley's phone number to coordinate with his men to keep everyone efficient and punctual for the burial.

As Jane sat in her kitchen sipping her lukewarm coffee she heard a strange moaning sound. "Sandy?"

Jane ran back to the bedroom and found Sandy on the floor, her mouth covered in a frothy yellow colored foam. Her eyes seemed glazed over. She was now drooling. She didn't appear conscious. She left Sandy on the floor and wiped her mouth. She could see that Sandy's had a major seizure. She ran back into the kitchen and called the operator. She requested an ambulance to her residence in Grand View. Jane explained the emergency. She said she had to get her friend to the hospital. She was unconscious. She explained her address was in the Grand View Cemetery. Imploringly, she ended with, "Please come quick."

Jane called Woody and told him about the emergency and that an ambulance would be heading to Grand View Hospital right away. He was trying to comprehend what she just said but replied anyway, "I'll be there."

She scooted back to Sandy and attempted to pick her up onto the bed. But she didn't quite have the strength to lift her up. She snatched a hand towel from the bathroom and wet it with warm water. She then covered Sandy's face cleaning off the vomit and foam. Her eyes were beginning to open. Her face was pale, the color was completely gone, she closed her eyes. Jane wiped sputum off of the bodice of her pajama top.

"Sandy... Sandy... Are you awake?" Jane was feeling frantic; Sandy wasn't talking at all. She was going in and out of consciousness and making a moaning sound. Jane could hear the ambulance and she cried, "I'm here Sandy. I'll stay with you." Sandy's eyes were closed but she was breathing and had a pulse. "Dear God, please help my friend and I promise to give back tenfold," Jane prays. The paramedics from the ambulance were coming in the house. She grabbed Sandy's purse along with her own and followed them out as they carried Sandy on the stretcher to the ambulance.

She rode in the ambulance with Sandy. The paramedics had given Sandy oxygen and had placed an IV tube in her arm. With their walkie-talkies they communicated with the hospital concerning her stats. The hospital responded they were awaiting her arrival. A hospital team greeted the ambulance when they arrived. The team carried Sandy through the double doors and into the emergency room.

Jane walked into a large, cold waiting room alone. She joined the many family members and loved ones that, like her, must wait for the okay to go in or receive information to relax their fears that their loved one was or wasn't going to be okay. Everyone here was in the same boat. Time just ticked by with no word forthcoming. Some folks flip through Good Housekeeping or Life magazines, but they, like Jane, were not really interested. They were just props to keep yourself awake. It was now seven thirty a.m. and so many people were here. The shift change must be happening soon, opening doors and crying babies could be heard. People cracking gum may be the worst sound while waiting. The

Janitor washing the floor with his big cumbersome machine was a close second.

Jane closed her eyes and hoped to hear her name soon. She was startled by a tap on the shoulder. It was Woody. "How did you make it so quick?" She stood up and gave him a polite hug.

He said the girl at the desk wanted Sandy's information, "Do you have her cards?" Jane reached for Sandy's purse and gave it to Woody who took it up to the reception desk.

Just as Woody returned to Jane's waiting area he heard the nurse call, "Dooley family..."

Woody turned and said, "That's us." He walked quickly around the corner and called to Jane, "Jane... We can go in."

Woody and Jane walked into the ICU and saw Sandy hooked up to machines and IV's. A doctor asked Woody, "Are you her husband?"

Woody answered, "Yes."

"Your wife is unconscious. I'm sorry to say she is unresponsive to tactile stimulation. Time will tell, but I believe she is dying. Her organs are shutting down. I am so sorry. Dr. Livingston will be in to examine her and will be able to brief you further."

Woody teared up and kissed Sandy's head. He walked over to a nurse and said, "We are going to step out and talk. Will you inform us when Dr. Livingston arrives?"

The nurse nodded. "We'll find you."

CHAPTER 33 The Banker

Jane and Woody were approached by Sarah, the nurse that was responsible for Sandy's care. "Hi Mr. Dooley. She actually woke up for a moment and was looking for you. She said your name, "Woody.""

All three of them walked back into Sandy's room. Woody moved close to Sandy. "I'm here Sandy. I'm with you."

Sandy blinked her eyes. She said, "David."

Woody quietly said, "I'll visit him. Don't worry."

Sandy looked at Woody and saw Jane from the corner of her eyes. "David."

Jane whispered, "We'll get David out of that place. I promise you."

Sandy closed her eyes. She appeared to be sleeping. Suddenly she seizured. The nurse used an intercom on the wall to call a code emergency. A crash team came running into the hospital room. The nurse led the two visitors to a waiting room where there was a chapel attached.

Whitey answered a phone at his house. It was *The Horse*. He wanted to give him an update on the figure he would have had to shell out each month to IRS and alert him that he would be getting a reminder every month when the payment was due. He would then be copasetic with IRS in one year. He also had good information about Woody, that the wrongful arrest for the murder rap had been expunged.

Whitey said, "Terrific, he'll be thrilled. I did get something in the mail. I believe I already got the payment book. I'll give it to Alice. She'll enjoy having something to do with her day. And by the way... Can I get a tax write-off for taking care of a homeless couple I've taken off the streets?"

Joe couldn't believe it. He said, "What did you do that for? They might be murderers. Are you crazy?"

"Joe, I felt sorry for them. I'll bet you've seen them before. They were always walking around with a baby buggy full of all kinds of shit."

"What's their name? I'll make sure they're not wanted by the cops."

"Their last name is Dooley, same as my brother. Isn't that odd?"

Joe said with seriousness to his voice, "Are they Clyde and Muriel Dooley?"

"Good guess! How the hell do you know that?"

"Because it was the biggest story in Westminster in the 1930's. Shit... Don't you realize who they are?"

"No, do you?"

"Yes, that's that guy... Um... Something Bromley, who embezzled God knows how many thousands... I mean *millions* of dollars from Dooley's bank during the Great Depression. Westminster Savings and Loan, was the name of the bank. The bank hung on through the Depression for a few years. Then they hired that guy who cleaned them out. Clyde was left flat broke. The bank went under. They had to close the doors. Isn't that something? They never found out what happened to the money. When Bromley went to prison he was given a furlough to go to his mother's funeral and he just took off. He somehow managed to slip away from the guard. They had him and then... He was gone. They blew it.. He took every last cent."

Whitey said, "Those people lost it all. They must be related to Woody. My father had an affair with a Wanda Dooley. I wonder if Wanda was somehow related to them. Wow, how do you know so much about them?"

Joe said, "When I was in Law School I wrote a report about this case. I'll see what I can find out about the family and let you know. I can't believe it."

Later on at the yard the phone rang. Whitey answered. It was Georgie. He would be home soon. Whitey erupted with excitement, he couldn't contain himself. He hollered to Jimmy to tell his mom that Georgie was coming home next week and he would be picking him up in Philadelphia.

Jimmy hollered, "Hooray!"

Early that evening, Whitey and Clyde arrived from grocery shopping carrying bags into Clyde's new home. Muriel walked into the kitchen to greet them. "My... My... My... Look here." She asked Whitey if he would like to come in.

"I'm just helping your husband with carrying the groceries."

"Miriam gave me a pair of glasses she didn't need. I can read now. I just read *The Good Earth*. What a sad book. Mr. King, can I get you a beverage?"

Whitey laughed and said, "No thank you Mrs. Dooley. I'm very busy today."

She said, "Well then don't be a stranger. You know they had a ballad for people like us. It was sad but true. We're grateful for what you've done. They don't have an almshouse anymore where people who run out of money can go."

Whitey listened intently. She said, "You know that song *Over the Hill to the Poor House*?" She sang, "*True, I'm not so supple nor yet so awful stout, but charity ain't no favor if you can't live without.* I'll think how the rest goes in just a sec. But years ago there really was a poor house in every city. They judged whether or not you were worthy of such help. I guess they just didn't have enough money for everybody. Anyway..."

Whitey rubbed his hands together and said, "I guess. I learned something. I really got to go though, Muriel."

Clyde shook Whitey's hand. "I can't thank you enough. I'm beginning to love Westminster almost as much as I once did." He walked over and sat on one of the chairs and looked at his smiling wife. "Well what do you think my bride?" Muriel nodded her head and sat on the other chair.

Whitey looked at Muriel and Clyde. "Now, some of that food should be put in the ice box." Clyde nodded. Whitey, quickly, before they distracted him, took off to finish up his work in the office.

Whitey was aware there's at least one customer walking around the yard. The kid asked, "How much for this tire? I was driving on York Road and got a flat... And no spare."

Whitey looked down, shook his head and said, "Where's your car."

The kid said, "I'm right out on York Road. Right beyond that sign."

Whitey looked at his watch. "Are you on foot?"

The kid nodded. He pointed in the direction of his car. Whitey quietly talked with the kid and patted him on the back.

The kid said, "Thanks a lot."

Whitey propped the *closed* sign up. He threw the tire the kid chose onto the back of his tow truck. They both jumped into the truck and off they went.

Burt, the owner of Big Stop, fed Clyde and Muriel at least once a week. He told Whitey he found out from talk at the diner that these two elders were Woody's grandparents. "Now that was just talk, but it is all making sense now. They were his mother's parents who suffered some hardships. So the matriarch of the Dooley's don't have many possessions. Just stuff that they stored in the carriage they pushed... It was probably rancid."

Whitey began bawling like a baby after talking with Burt. He also thanked him for his kind gestures. "Nobody realizes how close they are to being a 'Clyde and Muriel'. It could happen to anybody. When Whitey arrived back at his home, he and Alice rummaged through all their collected furnishings they'd stored in the basement. He was on a mission to share with Clyde, even his guest room sofa and a wooden chair from his basement. He would have Woody deliver it to them personally when he arrived back from the hospital. The Dooley's were so happy to now have a place to call their own.

Whitey was hoping Woody would be happy when he revealed their true identities. He would probably be suspicious of these new found family members. Hopefully Woody would be pleased that Whitey saved them. Anyway, Whitey was not going to watch them die on the street.

Jane and Woody had been sitting with Sandy all morning in her hospital room and there had been no change in her progress. She was having more seizures. From time to time she would say a word or two. The only sure thing was that, sadly, Sandy was dying. Jane and Woody held on to hope that she may have a few months.

Dr. Livingston took Woody aside and asked if he would like to bring her home. He explained that she would need constant care and it would be difficult, but such care in a hospital or even a nursing home would be very expensive. After a moment of thought, he added, "I've heard of an order of nuns in Bucks County... *The Sisters of Bon Secours* I think their called... that care for the extremely sick and impoverished. Perhaps they'd be able to help, although you may not qualify, income wise. You might want to check though. You never know. Anyway, a hospital social worker will be visiting very soon. Maybe you can work it out with her."

Woody thanked the doctor and sat down. He held Sandy's hand.

Bella stepped into Sandy's room. She looked at Sandy and said, "Hello Sandy. Remember me? I'm Bella, I have been trying for a week to get in touch with you." The animated social worker looked over at Woody and then at Jane. "Sandy. Can you hear me? She looked back at Woody. "You're Mr. Dooley, Sandy's husband... Or ex-husband, I don't know. She's told me about you. I didn't know you are back in her life."

Woody nodded his head. "She still lives with Jane, but I'm in her life now for sure. You can talk to her if you want. Do you need us to leave the room?"

Bella said, "No, please stay. I'm curious, are you and Sandy back together?"

Woody said, "Well... I thought about bringing Sandy to my house, but it's too small. Because Sandy is so sick she is better where she is with Jane. Jane had been taking great care of her. But we are still husband and wife."

Bella pondered the situation a moment, then said, "I visited with David. I found out that David can come home any time now."

Woody looked happily over at Sandy. He said, "Is that right?" He whispered, "David is coming home Sandy." He kissed her forehead. "I think she smiled."

Bella said, "David's a lovely child. He's a spitting image of his father."

Woody, a bit taken aback, asked, "Do you know David's father?"

She replied, "Why I was speaking of you Woody. I just assumed... And he *does* look just like you. You mean you're *not* his father?"

Woody stared at Bella, then turned and stared at Sandy. "I think he looks like Sandy." He put his head in his hands and began to cry. Sandy could hear Woody crying. A tear ran down her cheek. He got up and left the room. He was overwhelmed by all that was going on.

Jane looked at Bella and asked her to step out in the waiting room so she could speak with her in private. She explained to Bella that David actually was Woody's child;

that she had known this for some time, ever since Sandy's boyfriend took off. "The timing was such that David *had* to be Woody's. That's probably why the guy took off. He doesn't actually know yet. I just don't want to lay that on Woody after all Sandy put him through... Especially right now! Do you understand?"

Bella, looking very serious and sincere, replied, "You do realize that a father can appeal to the courts to bring him home to his house at any time. In fact, if he so chooses, I can make all the arrangements and handle that part for Woody while you break it to him."

Jane thanked Bella for her input. After mulling it over for a few minutes, she decided to take a different path... For now. She filled Bella in on her plan. She then found Woody and suggested he adopt David and care for him at his house while she was caring for Sandy at her house, if the courts would allow it. Bella looked on intently.

Woody said, "That would be great! Bella, if you can, please appeal to the courts to make it as quick as possible. I can handle taking care of him and getting him in school."

They all agreed to put the plan in action. Jane said goodbye to Sandy and that they would return in the morning. Woody kissed Sandy and said goodbye as well.

The three of them left the room and paused in the waiting area. Woody thoughtfully said, "First we have to find out if Sandy can come home." He took the nurse aside and asked her. She said, "Yes. She can come home tomorrow. You'll have to speak to Dr. Livingston one last time for her directives. He arrives at eight a.m."

An eerie almost blue daylight streamed through the eastside window of Clyde and Muriel's new cottage. They both sat up on the bed. Clyde stretched and said, "What a wonderful comfortable sleep."

Muriel looked over at Clyde. "Is this home?"

Clyde nodded. "I am finally happy. Yes dear, this is our new home."

Muriel's confusion persisted. "Where are we Clyde? I'm sad."

"We're in Westminster, where they don't have sidewalks Muriel. I'm happy now. Why are you sad?"

A large grey cat was sitting on the front porch and looking through the windowed door in the kitchen. There was snow starting to lay on the driveway and a chill was felt in the kitchen.

Clyde said like an excited kid, "It snowed Muriel. Not very much but I can see snowflakes coming down. We're home and no more snow for us. We're safe from those freezing cold nights. Remember that year that we had no place to go? We stayed under that railroad bridge. You cried and I finally rocked you to sleep. That was one of the worst. No more, Muriel... No more."

Clyde could see the cat from his bed. He reached out and held onto the chair, and painfully pulled himself up to a standing position. He called the cat, "Here kitty, kitty." He opened the kitchen door. A very pretty grey cat walked right in. "Look Muriel. You have a friend."

Muriel maneuvered herself up and sat on the chair, afraid to touch the cat. The cat walked over to her and rubbed up against her. Her body was still warm from being under the covers, sleeping. "What are you doing buster?" She looked a bit cautious.

Clyde smiled and said, "He likes you Muriel. You have to name him. He's your friend. How about Buddy?"

Muriel petted him. "He likes me Clyde. Buddy's a good name. I'll name him Buddy." They both smiled.

"We have milk. We can feed your new cat Muriel." Clyde stepped into the kitchen and found a single bowl. He opened the icebox and reached deep inside and pulled out the milk. The cat hopped up on the sink and seemed to know what he was about to do. Buddy purred and rubbed up against the milk container, meowing away. Clyde said, "Wait there Buddy boy. I'll get your milk, but you're not very polite. Hold on." He opened the milk and spills a small amount. Buddy began lapping it up. "Look at that Muriel. We have a pet of our own, just like that." Clyde set the milk on the floor. Buddy continued making meow sounds and loud purring could be heard. The cat was very vocal. "He's bossy Muriel! He wants me out of the way so he can have his breakfast. Isn't that something? This is Buddy's home too."

The bustling movements of a morning shift change in Grandview Hospital added to the manic confusion during a premature snow storm. A crew of county and hospital workers were spreading salt and announcing muffled messages about slippery conditions. Fortunately the snow storm began changing to sleet and a cold rain.

"Sandy, you're looking quite perky this morning," Carol the very friendly and sweet nurse that tended to Sandy yesterday said with a happy tone. "How are you feeling?"

Sandy smiled, but the medicine that was going through her veins was making it hard for her to talk much. She managed, "Blah... So so."

Carol said, "I'm going to take your vitals and then we're going to try and sit you up to have a cup of coffee or tea. Are you hungry?"

"No."

"Do you want coffee or tea?"

"Yes, coffee."

Sandy still had an IV going into her arm. She was now in a room with another woman. The roommate said, "Good morning."

Sandy looked over at her and nodded her head.

After Carol wrote down Sandy's vitals on her chart Dr. Livingston walked into the room. He read the chart, looked up smiling and said, "You are going home today."

Sandy responded with a smile that stretched from ear to ear.

As Dr. Livingston was leaving Sandy's room he met Woody at the door. Woody said, "Can I ask you a few questions? What kind of care will Sandy need?" Dr. Livingston smiled and pointed to Carol, Sandy's nurse, and replied, "She'll fill you in on all the details."

Carol took Woody aside and said, "She will need someone to help her do just about everything. Are you up for that?"

He replied, "Well, she will be staying with her best friend Jane who has been taking care of her for the past two years. I assume she can handle it."

Carol smiled, "Good. Is Jane here?"

Woody said, "No, but I'll be taking Sandy to her house in the country. Any instructions you want her to have you can tell me and I'll relay them to her."

Woody walked into the room and said hello to Sandy. He lifted her hand and kissed it.

Sandy said, "Hi." Goin' home..."

Woody replied, "I know. You get to ride in Bouncy Lucy."

Sandy smiled, "I love Lucy." She looked around the room. "Where's Jane?"

Woody said she had some work to do. "They had a funeral at the cemetery yesterday that her boss took care of so she could be here. Today she wanted to be here again, but had to get everything in order, I don't know... Clean up the gravesite or whatever. Funerals... You know... That's her job."

Sandy smiled, "Glad it wasn't mine." Sandy smirked sarcastically.

An hour later they were riding in the truck. Snow caught on the windshield wipers and vision was impaired a bit. Woody smiled as Bouncy Lucy's loud windshield wipers splatter and swished the sleet loudly all over. "The heater doesn't work, but if I drive fast enough we might get some residual heat from the vent. Sorry." Woody sped up a bit. He hit a slick spot. Lucy swerved and then righted itself. The springs were creaking at every pot hole in the road. It bounced on every bump, the truck continuing to ride up and down, feeling like the truck was flying, until the bounces slowly died out. Woody realized he'd hit the bump while going a little too fast. Again he said, "Shit... Sorry. You okay?"

Sandy chuckled. "This is fun."

They finally arrived in one piece at Jane's house and she greeted them, "Hi! How are you doing? Pretty weird having a snow storm like this in October."

Sandy weakly managed to reply what sounded like, "Too bouncy..."

Jane and Woody chuckled, then Jane said, "I have coffee ready. Let's get out of the snow."

Woody managed to get Sandy out of the truck and into the wheelchair the hospital had provided them. When they arrived at the threshold, he found that the chair couldn't fit through the doorframe. He lifted Sandy as easily as he'd lift an infant into his arms; she had become so thin and frail. She was petite to begin with. They went into the house leaving the door ajar behind them.

Jane said, "Please close the door. That snow and wind is freezing cold." The sleet was changing back to snow. It was covering everything in sight up on the hill.

Woody was occupied carrying Sandy, so Jane went to shut the door herself. She saw the wheelchair sitting on the stoop so she folded it and brought it inside. She shivered and slammed the door against the storm. Woody thanked her and carefully placed Sandy in the chair. He pushed her into the kitchen while Jane cleared a path to the bathroom. Woody turned to leave. He thanked Jane for everything she was doing and handed her an envelope with money in it. Jane thanked Woody and said, "I could never have done all that by myself. You're just wonderful."

He smiled, then left to tackle a job for Whitey that had been waiting.

As Woody pulled up to the junkyard he saw the old man sitting on a tire. He was bundled up in an army blanket. The *closed* sign was by the gate. Clyde held his hand up. Woody got out and walked over. He said, "Hello Clyde. Is Whitey here?"

"No, he is not... And who are you? I'm in charge and I am not letting anyone in today."

Woody, a bit surprised at Clyde's response, said, "I'm Dagwood Dooley. Don't you remember me? I work here too. I have a Job to do for Whitey but first, I need to talk with him."

Clyde looked at Woody and said, "You! You must be my grandson. I knew you were around here somewhere. What a fine young man you are."

Woody looked at the guy very surprised at what he just heard. He didn't know how to respond. He said quietly, "Grandson... Just go into the garage. You'll catch a death of cold, it's freezing. "

Clyde responded, "I'm fine." He stood up and walked slowly into the garage. The snow was piling up. It caused Woody's tires to spin as he left. He drove over to Whitey's house and found him in his truck, so they talked from window to window. Woody spoke loudly to be heard over the noise created by both vehicles running.

Woody said, "My heater isn't working. You don't want me to drive to Philly today do ya?"

Whitey laughed, "I don't think so. Go home and take the day off. Clyde is our watchman today."

"He said he's my grandfather."

Whitey said, "What? "

Woody hollered, "Grandfather."

Whitey said, "He is."

CHAPTER 34 The Adoption

Jane sat at her kitchen table with her coffee and newspaper. She picked up a red pen next to the phone. She circled something in the paper. She then began talking to herself, "Thank God... Good. at least you're going to have to stay there for a while."

A moan came from the bedroom. Sandy was waking up. Jane jumped to her feet. "I'll be right there." She scooted into the bedroom. Sandy was trying to get up, but she was too weak. "Let me help you sweetie."

Sandy's speech was impaired but she could say a few words, however, she was very limited. Sandy managed, "Pee." Jane guided Sandy into the bathroom and just made it. They both laughed.

"Whew," Jane whispered. With gaiety in her voice she said a bit louder, "We made it." They both laughed again.

Jane glanced out the window. She could see that Woody was there clearing the driveway. She said, "Your husband is outside clearing the driveway. There was a lot of snow out there."

Sandy mumbled, "Good." Jane helped Sandy wash her hands and face. Sandy said, "Teef."

Jane said, "Okay, we'll brush your teeth." She brushed Sandy's teeth trying to be careful not to hurt her gums. When she was finished she helped Sandy pulled on a clean pair of sweat pants. Jane said, "There you go. You're ready for the day."

Sandy weakly pointed toward the bed. Jane fluffed the covers, gave the sheets a sweep and helped her back into the bed. Sandy had to take her medicines and do leg stretches that she objected to, then... finally... she could rest. Jane smiled sympathetically and said, "You're all set my friend. I'll make us some eggs and sausage now."

Sandy responded by immediately falling sound asleep. Jane plopped on the chair smiling. Quietly she said, "Very well... I feel exhausted anyway."

Her mind wandered to that very special day. That kiss, that magical kiss. She wrapped her own arms around her body and smiled. She snapped out of her daydream. She suddenly heard a sound coming from the front door. She popped up and looked down the hall to the kitchen.

Step by step she heard someone shuffling up the steps. The door opened and Woody came in stomping the snow off his feet. Jane headed into the kitchen and greeted him with a jolly, "Thank you sir."

Woody said, "Now you owe me a cup of coffee."

Jane took a large, fat, porcelain mug down from the cupboard and poured him what was left in the coffee pot. "You have the best cup in the pot. It's Maxwell House; good to the last drop," she quipped and smiled.

Woody responded, "Good *to* the last drop, not *at* the last drop." They both laughed.

Jane looked at Woody and pointed to the article she'd circled in the newspaper that was sitting on the table. "Read that article I circled."

Woody took a big gulp of black coffee. He read the article and said, "Good! He'll be in the slammer for no less five years. Says here, aggravated sexual assault, with a weapon; a K-Bar knife... Wow! He's done it before Jane."

He asked Jane, "How is she this morning?"

Jane replied, "She is perfectly comfortable, clean, and sleeping. I have to try to get her to eat, but the directive instructions clearly say she may not want to eat. I have cream of wheat, applesauce, oatmeal and all kinds of soups. But... We'll see."

"Woody remarked, "Sounds like the right junk."

Jane smiled slightly and continued, "Bella should be coming sometime today concerning David. Since he's not allowed to live here, are you going to take him to your house?"

Woody looked at Jane with a bit of surprise. "Yes. That's what we talked about at the hospital. When he goes to school the school bus stops right at the corner of the property. That's handy, right? He would probably love living with me." Woody grinned. "I'll bring him over every evening."

"That's settled then. I hope they go for it."

Woody said, "I hope so too. After all, I'm not his blood father."

Jane looked away and changed the subject. "How does your truck drive in this mess?"

"I slid a bit. But the snow is melting as fast as it lands." The temperature was heading up this afternoon. He glanced around and said, "Someone is outside on your nicely shoveled driveway. I'll go see what's up." Woody stepped outside and saw it was the social worker, Bella. He walked over to meet her. "Hello Bella. Thanks for coming."

They went back into Jane's house. Bella took her wrap off. She laughed and said, "Brrr... It goes right through you."

Jane and Woody detail their plan to have David live with him while Jane takes care of Sandy here, at her house. They explained the necessity, not just because Sandy will require constant attention, but because Jane's lease didn't allow for children. Bella listened intently. When they were finished she glanced over at Woody and asked him, "Are you sure you can take care of a little boy?"

Woody said, "David and I get along so well already. I have visited him without anyone with me. We played a game, we sat and ate a piece of pie together and talked about how much he's always wanted a cat. And at the time I had a kitten." With enthusiasm Woody said, "We had a great time together. I can honestly say I love the boy."

Bella slowly smiled and said that she was completely on board with the plan. She dug in her briefcase and came up with a sheaf of papers. "This is the form required to adopt David and get him out of the Hope House. Please fill this out as completely and accurately as you can, Woody. And pay particular attention to the spaces where you state you reasons for wanting him and your living arrangements. I'll shed a positive light on everything when I present it to the court."

They discussed how they were going to arrange the transition for David. Jane made Bella a cup of tea. Woody filled out the arduous paper work for the adoption of David while chattering away at how great it was going to be.

Bella said, "You already sound like a proud father." Jane looked over at Woody and smiled. Bella then looked around slowly. "This is a very cute house." Jane nodded and thanked her. Bella anxiously asked, "So can I go and visit with Sandy now?"

Jane said, "Yes. Please do."

They all walked to the bedroom. Sandy was sleeping like a baby. Her snoring was puffy and they could see she was content. Bella whispered, "I don't want to disturb her."

An hour later Bella was leaving and said, "I have your paper work, I'll call when I get the court papers signed and then we'll be ready to go."

Woody and Jane waved. Woody walked Bella out to her car. He grabbed a broom that was leaning by the door as he passed it. He used it to brush the slush and icy mess off Bella's car. "Thanks." She backed out slowly but confidently.

Woody walked over to his own truck. It had more snow than ice piled on it. He brushed the driver's window. Slush made the snow heavy and it brushed off his window smoothly. He ran back in the house and gave Jane her broom. He then hugged her and said, "Thank you again Jane for everything." He kissed her softly on her cheek. As he left he hollered, "I'll be back about six." Jane vaguely waved. She was preoccupied by the lingering sensation of his lips, gentle on her cheek.

Thirty minutes later Jane was making soup from some chicken thighs she had in her ice box. It was almost ready when Jane heard a strange moaning sound. She turned the soup off. She hurried back to check on Sandy and found her lying in a pool of foamy bubbles which were coming from her mouth. Sandy started to vomit again. Jane reached for a towel but it was too late. A small amount of puke had reached her once fresh blanket.

Sandy looked at Jane and managed to say, "Sorry."

Jane smiled sympathetically. "No problem. It is what it is Sandy. This is nothing." She reached in a closet and grabbed a clean blanket. She removed and replaced the dirty one. "There. You're good as new." Her sweat shirt was still clean, her pants were clean and nothing else seemed to be tainted. Jane left the room and headed for the washer that was in her small kitchen. The blanket was thrown in with some other laundry of Sandy's. *The washer would be very active beginning today*, she thought.

The smell of chicken soup was enticing when Woody arrived. He could see all the way through the small house, so he could see Jane tending to Sandy. He called to the girls, "Hello!" He walked quickly to the back bedroom where Jane was feeding Sandy Chicken soup. "It smells delicious." He asked Sandy, "Is it good?" Sandy nodded her head and smiled.

Jane said, "She finished half the bowl. The first thing she ate since she came home. You know chicken soup is supposed to be a cure all. Jewish Penicillin, and all." They smile.

Sandy looked at Woody and said, "Good." Woody walked over to her and kissed the hand that had been resting on her lap.

CHAPTER 35 The Nun

David woke on a fun filled Friday morning. He was happy today, because he believed his mother would be visiting with his new found friend Woody. Also, it was the day before Halloween and he was hoping Mrs. Lee would let him dress in a costume. He got up with excitement and glee. *Would they let me wear a bed sheet with holes for eyes?* he wondered. *Should I cut holes in my sheet or would I get in trouble.*

He looked around the room. His roommate Grayson was awake and he was crying because the only relative he had in the world, Uncle Larry, might not visit today. David said, "Let's play checkers. You can visit with me, my mom and Woody, if he doesn't show up."

Miss Mary, the captain of the wing, was Mrs. Lee's daughter. She was a college student that lived at the Hope House as a floor monitor. She slept down the hall from David and Grayson. She had to go to New York for the week due to an invitation from NYU for graduate studies in the fall so she wasn't coming in to wrestle the boys awake today. David got up, quietly opened his door, and looked down the hall. The only thing he could see was Miss Bella and Mrs. Lee hovering over a desk. He said to Grayson, "Where is everybody?"

Grayson cried harder. "I hope I get to trick or treat with Uncle Larry tomorrow night."

David said, "Don't worry. He'll remember you Grayson."

Grayson stopped crying. "I'm so glad you're my friend David."

David reached under his bed and pulled out his checkers. "Let's play Grayson, you get to pick. Red or black?"

Grayson, whose eyes were puffy from crying, stopped sniffling and said, "Black."

They sat at a small desk and played several games until Mrs. Lee called them to the cafeteria for breakfast.

Bella was sitting in the cafeteria with Mrs. Lee. They were eating breakfast. Oatmeal and sausage links, coffee and orange juice. David walked in pushing Grayson in his wheelchair as Mrs. Lee asked the boys to join her. The boys sat across from Mrs. Lee. She had some good news for David and kind of good news for Grayson.

Mrs. Lee said, "David, you're going home. Bella will be transporting you to visit with your mother who, as you are aware, is very sick."

David jumped up from his seat and clapped his hands. "Goody... Goody... Goody!"

Mrs. Lee looked over at Grayson and told him he was going with his Uncle Larry for two days. And when he returned he would have a new roommate. Colton Thomas who had been transferred from a facility in Philadelphia to be near his elderly grandfather that lived in Ivy town.

Sandy was awake most of the night, alternately vomiting and seizuring. Jane, who slept next to her, clearly didn't get a very restful night either. Lately, Jane was getting used to her sleep regimen of getting five hours or less. She stretched and felt that same toe that cramped the other day tensing up. She said quietly, "No! Okay, just settle down toe." She closed her eyes, pictured her toe and willed that it relax. The toe relaxed. "Good."

Sister Marie would be visiting from The Sisters of Bon Secours today. Jane hoped she could help. She was beginning to have her own feelings of helplessness. This was taking its toll on Jane. Jane talked quietly to herself, "What are you going to do when she dies, Jane?" For a fleeting moment she thought of Woody then quickly erased the thought from her mind.

The phone rang. Jane scurried to her feet and headed to the kitchen to answer the phone.

"Hello Jane. This is Bella. I have David with me. We are on our way out to visit you and Sandy. He'll be heading to his new residence with his father right afterwards. He can't wait to see you guys. Is it okay?"

Sandy responded with excitement, "Yes... Yes!"

When they hung up Jane quickly made a pot of coffee. She scooted back into the bedroom and began to give Sandy a sponge bath in bed. Sandy was not very responsive but Jane told her David was coming anyway. She seemed to perk up a bit. Her eyes opened and a slight smile could be detected.

After Jane attended to Sandy she spruced herself up and finished her morning routine. She dressed in a typical pair of sweat pants and brushed her teeth. As she looked at herself in the mirror she saw a woman that needed some kind of help. She said, "Okay now... You can do this. It's simple. Just do what you have to do." She brushed her long brown hair and pulled it up into a tight pony tail. She heard a sound coming from the bedroom. She hurried over to Sandy's bed.

Sandy seizured again... And again. Her seizures were increasing and lasting longer. Jane sat on the edge of Sandy's bed and patted her arm. "I'm here honey. Relax my friend." Sandy appeared to go back to sleep.

Jane, in a new pair of slippers, shuffled her way into the kitchen and washed the dishes. She poured a cup of freshly brewed coffee. As she looked out her window she could see the snow had almost completely melted. A cold wind was blowing and the pine tree's branches waved furiously. She saw a car's headlights heading up her driveway. She surmised it must be Bella.

Woody stepped out of his truck with a bag of groceries. He opened the door and set the groceries on her counter. He turned and found himself walking into Jane's arms. They hugged for a long time. Jane said, "Thank God you're here. Your son is on his way." He smiled happily, especially at the reference to 'son'.

Woody looked at Jane. He asked, "How is she?"

Jane shook her head. "She's worse. She's had many seizures. The medicine is not working very well. She hasn't said much of anything. Let's pray David has a chance to see her." Someone was walking toward the door. "I think I see Sister Marie coming. She apparently found her way okay."

There was a knock at the door The person standing outside was short and stout. She was wrapped in a dark wrap that draped all the way around her and reached down to her feet. She was obviously Sister Marie, the nun Jane was expecting. She was dressed in a black and white very traditional looking habit. There was a rosary around her neck that had startlingly fat beads and a very heavy looking wooden crucifix. There was also a simple brown Scapular. Her little old face was peeking out from under a stiff, white crown and wrapped tightly in a form fitting coif that was part of the habit.

Jane said, "Good morning sister. I see you found us okay."

"My guarding angel found your house with no problem dear."

Woody walked back to Sandy alone and sat on the chair next to her. He heard the nun speaking with Jane and chose to stay in the bedroom with his wife.

Jane invited Sister into the house. *She appeared to be quite old* Jane thought as she unraveled her wrap which was really a large cape. It felt surprisingly heavy. She thought *My, my... How could she wear this thing. I guess it keeps her warm.* She carried the cape into the kitchen while escorting Sister Marie to the table. She sat on the small maple chair. Jane looked at the nun who was inspecting the table and chairs. The nun said, "My mother had a set like this. It's lovely. And her kitchen was a lot like this one."

Jane nodded at her remark. She asked her, "Would you like a cup of coffee... Or tea sister?"

The nun looked pleased at her request and quietly said, "Tea would be wonderful. Where is our friend Sandra?" Jane said she was in the back bedroom.

Sister nodded. She didn't say much to Jane at first. Then she began praying quietly. Jane set her tea in front of her. She also set a jar of honey with a spoon and a folded napkin on the table. She wondered, *Was this nun praying for Sandy... Or me... Or that the tea would be good?* Sister made the sign of the cross. Jane, who was not catholic, said, "Amen."

Sister drank her tea. Gulping... Not sipping. She then stood with her hands folded and her rosary beads interwoven in her fingers. She was thanking God for something; Sandy assumed for the tea. She then snapped, "Take me to her."

Sister followed Jane back to Sandy's room. Woody was rubbing Sandy's hand and was taken aback when he saw the short, heavy set nun began praying loud and confidently with both hands over Sandy's bed. "In the name of the father, and the son, and the holy ghost. I need your spirit dear God to help Sandra get through any fear or pain. Give her the ability to see your grace through the rest of her natural life on earth." She said, "Sandra can you hear me?" She then looked for a response. But there was nothing. Jane stood in the doorway with her hands folded. The nun quietly offered several prayers to Saint Camillus, the Saint that prayed over the sick.

Woody got up and positioned the chair for the nun to sit on. She graciously thanked him and asked, "Are you her husband?" Woody nodded his head. "I am going to sit with her while all of you tend to the chores. They must be overwhelming." Sandy thanked her. Sister asked her to make a list of all the things she needed that would help her in her everyday life to take care of Sandra.

Jane said, "I will."

An hour had passed and the nun was getting ready to leave. She walked into the kitchen. She could see Jane and Woody sitting very close on two maple chairs, side by side.

They were examining a list that they created for Sister. Jane got up and handed the list to Sister Marie who reviewed it, looked over at the couple and said, "I'm leaving now. But my words to you are: 'Stay true to Sandra and lay caution to the wind. Stay true to God.' You two are all she has. Make note. You have the power of our lord invested in her care. The supplies and assistance that you requested will be delivered within a day or two. God rest Sandra's soul. If you need anything else please call."

Jane thanked her. She brought her large cape over to her and began helping sister wrap up. Woody stood and walked with Jane and the nun to the door. They both watched Sister Marie get into her car and leave.

Jane looked at Woody and said sincerely, "I think she'll be a big help. At least I hope she will." Woody tried to keep his face neutral, but inside he was thinking, *I hope so.*

Bella's car drove speedily up Jane's driveway. Woody and Jane could see it from the kitchen window and walked out to the sidewalk in front of the house without coats. Bella came on fast, then stopped her car suddenly, kicking some loose gravel unto Jane's side walk. Jane and Woody looked at each other with a chuckle. They ran toward the parked car. David jumped out of the car and ran to Jane who caught him and swung him around once.

"Hello my friend," Jane said, "I've missed you so much."

Woody attempted to shake David's hand, but David grabbed him and hugged him, giving Woody a warm fuzzy feeling on a very cold day.

They all ran inside and out of the blustery cold.

"I don't ever have to go back Jane," David proclaimed.

Jane responded to David's announcement while corralling him into the kitchen, "Yes David. You are correct."

As they walked into the kitchen, Jane said to David, "Keep going... All the way back. I want you to see your mother."

David looked up at Jane. "Is she very, very sick like Miss Bella said?"

Jane said, "Yes, David. Very, very sick."

They entered the bedroom. At first, Sandy appeared to be sleeping, but then they noticed that her eyes were partially open.

David said, "Hi Mommy."

Jane said, "Sandy, look who is here to see you. It's David."

Woody said, "Sandy, your son wants to say 'Hi' to you."

David patted her hand and said, "I missed you Mommy."

Sandy's eyes slowly opened all the way. With a strained voice she clearly said, "David."

Woody said, "Right! It's David." To David he said, "She knows you're here David. You can talk to her."

David looked up at Jane. "Why can't she talk to me?"

Jane said, "Her brain isn't working correctly. We have to be patient with her. She's also taking lots of medicine. She can hear you, I believe, but she can't respond all the time."

David looked at his mother and began telling her that Halloween was tomorrow and he wanted to be a ghost.

Jane said, "There is only a cemetery here. No place to trick or treat. Unless you like ghouls." They all laugh.

Woody said, "I'll make sure you get to trick or treat. All the kids where I live will be dressing up and looking for candy. I guarantee. So you want to be a ghost, huh?"

Sandy sighed, "Boo..." David laughed and the others in the room followed.

Bella whispered to Jane, "She's in there." Jane nodded.

Jane and Bella left the room and went into the kitchen to talk. Jane said, "I can't believe how quickly you were able to bring David home. Thank you."

"I'll tell you about it some time, but we have to go now. Woody and I have to go to his residence. I have to report that he had registered David at the local elementary school. It's important also that the residence has at least one bedroom designated for the boy. So we will have to leave pretty quick and I have to follow Woody to his home. Then we have to make sure everything is in order. It's already getting late and I have to be back in my office by four."

Woody walked into the room with Bella and Jane. "Do you need to go inspect my home? I only have one bedroom. David will have that bedroom and I'll take the sofa."

"Yes. Can we go now? We have to make sure all is copasetic. In a nutshell, everything must fall into place."

"Okay. I'll go and tell Sandy and David. I'll be right back."

Woody, Sandy and David were alone in the bedroom. Woody said, "Tell your mother we're going to check out your new bedroom at your new home."

Sandy strained to say, "David."

David said seriously, "She said my name. She wants me to be with her."

Woody looked at Sandy, "Your son David *is* here with you Sandy."

Sandy groaned and in a barely audible voice said, "Your...son..." She trailed off, then said, "Woody."

Woody looked at Sandy and nodded his head. He looked at David and, confused, said to Sandy, "My son?"

Sandy, strained and exhausted, managed to utter with clarity, "Yes."

David looked at Woody and said, "Mommy's talking! She said I'm your son." He asked, "Does that mean you're my dad?"

Woody tearfully looked at David and whispered, "Yes... I think so."

Woody kissed Sandy and asked again, "Are you saying David is my natural son?"

Sandy, with quite a bit of difficulty, said, "Yes!"

David reached over and kissed his mother on her cheek. He was so excited he jumped up and down. He happily shouted, "Woody's my dad. Yea!" Woody and David kissed Sandy good bye and headed toward the kitchen.

Sandy closed her eyes to rest. She seemed to have accomplished what she wanted to. She had attained a sense of peace. She then drifted off to sleep.

Woody and David Joined Bella and they all left, waving to Jane. As Woody and David walked out of the house holding hands Bella looked at Jane and pointed to the hand holding. They both smiled. Bella called over to Woody, "Does that mean the two of you are driving in that truck and I'll follow?"

Woody said, "He has to try out Lucy... That truck. After all, everyone loves Lucy."

David looked at Bella with a smile, "Yep... I'm going with my dad."

Bella again looked back at Jane and said, "Wow! Do you believe this. As if they've known each other all David's life."

Jane waved laughing, crying and throwing kisses. "I love you, I'll see you tomorrow."

The next morning, stepping outside in the chilled air, wearing her pink bunny robe, Jane had not yet had her first cup of coffee. She didn't get much sleep; boy did she feel it! She gazed around feeling a bit woozy. She believed she could hear someone out on her old gravel road just sitting there with their engine running. It was barely eight a.m. *There it is*. She saw a large truck coming up the driveway. Supplies for Jane were expected today. Everything needed to care for a person who was immobile should be in that truck. The supplies were from The Sisters of Bon Secours.

The driver got out of his truck. He had a manifest in his hand. "Are you Jane Rathgeb?"

She looked at the driver, a polite older man with a beard and a smile. She said, "Yes."

He asked, "Where do you want all these boxes, ma'am? I have five large boxes for you."

Jane pointed to a small shed that sits behind the house. She said, "The side walk will guide you back."

He began removing the boxes from the truck and piling them up on the sidewalk. Jane lifted one of the boxes from the pile. She opened it. There were sanitary sprays for cleaning, creams, salves, a white woven blanket, pads for accidents, two large white terry towels and adult size diapers, along with several hospital gowns. The list went on. Jane had to figure out where she was going to put everything.

Today she was expecting a Grandview Hospital nurse to arrive and observe how Sandy's progressing. She hadn't realized how extensive the work involved in the care of one person could be.

The driver joined her while she was looking through the box. He said, "It was spooky looking at all those tomb stones trying to find your driveway. I didn't want to get lost in a cemetery on Halloween." He handed Jane the manifest to sign.

She said with a smile, "I've always loved cemeteries. My whole family is here. All but my father. And I never met him. Thank you for everything."

As the truck backed down Jane's driveway she could see a car that appeared to be waiting to pull in. "Who are you?" Jane asked herself out loud.

Jane managed carrying the opened box into her house. She set it on the kitchen table. She placed the coffee percolator on the stove then continued walking back to the bedroom. She heard Sandy breathing kind of choppy. It was difficult to tell if she could hear. Jane was not even sure she was at all cognizant. "If you need me just give me a sign... Anything." There was no recognition. Jane got the metal basin and filled it with warm soapy water. She added a sponge and washcloth. She set a trash bag on the floor next to Sandy's bed. She laid the towel over a chair and hung a hospital gown with a diaper on the end of the bed.

She heard a soft tap at her front door. She went to answer the door. The nurse she was informed was coming had arrived and was letting herself in. "Hi. I knew you might be busy so I let myself in. You must be Jane. My name is Myrtle Blunt." She appeared young. "I am here to give advice or help you in any way I can."

Jane said, "Pleased to meet you Myrtle. Please make sure that door is closed. It's cold out there."

Myrtle said, "Brrr... Closed tight."

Jane led Myrtle back to Sandy. Just when they started the sponge bath Jane had been preparing there was someone knocking frantically at the door. Jane looked at Myrtle. "Please do me a favor and stay with Sandy while I see who is at the door. I'm not expecting anyone."

As Jane went to the entrance she wondered who it could be. She approached with caution. She could see a woman looking through the window pane of the door. Jane opened it slowly and, a bit surprised, said, "Amy?" It was Sandy's sister. She was dressed only in a light sweater.

She said, "I'm freezing out here." Jane opened the door all the way and pulled Amy in and gave her a bear hug.

Jane noticed that Amy wreaked of cigarettes and booze. "Good to see you. I thought you fell off the face of the earth. Come in and get warm."

She led Amy down the hall to see her sister. Amy stopped in the bedroom doorway and stared at her sister. The nurse was drying Sandy off.

Jane said, "Myrtle, I want you to meet Sandy's sister Amy. Amy this is our visiting nurse Myrtle. She's checking on

Sandy's progress. You must have heard she was in the hospital."

Jane helped Myrtle dry Sandy and put a clean night gown on her. Sandy had not opened her eyes. She made a moaning sound. Jane, with some professional direction from Myrtle, put a diaper on Sandy. It was large and she was worried she might stick Sandy with one of the safety pins. They both attempted to pull up the plastic pants like covering that was supposed to keep everything dry.

Jane said, "Whew."

Amy said, "She has to wear diapers?"

Jane looked slightly annoyed by her question. "Yes, if you want your sister to stay dry."

Myrtle took Sandy's blood pressure and listened to her heart. "Her pressure is low, but she has a very strong heart beat."

Amy looked away, held her face, and began sobbing. "I heard she was sick but I thought it had to do with her drinking. I had no idea how sick she was until I got here." Her crying stopped. She looked at Jane and said, "I live in New Jersey. Do you realize how hard it was to find you? I was lost so many times. My boyfriend Stew's car is starting to make a funny sound. I left him at that bar in Willow Grove, Stubby's or something. I hope I can find my way back." She laughed, then cried.

Jane and Myrtle went into the bathroom to wash and sanitize their hands. When they returned, Amy asked, "What's wrong with Sandy?" and shook her head. She glanced apologetically at Myrtle.

Amy bent down over Sandy and very softly said, "Good morning. I made it." Myrtle saw that Amy was very animated; moving around nervously. Fearing Amy would make a mess if she knocked over the tub of dirty water that was still by Sandy's bed, left from her sponge bath, she snatched the tub and walked into the bathroom where she emptied it in the toilet.

When she returned, she and Jane pulled Sandy up on the pillow in more of a sitting position hoping to possibly help her be able to understand her sister's chatter. Sandy glanced at Myrtle. To Amy she said, "Amy, we're going to go in the kitchen for a while and let you talk to your sister."

"Wait, can she hear me?"

Jane ignored Amy. She and Myrtle left Sandy's bedroom and went into the kitchen. After they were seated at the table, Jane asked Myrtle, "Did you get her temperature?"

"Yes," Myrtle said, "It's high. One thing for sure... Her heart is beating like a loud percussion instrument. She's got a strong heart."

Jane smiled, "Yes she does... And a warm one."

Amy came out of the bedroom and said, "I told her I loved her and I kissed her. I think she heard me because she grinned slightly. I've got to go now. I have to find my way to Snubby's or Scrubby's or... Oh it's Stubby's. I'm pretty sure that's it"

Jane asked her, "You do know she's dying, don't you?"

Amy said slightly sarcastically, "I surmised that, but no, I didn't actually know for sure. I knew she was very sick. She's my only relative since my father died last year. No wait...

That's not true. My aunt is the only other one. She's the one who called me."

Jane said, "Before you go, why don't you write down your phone number in the address book next to the phone and I'll call if there is any news."

Amy looked down, "Or when she dies." Jane looked away. She glanced at Myrtle.

Amy said, "I won't be going to her funeral. I didn't go to my father's, my aunt took care of all that. I hate cemeteries. I don't know how you can live here." She smiled slightly. As she left she said, "Thanks for everything Jane." They hugged and Amy left.

Jane apologized to Myrtle and said, "Sorry, she's her sister. That's her only family member and that is what I have to put up with. That's the last I'll ever see of her. So sad."

Myrtle looked at Jane with a smile. "You are a true friend. There aren't many people like you Jane. You're a blessing."

Jane teared up and cried, "Thanks Myrtle."

Myrtle said, "It's time, Jane, she is probably not going to last twenty four hours. I could be wrong. She is lucky you're at her side." They hugged. Myrtle put on her Jacket and left.

Jane sat down at the table, feeling exhausted. She realized she hadn't offered anyone tea or coffee. She pondered the fact that Jane was really dying and said quietly to herself, "Jane, you can do this."

CHAPTER 36 Halloween

It was Halloween day in Westminster and the temperature had gone from a high of thirty three on October thirtieth to a balmy sixty degrees and no wind at all. The evening temperature was expected to only drop down to the high forties. Just the right temperature for Miriam's kids who generally trick or treat with some pretty ghoulish attire. The plan was the two older boys were taking Bobby and Dee Dee out trick or treating. Nancy and Sissy would stay together since they were old enough to be allowed out past seven p.m. on a Saturday night. Cassie was sixteen and not trick or treating. She was spending the evening with her boyfriend.

Woody had brought David over to Miriam's house to meet family members. The kids were thrilled to have a cousin who lived nearby and they dote all over him. Miriam was overwhelmed with the story about Sandy and her son. She invited David to have dinner with them. Miriam prepared hotdogs, baked beans and applesauce. After everyone finished they all began the fun of getting their costumes on. Billy created a Frankenstein face on Bobby. Dee Dee wanted to be a nun. That was easy because there was a black choir robe in the closet that was left there from last year. Nancy and Sissy were just going to be beatniks. They all decided to cross the main highway because it was on the other side of the street that they had the good candy and delicious candy apples. Woody would be walking the town with the older boys and joining in the chaperoning of David, Bobby and Dee Dee.

David, dressed as a ghost, was holding Woody's hand. The costume was made from one of Woody's sheets with holes cut for the eyes. The sheet moved around... Consequently he couldn't see very well.

He was now carrying a pillow case full of two city blocks worth of quality candy and he was thrilled. He decided he wanted to go see his mom, so Woody separated from the other kids leaving the older boys in charge. They hopped in Lucy and took off to Jane's house. As they drove and bounced they ate candy galore. It began to give David a belly ache. Woody realized this was a bit too much Halloween candy. Lucy was so bouncy David started complaining that he felt like he was going to vomit. Woody pushed on thinking *You can't really mess up this old piece of shit truck too much!*

They pulled up the driveway at seven p.m. Jane was standing at the door to greet them. David was still feeling sick but he wanted to scare Jane. He pulled the sheet over his face before he climbed out of the truck. Jane saw him coming and said with gradually increasing volume, "I wonder who is walking to my door. Oh no... **It's a ghost!"**

David pulled the sheet off. "No Jane... Don't be scared. It's me... David," He said soothingly. "I don't feel too good. I have to use the bathroom."

Woody walked David back to Sandy's room. She was sleeping. David went right into the small bathroom. He tried to throw up but found that he couldn't. When he came out of the bathroom he walked over to his mom, slipped into bed with her and hugged and kissed her. "I love you Mommy."

Sandy stirred. She tried to talk. Her eyes were slightly open. She said, "Daaaa..." Her eyes close.

David got off the bed. He looked at Woody and asked quietly, "Did she say my name?"

Woody nodded. "Yes."

Jane had softly snuck back to the bedroom and had been quiet, trying to avoid intruding. She was so touched by what she just saw she broke her silence and said, "She must be so happy to see and hear you David."

David said to Jane, "She said my name. Can I just sleep here? I want to be with my mommy." Before Jane or Woody could answer he ran over to Jane's bed; the twin bed next to Sandy's. He climbed in and pulled the cover's over his head. He appeared to fall asleep pretty quickly.

Woody and Jane walked back into the kitchen and sat at the table. Jane asked, "Would you like something to eat or some coffee?"

Woody asked for an Alka Seltzer and water. He could see that David brought the pillow case in. He showed Jane why they were both not feeling too well. Candy wrappers were scattered in with the candy. He said, "David and I both ate candy all the way to your house."

Jane chuckled. "Why don't you just lie on the sofa. I'll open that lounge chair. I can sleep there. We can let David sleep in my room with his mother. I was told she might not make it until tomorrow. I'll be mostly awake and checking on them throughout the night."

Woody winks at Jane and said quietly, "You're the best."

As the night progressed Jane found herself sitting on the chair in Sandy's room watching over the two of them like a lighthouse watching for ships in danger. She watched Sandy and guarded David. She knew that this was what Sandy would have wanted. Jane loved Sandy and was missing her already. She wanted the same things that Sandy wanted. She wanted to not waste a moment. She wondered if Sandy was in the hospital would she have passed by now. Especially since there was nothing in a hospital that could soothe or feed the soul. Our souls have to do with the depth of being alive and our memories, and especially loved ones that we feel we couldn't live without. Sandy and Jane had talked about this very subject. Sandy once said to Jane *I don't believe in the soul*. She said that it was all a bunch of mumbo jumbo. Jane looked at her friend lying in a bed next to her son David. He was beside his dying mother. This was the right way to say good-bye. Today was the day that his mother's soul was on a trip that we would all take some day.

Everyone but Jane had fallen asleep. Jane stared at Sandy. She was breathing small puffs and little David was snoring. Jane knew this was the way it should be and it was all serendipitous.

Jane woke up and attempted to get in an upright position. She had fallen asleep on the floor on a couple army blankets with her robe for a pillow. Her body ached all over. The room was still. All that could be heard were small, bubbly snoring sounds coming from David who was sleeping in the bed next to Sandy. Jane attempted to stay quiet. She arched her back then stretched and there it was; that damn toe! It was cramping up again. She pushed it on the edge of the bed post. "No... no." She realized she spoke too loud. She didn't want to wake Sandy or David. She pulled her leg up and reached with her hand to grab her big toe. And then the second toe started cramping. Now it was too late. She had a full on charley horse. "Owww." Her toes were punishing her for sleeping on the floor in a cramped position. She held the leg out and laid in that position for a moment. She said to herself, "Don't move Jane, you've got this." The toes slowly began relaxing. She was talking to them, and David heard her.

"Aunty," David said, "Where are you? I'm scared."

Jane, using Sandy's bed post, tried to pull herself upright. "I'm right here! I'm trying to get up but I'm getting old and I can't seem to make it."

David jumped out of bed, and walked over to her. He reached down to pull Jane up. She looked surprised. At five he was pretty strong. He had helped her and she managed to stand up. She looked at him and said, "Thank you sir. You saved the day."

David said, "Good, because I have to pee."

Jane had the same feeling, but David ran to the bathroom first. Jane looked at Sandy who appeared to be sleeping very quietly. She felt Sandy's wrist for a pulse and was shocked when she couldn't find one. She quickly headed into the kitchen crying, "Woody!"

Woody was sitting at the kitchen table reading a paper and drinking a cup of coffee. "Woody," she said quietly, "I can't get a pulse on Sandy."

Woody jumped up and scooted into the bedroom. He felt her wrist for a pulse and after a moment he said, "I got one. Listen now."

Jane felt Sandy's wrist again and there it is. "Whew! Loud and clear."

Woody put his head on her chest to listen for a heartbeat. "I believe I can hear her heart beating." He checked her pulse again and he looked over at Jane who was at his side. "She's fine, Jane. Where's David?"

Sandy said, "He's still in the bathroom."

Woody said, "I have to go to the bathroom."

Jane said, "Me too." Jane sat down with her legs crossed. She said quietly, "I really have to pee so bad... ."

Woody looked at her and nodded. Suddenly David attempted to open the door but he must have locked it. It rattled and rattled. Woody looked over at Jane. Her eyes had teared up. She said, "David? Are you okay?"

David said, "I think so." Finally the door opened. He walked out of the bathroom with his pants twisted but pulled up.

Jane made a quick dash into the bathroom.

"Hi Woody... I mean Dad. Can I call you Dad?"

Woody, with tears in his eyes, said, "Of course. We were worried about you for a moment. Will you please join me in the kitchen?"

"What for?"

"Well... I was wondering if you would like pancakes?" David nodded his head vigorously and said, "Oh yes!"

An hour later Woody, Jane and David had finished several stacks of pancakes with maple syrup. David said, "Dad you're the best cook in the world."

Jane looked over at David and said, "I agree."

Woody smiled and said, "Thanks. I hear someone coming up the sidewalk."

There was a knock on the kitchen door. Jane could see it was Sister Marie. She opened the door and said, "Come in Sister. I want you to meet Sandy's son David."

Sister looked down at David with a big smile and said, "God Bless you David. You look like you're about six years young." She took his hand and kissed it.

David said, "No, I'm five."

Sister said, "Oh, I was wrong. When is your birthday?"

"It's December eighteen."

"Well, that's why I was wrong. I only missed by forty eight days. So... Close enough."

Jane began putting the dirty dishes in the sink. "Can I get you some tea Sister?"

Sister Marie said, "No dear. I just had a big breakfast and two teas. Thank you."

Sister removed her wrap and handed it to Jane. She headed over to where David was sitting. She reached for his hand and said, "Shall we go see your mother?"

David looked at Woody. He said, "Yes." David led the way. Sister, Woody and Jane followed.

David asked, "Why is she a funny color?"

Sandy's color had changed. Her color was a pasty pallid grey. Woody said, "It's probably because the light in this room is so dim."

Sister Marie checked Sandy's pulse. She didn't say anything for a moment. She said a silent prayer.

Jane interrupted and said, "She hasn't had her sponge bath yet Sister."

Sister Marie held her hand up and turned around. "No need." She kissed Sandy's hand then opened an earthen vessel and put holy water on her forehead. She then took her rosaries and said a silent prayer. Then out loud Sister Marie while holding her rosaries over Sandy, said, "In the name of the Father, the son, and the holy ghost. God, thank you for being with us right now. We confess that we don't understand why things happen the way they do. We don't understand why illness comes into our lives, but we do know that you walk every path of life with us. Remind Sandra that you are walking with her right now. Remind Sandra that you love her, no matter what she is going through. I also pray for Sandra's family. Give them your strength as they have cared for Sandra. God, we thank you that you never leave us, that you never forsake us, but you love us. We trust you and pray this in your name. Amen." She then started praying the Our Father with David, Woody and Jane joining in.

Sister Marie hugged David and said, "Now listen my friend. You have to be a good son and pray for your father that he has strength and love to carry on. And you, sweet boy must keep your mother in your heart forever." She put her hand on David's chest. "Your mother is in Heaven now."

David gasped, "Does that mean she's *dead* right now?"

Sister patted his head. David looked at Woody. Woody with tears in his eyes nodded. "Yes."

Sister Marie said, "Who knows, She may visit with my mother who's also in Heaven. I'm sure she'll tell her what a fine young man you turned out to be."

David walked over to Jane and started crying. Sister looked at Woody. "God bless you. Take care of David, and take care of yourself." She looked at Jane comforting David and said, "You, dear girl, were a true friend and you'll be blessed for the loving care you have given Sandra Marie Dooley."

Jane began crying. Woody walked with Sister over to her wrap. He said, "Jane can arrange for the funeral director to take the body as soon as possible. In the mean time, thanks for coming." He helped her with her wrap and escorted her to her car.

"God Bless you Mr. Dooley. We'll come by later on in the week to pick up the unused boxes. Goodbye."

Sister Marie helped finalize the funeral. It was set at the small chapel next to the cemetery on November second, All Souls Day, commonly called *The day of the dead*. Roman Catholic doctrine held that the prayers of the faithful on earth would cleanse these souls in order to make them fit for the vision of God in heaven. It was like having a second chance for those in purgatory. The prayer was like a request to God to please allow them to find their way to heaven. So, the day was dedicated to prayer and remembrance. Requiem masses were commonly held. Many people visit and decorate their loved ones graves on that day.

As you opened the door of the quaint stone chapel, St. Francis of Grandview, your eye immediately followed the view from the nave through to the very back where a stone fireplace was burning. There was a chill but it was not bothersome. Flowers were everywhere flanking both sides of the fireplace. This small, cozy chapel felt welcoming. Sister

Marie was playing Amazing Grace on a beautiful organ next to the fireplace.

Open casket was Woody's one choice. He believed it would help offer closure for David.

Sandy's appearance was a surprise. Someone had put bright pink, maybe too pink, lipstick on her that didn't do her justice. Even with that flaw she looked lovely, like a china doll. Her stylish coifed hair draped her face with curls and softened the stiff look.

When David walked past his mother lying so peacefully he very carefully laid a blue bag filled with his Paw Paw's ashes alongside and right next to that he laid a red bag, Maw Maw's ashes. He had never met her but he said, "Maw Maw take care of Mommy." He threw a kiss and said, "Sleep good Mommy. I love you. I already miss you. Tell Paw Paw I miss him too."

David looked at one of the two stained glass windows and whispered, "Dad, that angel looks like Mommy." Woody examined the figure on the window. It was an angel with brown hair about the same length as Sandy's, but obviously a male angel. It did actually resemble Sandy. Woody nodded.

Jane was sitting next to Woody on the opposite side as David. She whispered to him, "I'm terribly nervous. I hope I can do this."

Woody said, "You'll do just fine."

David was asked if there was anything he wanted to say. He was sitting next to Woody and Jane. He kind of popped up and turned around facing everyone. He said, "God bless you Mommy. My mom was so funny. We used to tell each other stories and her stories were always funnier than mine. I love you Mommy." He sobbed, but continued, "Thank you for all the hugs you gave me. Thank you for giving me this rabbits foot for good luck." He held it up to show everyone. "And for being a good mom."

Cries and sniffles were heard. He started to cry. He turned around.

Jane stood up and spoke in place. She turned to face the few people that were there.

She said, "Today I say good bye to Sandra Marie Dooley. She was a wife, a mother, a sister, a niece, my best friend and a good human being. Like I, those of you who loved and ache from her passing will long remember her kind spirit. Her love of God, of family, especially one little boy, David. She had a degree in Kinesiology, a study in body movement. Her classmates at Temple who studied along with her said she was brilliant, making the dean's list almost every semester. Like me, she loved cemeteries. Living here at the cemetery with me allowed her to explore the beauty of living with the dead. Many tombstones have rich histories. This is where many of our ancestor's remains have since been planted. This cemetery is over one hundred years old. The two of us used to walk around and read the head stones and imagine what kind of life they must have led. Well, now I'll get to walk past her stone, already knowing that her life was full and happy and always changing for the better. She once gave a hundred dollar bill to a woman who had two children and who was flat broke, with no food. Sandy at the time had two hundred dollars to her name. She had bills to pay and an empty refrigerator. She handed the woman a hundred dollar bill. I tried to deter her from doing that. But she persisted and said, 'If I can give her the ability to feed her family, I'm going to do it. And no one is going to stop me.' That's my friend. My friend also had a bout of bad luck... But haven't we all. She pulled through her's just like many of us have pulled through ours. Sandy with her head held high made us all proud. May God Bless Sandra Marie Dooley and may she rest in eternal peace. Thank you Sandy for being my best friend in the world." She began sniffling. Jane sat down. There wasn't a dry eye in the house.

Woody whispered, "You did just fine."

More sniffles and nose blowing ended the eulogy.

The casket was closed and four men along with Woody placed it on to a gurney and walked it about two hundred yards. The grave site was ready for Sandy's pine casket. It was placed carefully onto a lift at her grave.

The grave site overlooked a magnificent view of East Valley Park. David threw the first handful of dirt on her casket while a deacon from a local parish said a prayer that was short, appropriate and sweet. David, Woody and Jane said their goodbyes to Sandy and thanked the group of people that were there for coming. Sandy's Aunt Martha gave David a big hug and kiss. He said, "My mom gave me Paw Paw's rabbit's foot. I hope it brings me good luck."

Martha began crying. She gave David a big hug. She said, "Come visit me and I'll show you my pictures of your Paw Paw and Mommy. I loved your mommy too."

One other person that was in attendance was Bella the Social worker. She said with tears in her eyes that this was one of the lightest, loveliest funerals that she had ever encountered and she hugged and kissed David, Woody and Jane.

Only sixteen people were at the small funeral. The wake consisted of Woody, David, Miriam, Billy and Cassie. Miriam brought a tray of rolls and deli meats and cheeses. She also made a large tray of bread pudding. Jane brewed coffee and made home brewed iced tea.

Miriam said, "Billy drove the whole way and didn't make one mistake. He's only had his license for a short while, you know. I'm very proud of him."

Billy piped in, "I didn't want my mom to drive all this way."

Miriam looked at him in disagreement. "What do you mean? I've driven this far before."

Everyone found a place to sit. Some sitting on the outside picnic table that was surrounded with chrysanthemums and roses.

A truck pulled up. It was Whitey. He walked into the kitchen without knocking. He began a nervous cackling laugh, "I'm so sorry I'm late, but I had to ask Clyde to watch the yard, but he had peed his pants." He tried not to laugh but it spurted out. "He went home to change in the only other pants he owned in the world. I think it took him almost an hour to get changed. Anyway, he came back with some strange looking cookies that Muriel had baked for the wake and of course I left them in the office. I'm not sure you would have wanted them anyway because they were a bit burnt on the bottom."

Everyone said, "Awww..."

Whitey went on, "I really forgot them." He laughed. "I really did." He stared at Jane, "I knew I wouldn't make the funeral but I am sorry to hear about your friend." He looked at Woody and said, "I'm sorry to hear about your wife." He hugged his brother. He then bent down to see little David sitting at the table eating a pickle. He reached in his pocket and pulled out his wallet. He searched and found a hundred dollar bill and handed it to David. "This is for you young man."

David said, "Wow! For me?"

Whitey laughed and said, "Yes it is."

David showed it to Woody and asked, "Can I keep it dad?"

His father said, "Of course. That's your Uncle Whitey."

David smiled and hopped down from his chair full of excitement. He gave Whitey a hug and said, "Thank you Uncle Whitey!"

The sun was out as everyone left. The temperature was warming up to somewhere in the fifties, which in Pennsylvania on the second of November was perfectly acceptable. As the last few people left, including Woody and David, Jane sat at the picnic table under the maple tree, looked over the grand view and said to herself. "We did good Sandy."

CHAPTER 37 Molly

The next day David was thinking that his mom dying was the worst day he'd had in his life. He was devastated by her loss. But there was no question he was going to have a better life than he could ever have had at the orphanage. He was very fond of Bobby his cousin, who was about five years older than he was but they loved to climb trees and play baseball together anyway. He would get to see Bobby whenever he wanted. However, something was missing that he couldn't figure out.

The first day of kindergarten at Westminster Elementary was fun and kind of exciting. He was the main event. Everyone wanted to be his friend or wanted to show him around and ask him what it was like living in a orphanage. The missing link he realized was that everyone else had a pet. Since he didn't have a brother or sister, a dog would be the perfect solution, he thought. But would Dad agree? That was the question.

His teacher, Mrs. Chanley, asked him if he would tell everyone a *want* he had and a *don't want* he had. That was easy. A *want* he had was to have a dog. A *don't want* was to be bullied or pummeled by someone who didn't like him. The whole class got involved. Loretta Jones knew of a cat that her friend wanted to give away because it peed all over the house. Gary Lane said he had four hamsters that his mom wanted him to find a home for because they stink. Mrs. Chanley's neighbor had a dog that was sweet but no one was around to walk her or play with her. The owner of the dog, Ben Smith, went away to college so he wouldn't be there to take care of Molly anymore. Ben's parents don't have time for the dog and want to find a good home for her.

That day was one of the best days of David's life so far, proceeded by one of the worst. While on the bus he sat with a new found friend Sidney, a neighbor from Ivy Street who engaged with him about lots of cool things. They spoke of dragons, worms, dogs and stuff. When the bus pulled up to his stop his dad was there awaiting his arrival. David hopped off the bus at Juniper Street and gave his dad a big hug. Sidney stayed on for the next bus stop at Ivy Street. He waved at David. "Good-bye. See you soon."

The first thing David asked his dad was, "Dad, can I have a dog?"

The answer was loud and clear, "Yes you can."

David thought it was amazing. He gets to have his own dog! Definitely this was a day to remember. Mrs. Chanley had written her neighbor's phone number on a piece of paper for David in case his father was interested. David gave it to his father who then called as soon as they walked in the door.

The woman who answered, Mrs. Smith, said, "If you can come over right away to get the dog, that would be wonderful. I'm leaving to go out of town tomorrow."

Perfect! David thought. The Smiths live only two miles away. They were there to see the dog within a half hour of the phone call. As they pulled up to the house David said, "Dad, I think I can hear my heart beating a mile a minute."

The house was a two story cinder block structure. It had a well groomed front garden and a dog fence that surrounded the large backyard. As soon as they get out of their car they could hear Molly. She was barking sharp little *barks*, as a good watch dog should when strangers approach. David became a bit panicky when he got close to Mrs. Smith's door as Molly's barks took on a more aggressive tone. Woody and David walked up to the door. They were both a bit apprehensive of knocking too loud. The knocking seemed to intensify Molly's barking.

Mrs. Smith opened the door and Molly's barking quieted down significantly. Mrs. Smith welcomed them in. Everyone was anxious to see if Molly was a good fit.

David asked, "Are you going to leave us alone with the dog?"

She smiled. "No dear. I'll stay with you to make sure you all get along. She loves people, but she's a good watch dog. The dog's name is Molly." Mrs. Smith said sadly, "We'll miss her. We just can't take care of her anymore. Our lives are getting too busy. She is five years old; young enough to want to play ball and have a buddy. We just can't give her what she needs anymore. She was my son's dog, but he's off to college... Penn State... We rarely see him now." She then asked David, "How old are you?"

David answered, "I'm five years old."

She said to David, "Would you like to meet her?"

David looked out her back window and could see a beautiful gold colored dog with flowing medium length hair anxious to come in the house. "Well, I think so. I'm sort of scared."

Mrs. Smith walked over to her back door and said, "I'll keep her on a leash. There's nothing to be afraid of, David."

Mrs. Smith got a leash and headed out to the yard. After a few moments she called to them, "Should I bring her in now?"

David and Woody peaked out the back door window at Molly. David looked at his dad. "What do you think dad?"

Woody peered out at Molly. He was pretty sure she was smiling. He said, "Let's go for it." He called out, "Okay..."

Mrs. Smith opened the door with one hand. Her other hand was holding a leash tethered to an amazing looking dog. He pulled a bit, anxious to get in the kitchen and check out the newcomers. He entered wagging his whole body, not just his tail. *He does look like he's smiling* Woody thought. Mrs. Smith asked David, "Would you like to take her for a walk?"

David was thrilled. "Okay."

As the leash was offered to David the dog started sweeping her large dust-pan-broom like tail back and forth like crazy. David apprehensively took the leash. Woody stayed close. They both began petting this marvelous dog and the dog strained to reach their faces so she could slather them with kisses. Woody and David took Molly for a happy, peppy walk around the block.

"Whew." David said to Mrs. Smith, "I love Molly already."

Woody smiled and petted Molly. Speaking under his breath he said, "What a fine dog you are, Molly"

Mrs. Smith said, "Well, she's yours."

David heard those words over and over again in his head. The words transported him to the day he and Gary Gleason sat in the cafeteria with the make-believe game they played... 'That family wanted me because I love dogs and they have one. They will want me for sure'.

Mrs. Smith said, "I think this is a match made in Heaven. You both look like you've always known Molly. Now... She's already had all her shots up to now. She might need some brushing and teeth cleaning, but other than that everything's up to date. Here is her record folder and food and water bowls. Her papers are in the folder. She's a purebred golden retriever; actually a very valuable dog." Mrs. Smith also gave them a huge bag of dog food saying, "This is the food she's on. It works best with her system; for good digestion and all... You know..."

CHAPTER 38 Thanksgiving

It was the end of a delicious Thanksgiving dinner. The floating aroma's of thyme, turkey and sweet potato conjure up in one's mind Thanksgiving itself. Single handedly Jane prepared all the popular dishes she was used to growing up, and then one. She labored without a thought of her self needs; she looked like Suzie Homemaker. Cranberry sauce with cherries, coleslaw, cut carrots and string beans. The flavors could almost be tasted when you entered the kitchen. It was a memorable holiday feast.

The prime side dish was creamed rutabagas that was suggested by Woody. He said his grandmother Muriel explained she always had them on Thanksgiving. Woody commented how wonderful they tasted. David was not a fan. Jane also passed. Muriel seemed to take only one bite even though that used to be her favorite when she was growing up.

Clyde and Muriel had been chatting at the dinner table in a huddle. They seemed to be very slow eaters and Muriel had not yet touched her turkey. The two had been so busy gabbing that Woody and David who had long finished their meal stepped outside to play some catch with their new dog,

Molly. Jane was standing at the sink washing all the dirty dishes, expecting to make room for dessert. She walked over to the couple and asked them if they needed anything. Clyde's eyes looked at Jane but shifted right back to his conversation with Muriel. Jane said disappointedly, "Well I guess not." Clyde looked over at Jane and shook his head. He mouthed the words *I'm sorry*.

Molly was circling the grounds with their ball. She was up to her usual pranks of ball snatching, sometimes retrieving, but today she was not giving it up for anyone.

Woody stepped inside and requested Jane sit down and relax. "That's not happening," Jane said under her breath. "They haven't touched the turkey. I'm sure it's cold by now."

Woody said, "Ask them if they want a cup of coffee."

Jane walked over to Muriel, bent down and asked, "Coffee or tea?"

Muriel looked confused. She said quietly, "No thanks." She convinced Clyde she needed to leave. She said to Jane, "Thank you, but I'm very tired and want to go home. You made such a lovely dinner."

Jane smiled trying to understand her request. She nodded, "Okay."

Woody said he would take them home. He had a busy day the next day so he said that he and David would be back tomorrow evening for the wonderful dessert. Although disappointed, he piled everyone into Lucy and off they went.

Jane would later learn Muriel was having an emotional breakdown, probably in addition to physical pain that may have plagued her that day. Jane was left wondering if Muriel may need to see a physician. It was an episode that affected

Clyde's well being also. He implied this happened regularly. This was a time that Jane wanted to speak with her best friend, Sandy. She missed their serious conversations, because they always led up to something to giggle about.

Jane daydreamed of Sandy and the fun they would have had by now, taking turns whipping the cream by hand, covering their pumpkin pie with it and one of them eating more than one serving... Then the tummy ache... Then telling jokes and old stories that only a best friend could bend-over-belly-laugh with. She talked out loud, "I miss you Sandy."

Jane sat at the table looking at all the mess and decided to leave it. She happily found her way to the sofa, propped the pillow and easily fell asleep.

Two hours later Jane woke up with a crook in her neck. "Owww." She slowly got up and scrambled her way to the filthy kitchen. She tackled the job and her kitchen became normal again. When the last dish was washed she headed to bed to hopefully get a good night's sleep.

As Clyde and Muriel lay in their comfortable bed with their special cat Buddy, Muriel began to cry, "We abandoned that boy Clyde. We forced Wanda to give him away. We don't deserve to be happy. He's turned out to be such a wonderful boy. Will he forgive us? Will God forgive us?" Muriel reached under her pillow where she kept her bible.

Clyde patted her head. "Dear girl... We are happy. We have a family again. Muriel. *Should a, would a, could a...* That has been our life for so many years. When we're alone, you cry. If we weren't so concerned about what other people thought we would not have forced Wanda to send him away like that. We're good people. We're just like everybody else. We only wanted the best or what we thought was the best for our daughter. We were just raised different then they raise them up now. Do you want a glass of water dear?"

Muriel cried softer and turned over. "No, I'm feeling so sick. I need to sleep." She cried herself to sleep. Clyde heard her weeping and didn't know what to do. He fell fast asleep with Buddy curled up on top of his feet.

It was seven a.m. Clyde attempted to wake up his wife. "It's time to get up now my dear. I have to go to work." She felt cold to Clyde so he put his coat over her blanket covered body. "Muriel you stay in bed, dear. I can have coffee with Whitey. Good bye dear." Muriel did not respond.

Clyde put a bowl of milk on the floor for Buddy. Buddy drank it and then followed Clyde to the yard. It was a very bitter cold day and Clyde had covered his wife with his only coat. After shivering along the path to put Zeus, along with his dog food container, into his pen, he scooted to the office to try and warm up. He found an army blanket in the office and decided to take it to his house and cover Muriel with it. He found Muriel sleeping very sound. He took the coat, exchanging it for the blanket. As he covered her he noticed she was not moving. "Muriel... Muriel." She didn't move an inch. He cried, "Muriel!" She didn't respond. Clyde felt her forehead. It was icy cold. "Oh my God! My darling wife... Don't go Muriel, Please don't go!"

Clyde ran across the street to Whiteys house and knocked rapidly. Alice answered. She yelled, "George... George... Come here George. It's that man... He's here."

Whitey came to the door with shaving cream on his face. "What in the world is going on? Clyde, what do you want?"

"I think Muriel is dead."

"What? What makes you think she's dead Clyde?"

"I tried to shake her once. When I touched her something felt odd. She's not moving and she's cold."

Whitey said, "Maybe you just need another couple blankets." He looked at Alice and said, "Get him some coffee and go get him two blankets out of the closet." Alice scurried out of the room. "Damn... Damn... Damn. I'll be right there. Come in." Whitey led Clyde past the living room, where all the furniture had clear plastic covers, and into the kitchen. He sat Clyde down on a chair at his kitchen table. Alice was nowhere in sight. "Sit there." He reached for a flowered cup and poured freshly brewed coffee in it. "I'm going to call Woody." George yelled loudly, "Damn! Where are you Alice?"

Within ten minutes, Woody was knocking at the door. Whitey was dressed now. He yelled to Woody, "Come in. Clyde believes Muriel is dead."

Clyde finished his cup of coffee and reached for a napkin to wipe his face.

Woody sat at the table and said, "Oh no! She looked okay yesterday."

Clyde got up and walked across the house to the door in the living room. Woody followed behind. Clyde nodded his head. His swollen red eyes looked at Alice. He nodded a gesture of thanks and left.

Whitey slipped on a light jacket and followed Clyde across the street to his new home. The three of them slowly walked in. It hit them like a ton of bricks. The smell was obvious. Muriel was lying in the bed with her bible in her hands. She had a safety pin pinned on her pajama top. The bible was bookmarked in blood, She must have used a safety pin, stuck herself and put a drop of blood on this verse:

*Be kind and compassionate to one another, **forgiving** each other, just as God forgave you. For if you **forgive** other people when they sin against you, your heavenly father will also **forgive** you. Bear with each other and **forgive** one another if any of you has a grievance against someone.*

Woody felt Muriel's wrist for a pulse. He couldn't detect one. Also, she felt stiff to him. Woody read the verse she had bookmarked.

Whitey said, "I'll call Dr. Perry. He'll come over to certify her death. Otherwise we have to get a coroner. We'll have to get her out of here so that Clyde doesn't have a nervous breakdown. Or *we* don't."

Clyde began crying. Woody hugged him. "I'll help you with this Clyde... I mean grandfather. Hold her Bible for her. She would want that." Woody saw the verse, and shook his head.

Clyde looked up at Woody and said, "She's my everything. What am I going to do without her?"

"I'm here. Don't worry Grandfather." He wrapped his arms around Clyde while he cried. "It's okay. She died in peace."

The rest of the day Woody and Whitey would not let Clyde go back into the house. He was to stay with them and they would keep him occupied throughout the day. Whitey's friend Jimmy Ferrie, a once funeral director, removed Muriel's body from Clyde's home after Dr. Perry left the death certificate next to her body. Ferrie then transported her body to the quaint church in Grandview.

Whitey and Woody closed the yard and took Clyde out to Willow Grove for a haircut. They went to Lit Brothers and bought him several sets of under garments, a few pairs of pants and two shirts, a pair of formal shoes, a dress suit for the funeral and a pair of work boots. After a long day out shopping and eating Woody and Clyde stopped at Miriam's home. The kids were watching Molly for Woody. Bobby answered the door, "Can Molly stay with us tonight?"

Woody, standing in the doorway, thought about it for a minute and said, "If it's okay with your mother."

Miriam asked Woody and Clyde to come in. Miriam looked at Clyde and shook her head. "I am so sorry for the loss of your wife."

Molly was showing super excitement and jumping all over Woody.

"Mir, if the dog is too much I'll just take her home."

She said, "No Woody. These kids have fallen in love with that dog. He's fine. I'm kind of getting attached to him myself. When is the funeral?"

He said, "It's going to be tomorrow afternoon. I think about two. Do you want to go?"

"If I can. The dog should stay. Where is Clyde going to sleep tonight?"

Woody said, "He's going to sleep in my bed. I'll take the sofa. Mir, If Molly stays the night I'll pick her up in the morning. If that's okay with you."

Miriam said, "Okay, the dog is staying."

Bobby jumped up and down. Molly wagged her tail, as if to say I'm happy too.

He said, "Thanks Mir."

Woody and Clyde left.

When they arrived back at Woody's home Clyde staggered to Woody's bedroom, completely exhausted, as if he knew where he was going. He stepped out of his old loafer style shoes and fell onto Woody's bed.

David spent the day and night with Jane at the cemetery. They ate all day long. They had pancakes for a late brunch. Then they made homemade pizza for dinner, and for dessert David wanted ice cream and homemade chocolate chip cookies. They were excited to watch The Wizard of Oz, but after the first half hour Jane was exhausted and she slumped into a deep sleep on the sofa. David attempted to wake her once, when the Wicked Witch of the West came on the TV screen. But it was impossible. He had to listen to those scary words of doom all alone, *'I'll get you my pretty, and your little dog too!'* When David said, "Jane," she sat up straight like she was interested, but then she flopped back over to a prone position. She was just not waking up. She mumbled something and went right back to sleep. David fell asleep halfway through the movie, cramped up next to Jane sardine style, making it difficult for either of them to move.

Muriel was not embalmed. Her funeral was to be was to be simple and quick. There were no known relatives or friends besides Woody and David and the King family. So it was quick but lovely. Nothing was even mentioned in the local newspaper. Burt, from Big Stop Diner, sent flowers and he gave Whitey one hundred dollars as thanks for the role he had played in helping the couple. When Whitey brought Clyde and Woody in that same day, Burt told Nancy their waitress not to take any money from their table. Clyde cried from all the kind condolences.

Muriel's funeral was a déjà vu moment for Jane. It was held at the same Saint Francis Grandview Chapel where Sandy's funeral had been. They had a reading that Muriel used to refer to when someone she loved died. Woody read the Psalm John 11:25-26 *Jesus said to her, "I am the resurrection and the life. The one who believes in me will live, even though they die; and whoever lives by believing in me will never die. Do you believe this?"*

When Woody Was finished Clyde stood up and cried, "Rest in peace my darling wife. I'll miss you dear. God rest your soul. My wife was my life." He sat down and covered his face with his hands.

The wake was held at Jane's house. It was a quiet affair. Whitey donated a lovely cemetery plot; a very generous gift. Whitey cried. He said, "She was a nice lady. I just saw her the other day walking around praying out loud. We thought she was in good health. We had no idea."

Alice made herself known by showcasing her new animal pelt coat surprising Miriam who then left early. She told Woody she would keep David until he made it home, since Molly was at her house anyway. They would stay until Woody got home in the evening. Just seeing Alice showing off her coat filled Miriam with disdain. She had to get out of there.

Clyde cried a bit more, soft sobs. but for the most part he was very quiet. He stood up and said, "Thank you everyone for coming. God Bless you. Muriel would have been so pleased."

That was it. No one was there from Clyde's family. Muriel had a sister, Ellen that was there but did not commiserate or visit with the family at Jane's house. How she found out was a mystery. No one even spoke to her. She had a glass of water. Clyde recognized her. Neither of them spoke. She left without a word, after looking over the picnic table at the grand view.

Turkey sandwiches were served with plenty of deserts, including pumpkin pie. Some were left over's that hadn't been touched from Thanksgiving, but they ate all the desserts and lots of turkey. As the last person left, Whitey and Alice took Clyde home in the truck. He heard on the weather report there may be a snow storm and he wasn't about to take the Cadillac out in snow.

When everyone finally left, Jane sensually tackled Woody... And he loved it! They headed straight to Jane's single bed. The two began kissing and disrobing until it happened: Woody's bum leg caught in the pant leg and his shirt wrapped around his neck. Jane was able to meticulously disrobed until she was totally naked. But before Woody could untangle himself, Murphy's Law asserted itself... The phone rang. It was David.

"When are you coming home dad?"

"Right now son," he said.

They hung up. Jane and Woody laughed. Their laughter continued as Jane tried unsuccessfully to dress him. She reached next to her bed for her bunny rabbit robe still laughing and the laughter became so intense she had to use the bathroom. Poor Woody was bent in a pretzel position and dressing was almost impossible.

He first asked Jane, "Are you okay with me leaving now?"

Her body was telling her no but Jane said, "Of course my love."

Woody, finally fully dressed, kissed Jane and left, shaking his head and still laughing.

While driving along in Lucy, Woody couldn't stop thinking about Jane and how he felt. He was now certain that she felt the same. He recalled looking into her eyes and he loved what he saw. Their love had been tested and what they both now realized was that *This was forever*.

CHAPTER 39 The Celebration

Two weeks before Christmas Woody's plan was to visit the Hope House with gifts for the kids and ten large pizza pies like he had in the past. He was anxious to have David help him with the details. Woody and David had fun picking out toys and even gifts for the staff. It seemed that doing it again this year would start a tradition. Everyone that worked at the Hope House referred to him as the Christmas Elf. Because they celebrated the same day as David's birthday it was a big deal for Woody, David and Jane. They brought a birthday cake for David. Everyone sang Happy Birthday to David and Mrs. Lee gave him a hug. This year they sang Happy Birthday and abruptly left. They didn't even eat pizza with everyone. Mrs. Lee seemed disappointed so they explained about Sandy's passing. Then she understood. This year was different.

After a bumpy ride in Lucy, Jane was wondering why Woody seemed to be rushing; hitting every pot hole. She was feeling sad for David. He didn't even get a taste of his birthday cake, but he was laughing and saying, "More... More." He enjoyed Lucy's bouncy ride.

As they arrived and hopped out of Lucy, they noticed Miriam's car was there. Jane walked slowly while David lead the way into the house. As they walked in there was Miriam and a tasty looking birthday cake for David. Miriam's kids were all inside. Everyone sang, "Happy Birthday to David."

"Wow," Jane said looking at David. "You're getting all kinds of birthday wishes."

David said, "Jane, we have a surprise for you too."

Woody looked at David. He placed his index finger on his lips in a *hush* sign, then made a motion as if locking his lips with a key.

David nodded his head and said, "I know... I won't tell her." He was holding a gift that Jane had brought for him. He said, "I wonder what it is?"

Jane noticed a sign written in crayon across the back window. It read *Congratulations*. Another one said *Happy Birthday*. Jane laughed and said to herself, "Maybe they were congratulating David late for the adoption, along with his birthday."

Bobby said, "Happy Birthday David."

The kids all looked at Jane and said, "Congratulations!" Miriam shushed everyone. That was very strange, Jane thought.

Then Jane noticed Molly walking around the house with something on her collar. Jane reached over and said, "What is it Molly?" It was a small pink gift box with a bow on it. There was a card attached. It read *To Jane*. Jane attempted to read the card.

David looked at his father and said, "Is she allowed to read the card dad?"

Woody smiled and said, "Sure."

Everyone started clapping prematurely. Jane read the card out loud, "To Jane. Open this and say Yes or No." *What in the world*, she thought. Jane could see that it was a small jewelry box. When she opened it there it was... A beautiful diamond ring inside and another small note said *Will you marry me?* The diamond ring was radiant; one single perfect stone. Jane looked over at Woody and said. "Yes... Yes... Yes!"

Everyone clapped louder and Woody walked over and took Jane in his arms holding her for the longest time. He said, "I love you Jane and I'm glad you said yes." They kissed a long awaited deep kiss. It was soft but sensual and made them feel tingly. They never wanted to be apart.

Everyone was clapping and then a *POP!* was heard. One of the boys had popped a balloon. It was Jimmy. He said, "Happy birthday David and congratulations Jane!"

A large pot of chili, one of Miriam's and the kids' favorites, was sitting on the stove. Whitey stopped by and brought Clyde with him. Clyde was timid but polite. he sat down at the small table and Cassie brought him a bowl of chili to eat. He bent his head over the bowl and never lifted it up until the whole bowl was devoured.

Jane was deliriously happy walking around, showing everyone the ring. She put the ring on and said to everyone, "David and I want to thank all of you for this wonderful surprise." She looked over at Woody and said in a mischievous manner, "Are you going to kidnap me soon?"

Woody looked at Jane and said, "I hope so."

Whitey congratulated the newly engaged couple. He handed them an envelope and wished David a happy birthday. He and Clyde then left.

Miriam asked David if he would like to stay the night at her house for a sleep over. David and Bobby were so excited. They both had so much in common.

David glanced questioningly at his father. Woody hugged David and said, "If you promise to be at your best behavior." He kissed him and said, "I love you to the moon."

David said, "I love you to the stars." David looked over at Jane and said, "I love you too Jane."

She kissed him and said, "I love you also."

David ran off with Bobby. Miriam and the other kids headed for the sleep over. The house was now empty except for Woody and Jane. The room was quiet. Not a sound could be heard except for Molly in the living room chewing a rawhide that Whitey had given him.

Slowly they found their way to Woody's bedroom. They were delightfully alone. They were happily surprised to see a bottle of champagne that was now sitting on Woody's night table with two plastic champagne glasses. Miriam had snuck in and placed it there earlier without them knowing. It was already opened. He said to himself, *Thank you Miriam.* They sat on the bed and Woody poured a small amount of the bubbly into both glasses and said, "This is a toast to my bride to be. I love you and I always will."

Jane said, "And I will be your bride with pleasure. I love you and I always will."

They both drank a good amount, put the glass down and fell into each other's arms.

It was seven forty five a.m. and Whitey was sitting at his desk in the office expecting Woody to pop in any minute. The coffee that he had brewed was very strong, seemingly thick. Clyde was sitting in his usual spot in the corner near Whitey's desk, like an observing troll, emotionally damaged and ready to pounce if need be. He sipped the hot coffee and exclaimed, "Whew."

Whitey picked up the paper and began reading the main story on the front page. He quietly gasped, "Oh Wow." and continued reading:

Headline news shows Edward Bromley caught in Saint Augustine, FL, after being on the run for over thirty five years. He's wanted for embezzling 5.5 million dollars from Westminster Savings and Loan in Westminster, PA. This bank was Westminster's pride. Everyone seemed to know everyone. A true family bank. The bank held their own during the great depression until Edward Bromley was hired as a loan officer to take some of the burden off of Clyde Dooley, the president. The bank had been solvent up until then. People were devastated. Many people lost their life savings.

Many committed suicide. The owner, Mr. Dooley, lost his own home and possessions. Bromley's shadowy past was hidden at the time Clyde hired him. Clyde's accounts payable and loan department was behind the eight ball.

Previously, Bromley had been convicted of two counts of grand theft totaling five thousand dollars. He had taken funds from a girlfriend's bank account and had stolen a diamond necklace from her home that had been in the family for years. He served five years. He was sentenced to ten but was released on good behavior.

The key to finding Bromley was a tip from a disgruntled partner who Bromley worked with in Florida. Bromley began shaving funds and purchasing boy toys that were clearly not from his own income.

Bromley has been known in the Saint Augustine area as "Dozer", his aka being John Dozer. He purchased a large, successful equipment manufacturing company, Choice Equipment, and has been doing business with a Johnstown, PA, branch. FBI agents have closed down both manufacturing companies and Bromley's bank accounts. He recently purchased a palatial retreat in the Johnstown area. His plan was to move back to Pennsylvania according to unidentified sources. FBI Agent Bo Lang from Saint Augustine said a deed to his new purchased residence was found in his brother's home. The brother, Jim Bromley, was recently arrested for theft at a sporting goods store. When his home was searched the deed was found by local authorities.

Bromley was brought in for arraignment at the Federal Building in Philadelphia. The case has been open for the past thirty two years while Bromley operated undetected. The FBI has not been able to locate bank owner Clyde Dooley. The Intelligencer would like anyone who knows of Clyde Dooley's whereabouts to contact the FBI at this number: 215-999-1199.

Whitey looked over at Clyde who was still sitting in the same position with his hands folded. His head was down like he may have been dozing off a bit. Whitey asked Clyde, "Why not have a magnificent cup of coffee? Aren't you a coffee drinker?"

Clyde smiled, "Sure I like coffee. I'm quite sure it is delicious, but no thank you."

Whitey looked at Clyde. "Where do you think Woody is?"

Clyde said with a distinguished look on his face, "Well, I don't really know for sure. He's probably taking care of Molly, his lovely new dog. He had to feed and move Zeus to his pen. Maybe Jane and he are... You know. Rumbling under the covers. Do you need me to go and check on him?"

Whitey laughed, shook his head, and said, "No, you're probably right. So you don't want another cup of my fine coffee?"

Clyde shook his head, "No. The way my insides work, that would not be a very good idea. Thank you anyway my friend. You have been very kind."

Woody walked into the office looking well rested and smiling. Whitey grabbed his arm and pulled him over. He whispered, "Read this article."

Woody picked up an old, slightly dirty coffee cup. He went into the bathroom and cleaned it out with his handkerchief. Then he poured the strong coffee into the cup. He found the old beat up chair that used to be a Studebaker's backseat. Carefully he put the cup on the garage floor, sat deep down into the seat, picked up the cup and took a huge gulp.

"Whoa." He shook his head. "Are you trying to kill me?"

Whitey laughed and said, "Just read that article."

Woody read the article, smiled and asked, "Grandfather. Can you read without your glasses? I saw them on your kitchen sink."

Clyde looked at the paper but he couldn't even read the headlines.

Woody excitedly said, "They found Bromley."

Whitey added, "And he's right in Philadelphia at the Fed building. He's where I was. It's the pits. He'll rot in jail and he deserves it. They're looking for you Clyde. They have closed all his accounts and so far the value of his wealth is millions of dollars. Now that's a lot of money."

Clyde listened but did not show much excitement. First he smiled then he shook his head, looked down and said, "I'm sorry Muriel. We could have finally been happy. You didn't have to suffer dear."

Whitey said, "I have to call *The Horse*. He'll help us if it means that green stuff... You know... That horses like."

Clyde looked at Whitey and said, "The horse?"

"We have to turn on the news." Whitey turned on the radio. It was eight o'clock.

Woody ran up to the front entrance and removed the *closed* sign and unlocked the gate. No one was waiting so he returned to the garage.

Whitey excitedly said to Clyde who could barely hear the broadcast due to the static, "Someone has already made their way to the Fed Building and believes they are your next of kin. A nephew named Raymond Dooley. He arrived with his son Brian Dooley who is eighteen."

Woody said, "What do you know. Relatives. They're coming out of the woodwork."

Clyde said, "They may be related to me, but they mean nothing to me. When Muriel and I lost our bank in Westminster and our beautiful home in Ivy Town no one wanted anything to do with us. We were blacklisted from all of them. They didn't know how to treat us so they avoided us like the plague. They knew we lost everything and suddenly we meant nothing to any of them. They never helped us one iota. They wouldn't even wave to us on the street."

Whitey patted Clyde on his back and put his hand up toward the sky. "Muriel did this for you. Listen to me will ya... I'm getting a bit tetched in the head. It's Saturday. Billy will be here by nine. Thanks to Billy we have someone to fill in. I guess I could close the yard... But it's Saturday and all those goofy teenagers are fixing or looking for a car. We can all pile in my new Cadillac Eldorado convertible. It's newer than Joe's. I haven't even put ten miles on it. I think it reads eight and something. It's been mostly in my garage."

Woody said, "What? You have got to be kidding. You never even mentioned it."

"I've been trying to hide it from Miriam. Alice thinks she'll want more money." Whitey laughed as he left and started walking down the driveway toward his house.

Billy came into the main entrance of the junkyard on his bicycle balancing a bag of donuts from Miriam. He dropped the bike in front of the office and ran inside. He said, "Mommy wanted me to make sure Woody and Clyde got one of these. Can I have one?" he asked Woody.

Woody nodded, "Of course."

Clyde said to him, "Why don't you pick two? Tell your mother I am very pleased, especially since cream filled is my favorite and I can see a couple peaking at me from the bag."

Billy said, "I love the chocolate covered and I saw one in the bag."

They both began eating happily and a lot of 'Ummms' and 'Ommms' were heard.

Whitey pulled up through the front entrance gate with a brand spanking new shiny silver Cadillac Eldorado. Woody stood there with his donut half in his mouth. Billy was on his bike eating a donut. He nearly choked shoving it into his mouth. He threw the remaining piece on the ground. Powdered sugar covered the bottom part of his face.

Clyde walked out of the garage to see what the fuss was about and said, "My... My... My. That must have set you back quite a bit."

Whitey said, "Don't say anything to Miriam."

Billy heard him and laughed quietly.

Whitey stepped out of his very own Christmas gift to himself and said, "After riding in *The Horse's* car I made my decision. But I didn't want everyone to think I copied. His is a different color and one year older. This is as new as it gets."

Woody and Clyde went into the garage bathroom and washed their hands. They piled into the car with Whitey.

Before they left, Whitey gave his son permission to eat as many donuts as he wanted while he mans the junkyard. And if he gets asked any questions that he can't answer have them come back this afternoon. Jane will be stopping by at Woody's house so that she and David could pick up Molly. She might be able to help you.

Billy was staring in awe. "Okay, pop. See ya."

Ivy town was small. Only about five hundred people live there. Almshouse Road ran along the perimeter and it also dead ended at the Hope House. As Woody, Whitey and Clyde, along with *The Horse*, left his office, they marveled again over the new car. *The Horse* couldn't celebrate with them today. He would only stay with Clyde for the arraignment. He would be driving his own Caddy and meet everyone there so he could leave for his next money making event.

He said, "Your case has been on my mind for a long time. We're going to get everything we can from that SOB. We'll shut him down and own his ass. He'll pay my mortgage for the next ten years. We'll be in line right behind the IRS. So don't panic. The FBI is very particular about how they prosecute. He'll be looking at four cold walls for a long time. I'm thrilled to represent Clyde in this case. But for now I'm pressed for time. Let's get going. I'll have to leave for a local court hearing in Willow Grove, which is ten miles away, right after."

He drove his own car and Whitey followed. The two cars parked next to each other looking very cool. Whitey walked backwards looking at the cars, proud as a peacock.

CHAPTER 40 The Homecoming

Georgie arrived home in his dress blues. He looked so dapper. Miriam was so proud she took pictures and made his favorite chuck roast dinner with mashed potatoes and gravy. He was now engaged to Margaret. Maggie was what he called her. She was from two streets away and with Miriam's consent he brought her to dinner in the new house and exhibited her new ring. It was a pretty blue sapphire, her birth stone.

Margaret was a slender not quite five foot prom queen. She was cute as a button and smart as a whip. She had recently started working at A&L Engineering, in Willow Grove, as a secretary. She had already been stashing away a hefty savings and a full hope chest while Georgie was in France where he was serving aboard the U.S.S. Springfield, flagship of the Mediterranean Fleet. They were in love and ready for the next step.

Whitey had given Georgie permission to move into the apartment above the garage when he returned. He dropped off his bags there. He saw that Cassie and Sissy had cleaned it so well that he gave them a small tip. He could actually move in. How exciting... Or was it? Woody left a teapot, a mattress, a table and two chairs. Woody had left it better than when he had moved in. Georgie moved in right away. He liked being independent. He already had most of his belongings there anyway. Although, that first night in his apartment he started to question how great this was going to be when he looked down the stairs and there was Pop heading up.

He said, "Hey pop, what's up?"

Whitey said, "Not much. I was wondering if you want to go to breakfast?"

Georgie said, "Sure. I'll be right down."

Now, normally that would be a perfect invitation. But today was his first day home and he wanted to relax and not have to work at the yard. But that thought was now gone. He was going to go get a nice hearty meal so Pop could get a full day of work out of him. The only issue he had was that he would be at his father's beck and call now that he was living in the yard.

Billy had already received his orders to report to boot camp at Fort Benning in two weeks. He was pretty sure he would be sent to Germany because the recruiter had said so. His wishes were anywhere away from the yard. Miriam knew that, but of course he didn't express that to Whitey.

Jimmy was still in school but flunked back a year and he was hating the idea of returning with kids that seemed like babies to him. Pop made fun of him and said he was left back because he still wet his pants. Cassie and Sissy felt sorry for him and booed Pop when he taunted him.

Jimmy also was running around with kids that were up to no good. They weren't exactly kids. One was twenty one but he couldn't read or write. The other one was just a product of living with an older grandfather, because his parents couldn't handle him. The old grandfather had lost his eyesight. The kid quit school and enjoyed burglarizing homes where he knew couples that worked during the day wouldn't be home. Then he would sell the goods. Whitey called them the criminals. He'd see them and say out loud so everyone could hear, "Jimmy the 'Criminals' are here." Jimmy would apologize to them and say he hadn't meant it. But they were petrified of Whitey. They never wanted to talk to or about him.

Jimmy was planning some sinister money making schemes having to do with scrap metal so he could feel cool like them. He didn't seem to care that they both had been incarcerated at one time or another. None of his friends, if that was what you want to call them, wanted to get a normal job. Whitey didn't trust them as far as he could throw them. When they walked around in the junkyard he made sure he knew at all times exactly where they were. They were not allowed to touch anything of his or go into the office... Ever!

Cassie, who was sixteen, went away for the week-end. She said she was staying at her girlfriends house. Miriam had no reason to believe otherwise. Lo and behold she and her boyfriend Rich eloped to Maryland. When she returned she announced to Miriam she was married and three months pregnant. Pop seemed upset over Cassie's pregnancy but of course he never mentioned how his marriages started.

That was not that much of a surprise. They were lovebirds for over a year. Kissing and hugging every chance they could. Cassie moved into her strapping young boyfriend's home, just blocks away, where they'd have their own bedroom. Her husband Rich was a fine young man that had joined the Air Force. His plan was to head to college when he's discharged and Cassie was seemingly thrilled.

Sissy had a boyfriend but kept it a secret because he was much older than she was. When Miriam finally found out she tried to put an end to the relationship saying there was absolutely no way that Sissy could continue seeing him! That was when Sissy showed her she had a pair. Miriam might put both feet down, but it didn't change Sissy's love for the guy. They sneaked around for several months. Other family concerns seemed mild.

Miriam was of the belief that her working two jobs and not able to keep a watchful eye on anyone was the reason there was so much chaos in her family.

Nancy was a pre-teen and becoming more obstinate about chores. She had adopted her big sister's sarcasm and wanted to visit her friends more and not have to tackle everyone else's chores. Cassie was gone now, leaving her chores for whomever was home.

Bobby and Dee Dee were happy to be living in a community where there were families with kids their ages. The neighbors, the Desches, were their best friends. They played baseball, climbed trees and played board games as often as possible. Mr. Desch was a hairdresser and cut their hair whenever it was time.

EPILOGUE

After a quiet wedding Jane moved from the cemetery and into Woody's house in Westminster. It was expanded to fit Woody, Jane, David and Clyde. They also created room for Zeus who they adopted as a companion for their sweet Molly. Zeus and Molly fell in love at first sight. Whitey gave up Zeus and was sad to leave him but he had no way to care for him properly, especially with a fourth child now added to his new family.

Whitey sold the junkyard to Clyde who turned most of the yard into Westminster Park. The family now had a busy schedule. Woody was writing a book and Jane was working out of Willow Grove as a Social Worker. Clyde became an avid gardener. He stayed with David when he arrived home from school.

Woody and Clyde awakened a relationship that should have been there all along. David called Clyde Pop- Pop. They truly became best pals.

Whitey sold most of the flattened cars to the scrappers. With the junkyard now out of Whitey's possession he purchased a new junkyard up in Appleton. He built Alice and their four children a five bedroom home. Twenty acres of a thirty acre property was converted to a junkyard with a backdrop of a beautiful swimming hole... The Appleton Dam.

Miriam's house was painted and the upstairs apartment was given to Georgie and his new wife Margaret. Cassie and her husband Rich had a beautiful baby boy. Sissy eloped with an older man that everyone liked. Nancy graduated high school and was in charge of the younger kids. Billy was sent to Germany where he met his wife.

Jimmy... Well he was last known to be languishing in jail. His career of burglarizing homes had caught up with him.

THE END

9 781736 947302